Overdrive

ALSO BY DAWN IUS

Anne + Henry

oVerdrive

DAWN IUS

Simon Pulse

SIMON PULSE

An imprint of Simon & Schuster Children's Publishing Division

1230 Avenue of the Americas, New York, New York 10020

First Simon Pulse hardcover edition September 2016

Text copyright © 2016 by Dawn Ius

Jacket collage photographs copyright © 2016 by Getty Images

All rights reserved, including the right of reproduction in whole or in part in any form.

SIMON PULSE and colophon are registered trademarks of Simon & Schuster, Inc.

For information about special discounts for bulk purchases, please contact Simon & Schuster Special Sales at 1-866-506-1949 or business@simonandschuster.com.

The Simon & Schuster Speakers Bureau can bring authors to your live event.

For more information or to book an event contact the Simon & Schuster Speakers Bureau at 1-866-248-3049 or visit our website at www.simonspeakers.com.

Jacket designed by Karina Granda

Interior designed by Mike Rosamilia

The text of this book is set in Adobe Garamond Pro.

Manufactured in the United States of America

2 4 6 8 10 9 7 5 3 1

Library of Congress Cataloging-in-Publication Data

Names: Ius, Dawn, author.

Title: Overdrive / by Dawn Ius.

Description: Simon Pulse hardcover edition. | New York : Simon Pulse, 2016. |
Summary: Seventeen-year-old Jules Parish turned to stealing cars to try to get her sister out of foster care, but after she is caught, a wealthy eccentric offers a promising—but perilous—solution.

Identifiers: LCCN 2015051102 | ISBN 9781481439442 (hc) |
ISBN 9781481439466 (eBook)

Subjects: | CYAC: Automobile theft—Fiction. | Stealing—Fiction. |
Juvenile delinquency—Fiction. | Sisters—Fiction. | Foster home care—Fiction. |
Las Vegas (Nev.)—Fiction. | BISAC: JUVENILE FICTION / Law & Crime. |
JUVENILE FICTION / Family / Orphans & Foster Homes. |
JUVENILE FICTION / Love & Romance.

Classification: LCC PZ7.1.I97 Ove 2016 | DDC [Fic]—dc23

LC record available at https://lccn.loc.gov/2015051102

For Kitty.
Your appreciation for muscle cars pales next to
my appreciation for your unwavering love and support.
Eleanor is mine, but Nick is for you.

1

KEVIN JAMS HIS TONGUE IN MY EAR.

Yeah, gross, but I've got a roll of electrician's tape clenched between my teeth and the butt end of a live wire hovering over an exposed battery line. Best I can manage is a stifled grunt.

The scent of cheap beer makes my stomach roil. It's not just my boyfriend's alcohol-infused breath making me queasy, though. Thirty thousand people linger in the Las Vegas Arts District just a couple of blocks away.

Too close.

Kevin slides his hand up under my damp T-shirt. "Come on, Jules."

I spit out the tape, cringing as it clunks against the brake pedal and rolls farther under the dash. The soft thud is loud enough to hear over the drizzling rain. Steam rises off the asphalt. "You're going to make me blow it."

He laughs, but his cool hand continues to creep across my skin. When his finger hooks under my bra, I flinch. "Seriously, Kev. Stop it." I squirm to break contact. "Focus."

My heartbeat stutters. I'm one exaggerated twitch away from zapping more than this car's engine to life.

His tongue circles around my earlobe. "You got this, baby." A shiver runs along the back of my neck and I scrunch my shoulders. "That's why they call you the Ghost, right?"

I grit my teeth. "Invisible, not invincible."

It's a stupid street name, but after forty-two successful boosts, I guess I've earned a label. Thing is, I'm not cocky enough to believe my luck won't run out. The odds are always in favor of the house.

Kevin gets all whiny. "I really need this."

Jesus. It's not even a hot car.

A 1995 Mazda RX-8, midnight blue, standard stick. But judging by the interior—tricked-out stereo, new covers for the scooped racing-style seats—it's gotta be someone's baby.

Except that it's parked under a streetlight in a dark alley in one of the city's peak theft districts, which makes no sense. Guys who own cars like this know streetlights aren't deterrents for people like us, like *me*. No slinking in the dark, no flash-light, easy access.

It's too simple.

"I've got a bad feeling about this, Kev."

He gives me a wolfish grin.

Annoyance shakes through me. I get that he's got this whole Bonnie and Clyde fantasy going on, but his slurred encouragement isn't doing much to inspire confidence in *his* skills. This is a mistake.

I touch the starter wire to the battery cable and *zzzzt-zzzzt-zzzzt*, the engine sparks. A couple of revs later and the RX purrs.

Kevin hisses out a "yes!" as I sit upright and pull the driver's-side door closed. He practically climbs over the console for a congratulatory kiss. Of course I give in.

"Knew you could do it," he says, nibbling on my lower lip. And damn if my adrenaline isn't jacked. I know it's not right, but the truth is, I'm addicted to it—the danger, the rush.

Kevin kneads my right breast. "You're so hot, baby."

Sweating, actually.

Something still feels wrong and it's more than Kevin's overly obnoxious drunk-guy pawing. I yank his hand off my chest and shimmy up in the seat for a better view. He's supposed to be my lookout, but clearly he's using the wrong head. Figures.

I squint into the rain-soaked shadows, looking for something—some*one*—out of place. Vibrant graffiti slashes across Dumpsters overflowing with trash. A single lightbulb flickers at the back door of a run-down apartment complex. If the owner of the RX is out there waiting for me to fuck up, he's keeping it low-key.

Time to move out.

Kevin folds the passenger seat back, stretching out his long, scrawny torso, legs drawn almost up to his chest. I've pulled my trademark white hair up into a bun, but one police-issue flashlight pass over my alabaster skin and I'll go from the Ghost to living, breathing criminal. My saliva turns to paste.

His fingers skim the inside of my thigh. "Let's blow," he says. "We can get five large for this, easy."

Five thousand dollars.

It's not my biggest boost and the cash won't last long—especially when we split it. I gnaw on the inside of my cheek. "And then what?"

Kevin's fingers dance across my knee. "I didn't think you were into dirty talk, but I'm happy to give you a play-by-play." He yanks the seat upright with a jolt, leans over, and brushes his lips against my neck.

"That's not what I meant," I say, rubbing off his spit. "Like, after this grab . . ."

"You wanna get a burger or something?"

I punch the side of his arm. "No, you dick. I'm talking about the future. We can't steal cars forever."

At least *I* can't. Not if I want custody of my little sister someday.

Kevin's face blanks. "Shit, Jules. You're not thinking about dipping, are you? I'm just getting my feet wet here. What about Ems? Isn't this all about her?"

I doubt Kevin and I are on the same page, but I'm *always* thinking about my sister and her slightly crooked front teeth, the jeans that fit a little too tight, her bedroom in our foster parents' run-down trailer, the size of a broom closet.

I've tried legal life, but boosting cars is the fastest way to get Emma away from the Millers, out of the foster care system for good.

My moral equilibrium shifts out of gear.

I swat Kevin's hand away from my crotch, give the whiny engine another rev, and twist the wheel to unlock the steering. He's right, now's not the time for second-guessing.

My pulse thrums.

Hit the gas and I'm doing this. Again.

Jesus. It never gets easier.

I catch movement from behind a garbage bin and my hesitation drains like a deflating Goodyear. Clutch engaged, I step on the gas and the car shoots forward. I quick-shift into second. The back end twists, the tires squeal. *Holy shit!*

This thing's got guts.

Kevin lets out a loud *whoop* just as the warning siren in my head becomes ominous and real. Blue-and-reds blaze in my rearview, two cop cars gaining on me, on this now stolen RX.

Sweat pools in my palms and my hands grip the steering wheel so tight they've almost gone translucent. One glance at Kevin and I know he's spooked too.

"Floor it," he shouts over the thunderous rumble in my

chest. "I get pinched and it's no juvey for me. I'm doing time."

I shift into third, crank the wheel. The car careens around a corner and skips across the asphalt. I'm terrified and I can't shout, can't remind Kevin that this is bad—real bad—for me too. An image of my sister shimmers across the water-streaked windshield and I choke back a lump of terror.

I cannot, cannot, *cannot* get caught.

At the intersection of Hoover and Las Vegas Boulevard, I take a sharp left. Water rolls off the tires and splashes across the glass, blurring my vision. For a second, I think we'll hydroplane, but then the wheels smack against the road and we surge ahead. Kevin's head snaps back.

"Fucking buckle up!" I scream over the wailing sirens.

His face is almost green when he glances over his shoulder. Cop lights reflect off the Mazda's black polished interior. "I gotta jump, Jules."

I crank the RX up to fourth, then fifth. "Like hell."

One gear left, but even with it, I know there's no way I'll outrun the cops. I don't want to—I am *not* a cop outrunner. I've never had to before.

Kevin reaches for the door handle.

I swerve to avoid an oncoming BMW and the driver lays on the horn.

The police are up my ass now. I should pull over, stop the car, take the heat—*I'm underage, what can they do?*—but it's like the fuel line to my brain is clogged with motor oil. Everything is muddy and out of focus.

"Don't do it," I say. My voice cracks, tears brim, and I'm pissed that I sound desperate.

Kevin turns to me, his catlike hazel eyes wide and bulging—scared sober. And suddenly I've forgotten what I ever saw in him. The day-old stubble, the ripped jeans and eighties-style leather coat. He looks homeless, not badass, and I can't believe I ever let myself stoop to this. We were never going to be a team. A boil of emotions roll along the back of my throat.

"If I go to jail, I'm finished," he says. "*We're* finished."

But I already know we're done. I thought we hooked up because we both needed something—companionship, connection, more than a partner in crime—but I should have known better. I'm worth so much more than this.

Buildings, bystanders, palm trees pass in a blur. The hot Vegas Strip pulses like a lighthouse beacon ahead. I crank the wheel and spin a one-eighty, my guts practically projecting out of my open mouth. Somewhere in my subconscious I hear myself scream.

The tires hit the curb and we bounce into oncoming traffic.

I take a hard right into an alley. My stomach flips over. It's a fucking dead end.

"Back up!" Kevin yells.

Blood rushes to my head as I work to get the RX in gear.

It's stuck. No matter how hard I push in the clutch, I can't hit reverse. The car lurches forward.

"Reverse, Jules! Reverse!"

Panic seizes my vocal chords. "It won't pop into gear," I screech.

Lights flash-blink-flash in my eyes.

Sirens roar.

I ram the stick shift left, up, left again, and stomp on the gas. The RX sputters and then pitches forward. Fast. Too fast. I slam on the brake, lift my foot off the clutch, and jam the car into neutral. It stutters to a stop.

Kevin's curse pinballs off the dash, and before I can even register what's happening, there's a sharp rap at my window. I'm surrounded by cops and staring into the barrel of a gun.

My stomach begins a downward spiral.

I turn to Kevin for some kind of assurance, for him to tell me he'll stick with me on this. But the passenger door is slung open and somewhere in the distance I catch a glimpse of my ex-boyfriend's retreating ass.

My heart stalls with a twinge of pain. I shouldn't be surprised he bailed—everyone does. Still, nausea coils in my gut.

I swallow a dry heave and slap my hand over my face.

Fuck my life.

2

ELEVEN SCUFF MARKS ON THE CHECKERBOARD FLOOR.
I missed a couple on first count—two black streaks under the
far side of the table. They're important. Part of the interroga-
tion process.

I picture "bad cop" yanking back the chair, metal legs
screeching across the vinyl. He sits, stares, passes me a smoke
like they do in the movies. Or maybe that's just for big-time
criminals, like murderers and shit.

My stomach pirouettes.

I rub my wrists, red and raw from the handcuffs. Truth is,
I didn't make it anywhere near the slammer. "Good cop" threw
me in this room instead, leaving me to stew about Kevin, my
stupidity, my very bleak future.

I should be at the chop shop collecting my cash and hitting
up In-N-Out Burger with my boyfriend. Instead, I'm staring

at four beige walls and a fist-size hole I bet one of the *big-time* criminals made after "bad cop" delivered "bad" news. My fingers curl until they form fists.

Ineffective anger management, my social worker's voice plucks in my subconscious.

I can see her and the two officers in another room on the other side of the window. She paces while "good cop" sits at a round table pawing through a file. *My* file. "Bad cop"—I've decided to call him Frank; all the Franks I know are dicks—leans against a counter, sipping coffee between intermittent scowls. He's got one of those resting asshole faces.

Everyone's lips move but it's like I'm watching *CSI* on mute. There's shrugging, a what-the-fuck type motion from Frank, and then all eyes land on me, like they think they're invisible on the other side of the glass.

I'm a maggot under a microscope.

I shift my gaze before they catch me squirming. Begin re-counting the scuff marks on the floor to distract myself from thinking about how much shit I'm in. It's not just this stunt—more than eight thousand cars in Vegas are jacked every year. But by now, Frank over there has probably figured out I'm the infamous Ghost. No wonder his lips are twisted into a perma-smirk.

Movement outside the door pulls my attention.

The handle turns.

I fold my arms across my chest and steel for confrontation.

Whether they throw me in juvenile detention, dish out community service, or stick me with a stuffy, twig-up-his-ass probation officer, I'm done. My foster parents will never let me back into their doublewide shit-hole.

And Emma.

My breath hitches. We've spent the last four years bouncing from one shitty place to the next. Together. If we're separated now . . .

I swipe away a tear with the back of my hand. Not if I have anything to say about it.

The door wedges open. I roll my shoulders back. Sweat beads across my forehead.

Muffled voices.

Terse good-byes.

And then the *click-click-click* of my social worker's heels.

Vanessa, as she likes to be called, stands in the doorway, the hall light glowing around her white pantsuit like a damn halo.

I shift to take some of the pressure off my ass.

"Julia." Her voice tenses, just like her expression. "Or perhaps I should call you Ghost?"

My mouth glues shut.

Vanessa closes the door and makes her way over to the table. She opens her briefcase, reaches inside, and drops my file in front of me before dragging her chair across the vinyl with an extended *scraaape*. Two more scuff marks.

My bottom lip trembles. "It's bad, right?"

Vanessa sighs, folds her hands on the table, and crosses her legs. A thin blue line streaks the side of her pants. Probably ink. Her left hand is covered in it, little nicks and dots where her pen missed the paper. It's the jarring inconsistency of her otherwise perfect demeanor. I zero in on a leopard print heel that screams middle age.

"The police suspect you are linked to more than forty car thefts in the last nine months."

Forty-three, but who's counting? "Am I going to jail?"

Vanessa lifts one eyebrow. "The typical sentence for tonight's crime is about five years."

Unease winds around my neck like a noose. Even though it's my first time being charged, I'm still looking at two years, maybe three.

"But . . . ," Vanessa begins, and a small balloon of hope swells in my chest. My teeth sink into the side of my cheek and start gnawing until blood tickles my gag reflex. "The owner of the vehicle has decided not to press charges."

I blink. "That doesn't make sense."

The RX is basically trashed. Stripped wires dangle from the dash and the right side rims are gouged where I bounced off the curb. Shit, the transmission will probably fall out with the next sloppy gearshift. This guy should want my scrawny ass behind bars—or worse. He's clearly a crook. Maybe the car's stolen, not insured, something, because there's no logical reason for him *not* to press charges.

"I'm afraid the law isn't quite as generous," Vanessa continues. "You eluded police and put their lives, the *public's* lives, in danger. That's not a misdemeanor. There will be charges for that high-speed stunt, and because you're almost eighteen, there's a chance you'll be tried as an adult." She blows out a long breath. "Jesus, Julia. What were you thinking?"

Solid question.

It's also rhetorical because Vanessa has that look on her face, the what-the-hell-am-I-going-to-do-with-you expression that makes the Grand Canyon look small compared to the crevices spider-webbing across my heart.

I could blame a lot of things. Claim I panicked. Make her believe Kevin made me do it. But the excuses are just a smoke-screen for the inexcusable truth: I *wasn't* thinking.

Rookie move.

"You won't be charged with theft—God only knows why—but you've broken more than one law . . . tonight."

Her hesitation on the last word doesn't go unnoticed.

Vanessa flips open a manila folder and the pages of my sister's and my clichéd history spring to life. Four years of memories swipe back and forth like windshield wiper blades.

I was ten—Emma's age—when we moved to Vegas, twelve when Dad bet our lives away on the slots, and not even a teen when Mom threw him out on his cheating ass. Go, Mom! Too bad she couldn't hack the single life. She spiraled out of control faster than a Nevada dust devil. Classic Vegas.

13

Vanessa's been our caseworker for almost four years, ever since Mom lost custody after choosing her bong—or latest boy toy—over our basic needs. Again.

I'm over it.

But Emma. My insides twist at the memory of her face streaked with giant tears, her tiny fingers wrapped around her Princess Barbie with the strength of a socket wrench. Terrified and confused. Six years old and abandoned by a mother she was better off without. But how do you tell that to a kid?

I zero in on the picture of her paper-clipped to the corner of the file. The lump in my esophagus swells to the size of a softball. I rub under my eyes with the back of my hand and avoid Vanessa's gaze. She's seen me at my worst. This is different. We both know it.

Her voice softens. "If you provide some information about your boyfriend . . ."

"Ex-boyfriend," I say, my voice thick. "I'm not a rat."

Vanessa nods and I'm glad she doesn't push. I've run out of reasons for my misguided loyalty to Kevin.

"And then there's the matter of the Millers."

My stomach plummets so fast I jolt forward. "They don't want to foster me anymore."

Not like it's A-plus living anyway—Mr. Miller drinks too much and his wife's too dumb to see her husband's a cheat. The roof leaks, the trailer reeks of old people and stale beer, and Mrs. Miller couldn't bake a decent chocolate chip cookie if Pillsbury force-fed her step-by-step instructions. But it was a house, and more than that, Ems and I were together. At the thought of being separated from her—

Fuck that.

"I'm afraid it's more complicated," Vanessa says, cheeks pink. Her frustration transforms into something sympathetic and raw.

Discomfort.

The tension in the room thickens.

"Emma's out too," I say, filling in the gaps.

Vanessa takes my hands in hers. They're cold, like she's got antifreeze pumping through her veins. My whole body goes numb. "They warned us, Julia. They're not wired for this."

I snicker at her choice of words. "Why'd you have to go and tell them, anyway?"

Anger fuels the question, but the emotion bubbling beneath the surface is something stronger, something foreign.

Desperation.

My gaze flits to the hole in the wall and I imagine my knuckles making contact. I never should have taken this boost, never should have trusted Kevin. I let my guard down—*for what?*—and now everything's fucked.

"I know it looks bleak," Vanessa says. "But there are some options."

At this, she actually brightens, and a faint glimmer of light shines through the thick fog of my dismay. Vanessa is a kind, practical woman with the patience of a saint. But unless she's working miracles on the sly, I can't piece together a Happily Ever After here.

I yank my hand away and slide the chair back. My heart hammers like it's mainlining nitrous oxide.

"Think about it, Julia. You're almost eighteen," Vanessa says. "You have no legal"—she levels me with a knowing look that shrinks me to the size of a dashboard bobblehead—"income. I know you want to support Emma, but you don't have the means. Is this the kind of role model you want to be? What if Emma found out what you've been doing?"

The lump swells.

My sister's jaded, but somehow still innocent despite the shitty life cards we've been dealt. I've kept this—my not-so-legal side job—from her, but for how long? The lies are stacked so high I'm practically tripping over them.

"Isn't this supposed to be the part where you tell me everything's going to be fine?" I snap. Sarcasm comes second nature to me, but the question sounds harsh even to my trained ears. I feel my eyes start watering. Truth is, Vanessa's touched a nerve.

"There's a man," she says, cautious. "Roger Montgomery. A local art dealer and a philanthropist. A bit of an eccentric." When I don't say anything, she continues. "He checks out."

I actually *harrumph*.

Vanessa worries her wedding band and I know what's on

her mind. The Millers "checked out" too, but they weren't exactly up for Foster Parents of the Year.

I press forward. "What's the catch?"

She tilts her head and offers me one of those sad, sympathetic smiles I've come to associate with personal disappointment.

"This life . . . it's got to stop." She licks her lips. "If the police had enough evidence to link you to those other stolen cars, this would be a very different conversation."

"I meant, what's the catch with *Roger*?"

Vanessa sighs. "I can't find one." She flips over the paperwork in my file until she lands on a picture of a dude in a beige fedora, thick Coke-bottle glasses, and a brown leather coat buttoned up to his neck. A black scarf looks like it's choking him into a smirk. Dark patches of hair dot his chin and upper lip.

Gross.

"I can't trust anyone that wears a fedora."

Vanessa trips on a light chuckle. "You don't trust anyone."

True, but can you blame me? My parents, foster parents, Kevin, even Vanessa—they've all betrayed me somehow. Emma's my only constant, the only one who's never sold me out. My heart aches. For her, I need to make this work.

I exhale slowly. "What's his wife like?"

Vanessa shakes her head.

"So, he's some kind of creeper?" Call me paranoid, but something doesn't feel right here.

17

"He lost his wife in a tragic accident," Vanessa says with quiet admonishment.

Tough break, but I still don't like the idea of me and Ems being alone with this guy.

"You won't be," Vanessa says, when I tell her as much. "Mr. Montgomery has a soft spot for teenagers—he's already taken in three kids about your age."

"Perfect. Insta–Brady Bunch."

Vanessa smooths out the crinkles in her pants. Maybe I imagine it, but when she finally meets my gaze, her eyes have gone all glassy, like she's teetering on tears. "You know the drill here, Julia. It's this, or separate group homes for you and Emma, and I know you don't want that." Her cell rings and she jumps to silence it. "You're basically a good kid, but you've committed a felony. I can't sweep it under the carpet. I'm sorry. This is a great offer—better than you deserve. You need to think about what's best for your sister."

Emotion strangles my voice. "Because I don't all the time?"

"Roger checks out," she says again, softer now, not answering my question. My stomach does a slow roll of acceptance. "He's kind and generous. At least give him a chance. Because if this doesn't work out . . ."

No need to elaborate. Her underlying threat hits me with the force of a head-on crash.

3

EMMA'S BLOND HAIR FALLS LOOSELY ON HER STIFF shoulders. Her chin juts out, her spine straightens. She's trying to keep it together, but her fingers are wrapped so tight around the handle of her suitcase that they tremble.

A red flush creeps up the side of her neck.

"Deep breath," I say through the corner of my mouth. "You got this, Ems."

I get why she's anxious. It's a miracle I'm not speechless after our long trek up Roger Montgomery's cobblestone sidewalk to the enormous brick entrance of his mansion. Two dog statues stand as sentries on either side of the door. It's an absolute beast of a house—sharp-angled walls and round turrets, giant windows, interlocking marble blocks, and limestone siding. My insides squirm.

We can't possibly live here. It's too big, too showy, too . . .

Not us.

A couple of cars loiter in the cul-de-sac driveway—an expensive-looking Audi and a baby blue Chevelle with white racing stripes across the hood. I lick my lips. That muscle car rates high on the black market—probably worth $50K in mint condition. My mind starts working out logistics, checking security, drafting a plan.

Emma catches me and narrows her eyes in disapproval. Jesus. Sometimes it's like she can read my mind.

Behind us, Vanessa fidgets. Her suit jacket rustles as she reaches over Emma's head to press the doorbell. The resulting chime warbles like it's badly in need of a tune-up. She coughs. "Quite the place."

"It's like a castle," Emma says.

The door opens before I can spit out a response.

Roger Montgomery peers through thick, black-rimmed glasses that rest tight on the bridge of his nose, zeroing in on me with eyes the color of milk chocolate. His black goatee and mustache are trimmed almost to perfection. No doubt there's something quirky about him, but I sense behind his nerdy appearance he's—*distinguished? good-looking?*—something.

"Hi," Emma says in a swoosh of air, and my chest constricts. My sister wants this so badly, *I* hurt.

Roger drops his gaze to her. "You're shorter than I imagined."

Her face goes red. "You're older than I expected."

At this, they both laugh—Ems with a bit of a nervous hitch, Roger with a confidence that feels forced. Or maybe that's just my nerves kicking in.

I scope out the foyer in the background. The scent of *old* is cloying. Like we're in a museum past visiting hours and there's an invisible screen covering the flashing signs warning us to KEEP OUT!, DON'T TOUCH!, GET LOST! As though our greasy fingerprints might mar the polished gold finish of the gilt frames or the glossy wood.

What a joke.

Roger waves us all over the threshold. "Please, do come in."

We've barely stepped in the door before some dude in a penguin suit swoops by to grab Emma's suitcase and my duffel bag. He's halfway up the wooden spiral staircase before I can mumble out a halfhearted protest.

Roger turns to my sister. "Well then, you must be Emma."

"Ems," she says, and gives him a look that's been known to bring parental types to their knees. Not quite, but Roger bends a little to shake her hand.

Our life has always been about extremes—people who don't give a crap, or those who try too hard. Roger is clearly the latter, and maybe I should be grateful, but frantic energy bubbles through me.

"I'm Julia, if it matters."

There's a split second of hesitation, and I think I catch a flash of annoyance before Roger acknowledges me with a smile that doesn't quite reach his eyes. "Of course. Do you prefer Jules?"

I shrug. "Whatever works."

Sunlight cuts through the windows, reflecting off a giant chandelier. Dozens of rainbows dance on the walls. I shield my eyes with the edge of my hand and look up. "That thing looks like it's straight out of *Phantom of the Opera*."

Roger twirls the end of his mustache. "It is."

My jaw goes slack. The chandelier hangs from the vaulted ceiling by a gold interlocking chain I'm sure can't hold it. Maybe it's symbolic. Like, if it shatters to the ground, everything else does too.

"So, Mr. Montgomery," I begin.

He cuts me off with a grimace. "I'm not much into formalities. Please, just Roger will be fine."

Roger, Roger. "What's the deal here?"

He blinks.

"Nice digs." My sarcasm spews like antifreeze from a cracked radiator hose. "But it's not exactly teen-friendly. Want to take us out to the dog shed or wherever you keep the rest of us hoodlums?"

Vanessa admonishes me with an out-loud *tsk*. I expect smoke to steam from Roger's ears any minute, but he masks whatever he's feeling with a soft expression of sympathy. My spine stiffens. Screw him. I don't need his pity.

"I can show them around, Rog," comes a voice from my right.

22

A willowy redhead glides into the room, flashing a smile I'm sure has fired up a few engines. The outline of her bathing suit shows through a sheer cover-up—a flashy bronze and brown one-piece with strategic cutouts. Something I could never pull off.

I gather my hair to the side of my neck and knot it around my fingers. I'd give anything for a brush, shampoo. Scissors.

"Chelsea," she says with a tilt of her head. "You must be Julia."

I nod, drawn to her hypnotizing coffee-colored eyes.

"And I'm Emma." My sister's cheeks glow pink. "You're *really* pretty."

"And you"—Chelsea pokes Emma's chest—"are my new favorite person."

My sister rocks back on her heels, proud, while quiet jealousy pulses at my temples. It's not just my sister's reaction. Everything about Chelsea is intoxicating, even her laugh, like it's infused with champagne. I swear she radiates confidence.

"Go on, then," Roger says, nudging his chin toward the spiral staircase. "Vanessa and I will finish up the necessary paperwork and be up in a few minutes."

Emma bounds up the stairs like a turbo-boosted pace car. At the balcony landing, she leans over the edge, face beaming, and shouts, "Jules! Check this out!"

This is a long, narrow hallway peppered with framed artwork. I'm no expert, but it reeks of the big names—Monet,

Picasso, and something that reminds me of a Van Gogh at the end of the hall. I pause and tilt my head sideways to study the image. It can't be real.

"You're a fan?" Chelsea asks.

Not really, but I shrug to avoid sticking my foot in my mouth, remembering that Roger is the reason Ems and I are still together. Besides, I'm more intrigued by a series of hanging wood carvings that look suspiciously like weapons.

"Cannibal tools," Chelsea says. "From Fiji."

"Charming."

A shy smile tugs at her lips. "Roger likes to collect . . . things."

I'm mid-wondering where Ems and I fit in Roger's collection of misfit toys when Emma's high-pitched squeal ping-pongs through the hall. My pulse spikes with a split second of fear, until she peers out from a doorway, giant grin stretched across her flushed face.

"Jules," she breathes. "This room is . . ."

A preteen girl's wet dream.

The walls, the bedding, the furniture, even the ceiling, is splashed with neon—pink, green, orange, yellow. It's enough to give me a headache. Behind an oversize bed overflowing with pillows, graffiti covers a charcoal brick wall.

Emma runs toward a giant keyboard set in the floor in the corner of the room.

I want to scream at her not to touch it. Not to touch

anything. But she's already planted her feet on the alternating black and white keys. A deep musical note erupts from surround-sound speakers. We both jump in surprise.

Chelsea laughs. "We should probably turn down the volume on that."

Fuck, yes. "This entire room could use some toning down."

Emma jumps onto her bed, burying herself into a mountain of pillows. When she emerges, one is tucked against her chest, her hands wrapped around it so tight, it's now in the shape of an hourglass.

My heart races so fast I'm sure it will redline. I'm on the verge of tears and I don't know if it's because I'm scared or happy or pissed right the hell off. Mad because even though none of this makes sense, it *has* to. Emma needs this.

Maybe I do too.

I conjure up a smile. "However will you sleep in here?"

She flops back onto the mattress with a sigh. "Perfectly."

Her response twinges something in my subconscious and a shiver of unease trickles across my spine. Emma's entire room is perfect—too perfectly Emma.

I drop my voice to a whisper. "What's Roger's deal?"

Chelsea raises an eyebrow.

"All this"—I scan the room—"seems a bit much."

It's like a lightbulb goes off in her head. "Right? You'll get used to the way Roger spoils us. . . ." She holds out her wrist and a heavily jeweled bracelet blinks at me. "He gave me this for my birthday."

"Nice," I lie. Am I the only one that finds this all a bit . . . ick?

My sister flings opens the French doors that lead to an en suite. Her gasp rebounds off the gleaming tile and punches me right in the solar plexus. "Oh my goodness."

It's more spa than bathroom. Dozens of shampoos, soaps, bubble bath containers, and pedicure tools overflow from a basket propped beside a deep claw-foot tub. The jewel-framed vanity mirror sparkles like it belongs backstage at a burlesque.

Air catches in my lungs, causing me to choke. "It's a little over the top, no?"

"Only the best for my children."

I spin around to find Roger staring at my sister with shimmering dark eyes. The guy creeps me out in an I-need-to-take-a-shower way, but I get what's at stake here. Emma and I have one shot to stay together. Roger's it.

"Do you like it?"

I sputter out a huff of disgust. "How could she not?"

Emma's face glows. "It's the best room I've ever had."

Roger may not know the significance of her words, but his chest still puffs with pride. And while I'm not convinced he's quite the White Knight my sister has inadvertently labeled him, I confess there may be some silver armor beneath that stuffy tweed vest.

But when the smile begins to fade from my sister's face, I

know her anxiety is threatening to smother this new excitement.

"Do you want to have a sleepover?" she says, and my heart cracks a little.

My room at the Millers' was barely larger than a storage closet, the hard futon no bigger than a twin, but when Emma woke with night terrors, I'd curl her into my arms and whisper, "Come on, let's have a sleepover."

Chelsea puts her hands on her thin hips. "How do I get invited to this slumber party?"

Annoyance flashes through me, but I mask it with a forced smile. "Maybe I should check out my room first. It could be even cooler than yours."

Emma's eyes widen. "I bet it's perfect."

Probably not. And yet, my stomach clenches as we all make our way down the hall. Emma's room is slam-dunk perfection. That can't be coincidence. So does that mean my bed will be covered in satin, like my old ballet slippers? Will dance posters cover the walls?

The idea is obviously ridiculous because I doubt Roger sees past my scuffed running shoes and oversize hoodie. Doesn't matter anyway. Unlike Ems, I won't be so quick to get caught up in this fairytale.

At my bedroom door, I straighten. Take a deep breath and flick on the lights.

My stomach sinks so fast I'm rooted to the floor.

"Oh."

Plain black furniture spots a room that is otherwise blanketed in white—the curtains, the bedspread, even the carpet. I curl my toes into the floor for balance.

Emma jumps on my bed. "Wow! It's so . . ."

White.

White and cold and impersonal.

I rub my hands over my jeans and then wrap them around my upper arms. Goose pimples cover my skin. I catch Roger staring at me, and for a split second I get a solid view of what's behind those brown eyes—the design of my room is absolutely deliberate. A silent signal.

White as a Ghost.

And then, whatever malevolence I envision is replaced with deceptive charm. He has the arrogance to look sheepish. "I admit, it's a bit of a blank canvas right now."

I steady my voice. "All good."

Chelsea butts in. "Roger seriously knows nothing about teenagers. We'll get this place fixed up in no time."

A sly smile tugs at Roger's lips. "Please, order . . ." He pauses. "Anything you'd like."

Emma gasps. "Anything?"

"Of course." Roger winks at her before leaving the room with a likely unintentional plié.

"See," Chelsea says, nudging me with her hip. "Harmless."

Not quite my assessment, but I need to get my bearings before I tackle that debate. "So, there's three of you, right?"

"Yeah. Mat's in the pool and Nick is . . ." Her gaze flicks over my shoulder and mischievous flecks of hazel twinkle in her eyes. "Nick, say hi."

I spin around and freeze. A guy stands in the hallway wrapped only in a towel that rides low on his hips. Tattooed angel wings stretch across his broad chest and feather downward to muscular arms marked with black tribal ink. My pulse picks up speed.

He's not the biggest guy I've ever seen, but his presence somehow fills the space. Commands attention. He is . . .

Dangerous.

Sirens go off in my head and I should break the stare. Something pulls me in. Makes me hold on a little longer than I should.

Hit the brakes, Jules.

His eyes are blue. Not the kind of blue that makes my knees buckle or makes me start planning our wedding, but a blue that sends vibrations of unease up my spine. A cold, ice blue that growls, *Back. The fuck. Off.*

Nick scrapes his teeth along the corner of his lip. Jesus. There's a piercing.

The tension between us is so thick, it practically crackles. Instinct tells me to steer clear of this bad boy, but then I remember the promises I made to Vanessa, to Emma. I can't screw this up.

I force nonchalance. "Hey, I'm Jules."

A hint of laughter plays on his lips just before they twist into a bone-chilling sneer.

4

A RED FERRARI ZIPS ACROSS THE GIANT FLAT-SCREEN. Nick shifts while his thumbs easily work the knobs on a game controller. He leans left, a quick right, and then sends the car hard into the corner. It spins out of control, slamming into the virtual sidewall. A fiery explosion blows through the surround sound, rattling the bookshelves against the wall.

I flinch, but no one notices me hovering on the sidelines of the enormous games room. The place is obnoxious, like a kid's toy box on high-grade nitrous.

The guy next to Nick throws his hands up. "Crash and burn, *pendejo*!"

If that's Matias, I already like him. My Spanish might be rusty, but I'm pretty sure he's just called Nick an asshole.

Nick tosses the controller and grunts. "Think you can do better?"

The two of them are stretched out on a leather sofa that floats in the middle of the room. An antique jukebox in the corner pumps out a Maroon 5 tune, while Chelsea hip-checks the right side of a pinball machine into submission. The overhead light flashes, sirens wail. She fist-pumps the air. "Take that!"

Matias leans forward to push the reset button on the Xbox. Need for Speed splashes onto the screen, the intro music drowning out a crooning Adam Levine.

"Check this." Matias's thumbs work in tandem to move a Lamborghini onto the virtual track. "Control. Vision. Determination. These are the fundamental components of a race car dri—"

Nick snorts. "Fuck you, man."

To my left, a small stage backs up against a wall cluttered with framed photos—The Doors, Jim Morrison, a bunch of famous people I barely recognize. My eyes are drawn to an autographed picture of an actress who looks vaguely familiar. She's stunning.

Beneath the collage, a pink karaoke machine blink-blink-blinks, like a slot machine at the Flamingo.

Ugh. I'm so not into this.

I start to back away when Chelsea traps me in one of her high beams. "Jules!"

Busted.

"Guys, Jules is here!"

31

Matias shifts around on the sofa and grins. Loose, dark brown curls frame his naturally bronzed skin. "Mat," he says, raising the controller over his head in a half-wave of introduction.

Nick doesn't bother acknowledging me, and for some reason it stings.

"Need for Speed," I say, a weak attempt at conversation. I hate how awkward this is. "I'm more of a Grand Theft Auto girl."

Nick mutters under his breath. "Shocker."

My stomach clenches.

Chelsea waves her hand in dismissal. "Ignore Mr. Grumpy Pants over there. He doesn't like to lose." After an exaggerated eye roll that suggests boys-will-be-boys, she motions to the pinball machines spaced evenly against the wall. "Wanna play? We've got the classics—like Pac-Man, baby—and a few newer games." She clucks her tongue with mock cockiness. "Currently, I'm kicking the crap out of Lara Croft. This Tomb Raider chick's got nothing on me."

"You probably rigged the machine," Mat calls out over his shoulder.

"That's more your style," Chelsea quips.

I wet my lips, hesitating. "Think I'll just go to bed. I'm kind of beat."

"Don't let the door hit you on the way out," Nick says.

Anger shoots through me. "What's your fucking problem?"

I spin around to glare at him, but his eyes are glued to the TV, stony profile unwavering. The Lamborghini crashes and explodes in a ball of flame. Mat tosses the controller aside with disgust.

Nick retrieves it and grins. "So much for waxing my ass, *pendejo*," he says, with an emphasis on the slang. God, what a dick.

A handful of popcorn kernels fall from Mat's lap when he stands. He slaps Nick on the back. "You win this time, *pajero*."

I cup my hand over my mouth. "Did you just call him a masturbator?"

Nick freezes, looks back, and scowls. "Up yours, bro."

The two launch into a friendly push and shove war, punctuated by insults and laughter. I deflect a pang of jealousy with the acceptance that I'll probably never fit in with these guys. Clearly I'm not gaining any mileage with Nick. Not that it should matter.

Chelsea comes closer. "Emma fall asleep okay?"

"Zonked as soon as her head hit the pillow."

"Roger went *all out* on that room," she says.

There's a wink in her voice but I don't like the implication. Emma's room is more than simple decor math—it practically *breathes* with her essence. Something about it doesn't feel right.

"So what's his angle?"

Chelsea frowns. "Skeptical much?"

When I don't answer, she keeps talking. Her eyebrows knit with annoyance. "I get it. Roger can come off a bit . . ."

"Scattered," Mat fills in.

"He's definitely not firing on all pistons," I add, a little under my breath.

Nick huffs. "Harsh."

My face goes hot.

Chelsea shrugs. "It'll just take time, you know?" At my hesitant nod, she brightens. "Forget it for now. How about a dance-off?" Her arms and legs twist into some fucked-up side-shift-lunge move. "Bet you could kick my butt."

"I'm not much of a dancer." The lie gets caught in my throat.

Nick ejects Need for Speed and slips another disc into the Xbox. Blood whooshes to my head when the Grand Theft Auto logo pops onto the screen. Fuck. Me and my big mouth.

He holds out a controller. "Come on, hotshot. Let's see what you're made of."

The edge in his voice is as sharp as steel. I take a step back, bumping into the wall. A hanging African-style mask tilts sideways. I note the plaque beneath it—another movie prop—and adjust the mask, stalling. "No, I couldn't . . ."

Nick slumps back against the sofa cushions. "Shoulda known you're all talk."

My skin suddenly feels too tight on my body. I snag the controller and flop down next to him. Our thighs touch. The couch practically shakes as his muscles tense. Good. I want him on edge. "You asked for this."

Chelsea pulls a stool up alongside the sofa and winds

her finger through a lock of red hair. "Well. This just got interesting."

While the game scene sets up, Mat and Chelsea make fun of the characters that flicker across the screen. I try to focus on deciphering Mat's words, but I'm hyperaware of Nick. The way he slouches on the sofa, the smirk in the corner of his lip. Maybe it's me that's on edge.

Gunfire spits through the speakers and the next thing I know, I'm in the midst of a virtual shoot-out.

Chelsea leans forward on her stool. Her voice raises a full octave. "Get out of there!"

"Grab the cash first," Nick says, a little under his breath.

I scrunch up my face. "I'm not a moron."

Mat slides a stool next to Chelsea and cracks open a can of soda. I toggle through a series of hallways until I find the bank vault. Collect the money. Outrun a security guard. Meet up with—

Seriously?

"Uh, she's . . . interesting," Chelsea says.

Mat whistles low. "Whoa, get a load of those *chichis.*"

Ignoring their commentary, I gun my way through an obstacle course of police cruisers and cops, while bikini girl runs behind me screaming like a damn banshee. "God, someone ought to just put her out of her misery."

Chelsea points wildly at the screen. "Oh! Oh! Go left!"

One of my thumbs slips off the controller, spinning my character in a one-eighty.

"Your other left," Nick mumbles.

Screw you.

I regain control and my character starts outrunning a couple of cops on foot—as if this entire scenario wasn't already giving me epic déjà vu vibes. My heart thumps as I search for a set of wheels.

Mat hoots with laughter. "My *abuela* is faster."

"I doubt your grandma is hot-wiring cars," I say, smirking.

Nick's voice drops to a low growl. "Everyone's got their secrets."

I duck my head so that my hair covers my blush. Maybe it wasn't personal, but the dig burns a little hole inside me. What? Roger told them all I'm a car thief so I'm a household pariah? Fuck this.

Mat grabs Chelsea's water and chugs. "Things are really heating up now." He wipes the back of his mouth and hands back the bottle.

"Didn't you just open a soda?" I say.

Mat shrugs. "Chelsea's bottle looked better."

"Gross," she says. "Now I've got Mat germs."

Their laughter cuts through the thick tension that's settled on the couch. I try not to think about it as I guide my character through a series of rapid lunges, kicks, and sprints, then dart into a dark back alley.

Mat points at a lone Mustang under a virtual spotlight. "There's an easy boost."

Not always. "Nah, I need something with more guts."

Nick shoots me a dark glare. "It's not what's under the hood that matters."

Experience tells me that most new Mustangs run a stock engine—enough torque to stoke male pride, but not much in the way of a serious getaway car. Launching into this discussion with Nick feels like social suicide, though, so I ignore the bait.

I spot a Camaro tucked behind a garbage Dumpster and toggle my character forward. My adrenaline surges. Seconds later, I've virtual hot-wired the car, and bikini girl and I are set to ride into the smog-filled horizon.

Mat reaches across Chelsea to give me a high five. "Impressive."

I slough off the compliment with a half-assed shrug.

"No really, you totally knew what you were doing—in and done. Practically invisible or something. . . ."

Nick snorts. "Or something . . ."

My breath catches, but Chelsea doesn't miss a beat. "You've obviously done this before."

I set the controller on the coffee table, so not liking where this conversation's headed, grab a handful of Chelsea's popcorn, and stuff my mouth to stop from blurting out something I don't mean.

"Thief!" she shouts with a laugh.

The word lands hard. Over the thundering roar of my heartbeat, I swear I hear Nick snicker.

I stand on shaky legs. "I'm heading to bed."

Chelsea's pink-frosted lips form a pout. "Oh, hey, hope I didn't hit a nerve there. You know I was just joking around, right?" Two worry lines knot above her perfectly groomed eyebrows. "Like Nick says, we've all got a rough past."

"Don't let the bedbugs bite," Nick cuts in.

Jesus. Just how far is that joystick stuck up his ass?

I'm itching to continue a conversation with Chelsea, but one look at Nick's scowl and my curiosity shrivels like an overripe grape. And of course I'm so flustered and pissed off, I trip on the edge of a throw rug and pitch myself into the hall.

Right into Roger.

Like things could get any worse.

He tilts his head. "Somehow I thought you'd be more graceful than that."

I bite down on my lip hard enough to draw blood. Tears brim in my eyes and that sucks because I'm already tired of crying. Tired of trying to understand Nick, this place, Roger, all of it.

"I'm sorry. That was uncalled for."

His apology draws out a strangled sob.

"Oh dear," he says. "I'm sure this is all quite overwhelming."

His tone is soft, comforting, like a Toyota Supra after a fresh tune-up. I'm not buying it.

"Give it some time," he goes on. "You'll feel at home before long."

Home.

My chest fills with air so fast I think it might explode. "I just need to blow off some steam."

Roger's mustache lifts with a fake smile. "I have the perfect solution. Come."

The animated chatter in the games room fades as I respond to Roger's command. I scope out the rooms down the hall—a cherrywood desk fills an office, a hot tub in the spa overlooks Mount Charleston, and a life-size knight in polished armor guards another room with a stocked bar and two pool tables. Something about the statue looks familiar.

"What's with all the movie props?"

Roger doesn't answer.

"Right, you collect things. But half this stuff looks out of place."

"They belong right where they are," he says.

I must have struck a nerve.

Roger pushes open a door at the end of the hall and motions me forward.

A blast of cool air blows my hair back. I blink at the bank of overhead fluorescents, until my eyes adjust to the light. The first thing I see is a row of treadmills and elliptical machines. Behind it, manual equipment and several rows of free weights.

"Little late for cardio, Rog."

"You mentioned blowing off steam—I thought this would suit."

Not quite, but I can't exactly tell him what I really want is to boost the Chevelle in his driveway, kick it into gear, and tear up the Strip on the way to the Gold & Silver Pawn Shop. I'd bet my last buck the *Pawn Stars* guys would take it.

Something inside me snaps. "Guess you don't know me after all."

His eyes go glassy. "Oh, I think you're wrong about that."

He pulls out a tiny remote control from his vest pocket and pushes a button. At the far end of the gym, a wall slides left to reveal a "secret" room. Blood pounds through my veins, and my heart is a drum beating a war chant of protest. It can't be—

But of course it is.

Soft light shimmers off the shiny polish of a long ballet barre.

Roger clears his throat. "I had this installed for you yesterday."

His words turn to white noise and tangle inside my head, like a tape recording played back at slow speed. Snippets of conversation cut through the muddle.

". . . gave up dance to support your sister . . ."

". . . inspire you . . ."

". . . join ballet again."

Emotion bubbles up inside me as I allow the dreams to unfurl. My toes itch to point. The muscles in my legs begin to unwind. I squeeze my eyes shut to block the images of the past, forcing myself not to wish, not to dream. This can't be real. None of this is.

I swat at tears gathering in the corner of my eyes and suck in a deep breath. Clear away the nostalgia that's sure to cloud my focus. My face grows hot with anger.

What a fucking joke.

Does Roger think I'm an idiot? Obviously the barre is nothing more than a smoke screen for Roger's true ruse—there's no other explanation.

I spin around to face him, my teeth clenched. "I see right through you."

At his shocked expression, I keep going, renewed conviction fueling my words. How stupid to have let my guard down, even a little. "Cut the crap, Roger. What are we really doing here?"

5

RESTLESS ENERGY THRUMS THROUGH MY SYSTEM.

Trouble is, I can't tell if it's because Nick's thigh pressed up against mine is doing something to my equilibrium, or I'm scared shitless.

Instead of answering my question, Roger asked the butler to stay with Emma and ordered the rest of us to get into his Town Car. I'm stuffed between Nick and Chelsea in the backseat, where the tension's so thick you couldn't four-by-four through it with a Hummer.

I angle my body away from Nick, which only wedges my ass into his hip. There's room for him to move closer to the window, but he doesn't. He's a damn brick wall. Except warmer. Heat radiates through two layers of denim.

Mat shifts in the front seat. "Where we headin', Rog?"

No response.

The gravel road bends and curves. In the limited range of the headlights, I can tell the side ditches are nothing more than desert sand and sagebrush, silvery under the glow of moonlight. Behind us, the pulsing Vegas Strip fades to a dull throb.

The rhythm of my heartbeat clashes with Roger's music. It's classical. Ominous. I almost expect some dude in a hockey mask to jump in front of the car and go all *chee-chee-ha-ha* on us. Which is kind of ridiculous.

"Let's play twenty questions," Chelsea says. She presses her face up against the glass. "I'll go first. Are we—"

Roger puts a finger to his lips, then turns up the music. The orchestra hits a crescendo. He waves his right hand through the air like a conductor, vibrating it on the last note for ten startling seconds. Clearly the guy's a sociopath.

Our eyes meet in the rearview mirror and I quickly look away. Focus on the passing desert landscape. I count the sagebrush. Five, six, se—

Roger's headlights skim over white bone. A skull. I can see the empty eye socket, the sharp teeth.

My tongue grows paralyzed.

"Coyote," Nick says. "There's a few of them around."

Sweat rolls between my shoulder blades. I stretch across Chelsea to crack open the window and a cloud of hot dust blows up in my face. My chest constricts. I can't get enough air.

Ahead, a giant building emerges from behind a rolling hill like some kind of sand creature. I lean forward for a closer look.

43

Wind and heat have stripped the paint, giving the exterior an eerie sandblasted appearance. Wooden planks crisscross each window and a chain-link fence at least ten feet tall surrounds the perimeter, barbed spikes glinting like razor blades.

Cautionary signs pepper the entrance: KEEP OUT! PRIVATE PROPERTY! VIOLATORS WILL BE PROSECUTED!

My skin prickles. "What is this place?"

"Stay here," Roger says. He gets out of the car to unlock the first gate. Behind it, another, even more complex lock protects the ramshackle building in the background.

"Holy crap, this place is tighter than Fort Knox." Chelsea tucks her feet under her butt and peers over the driver's-side seat. "Looks like an UltraSafe electric strike from here."

"Doesn't make sense. Should be a keyless entry," Mat says. "Unless there's some kind of wind interference that would mess with the connection."

My eyebrows raise. "Electric strike? Wind interference? Is that code for *we're fucked*?"

For some reason, this makes Nick laugh. "Nah, they're just showing off."

Roger climbs back into the car, an unlit cigar dangling from his lips. He drives through the first gate and stops at a keypad just inside the perimeter. Four obscured digits later and we're through.

My insides twist like a Rubik's Cube.

What is this place? Maybe I've seen too many B-grade horror flicks, but my imagination has started working up a few bloodcurdling explanations.

Torture chamber.

Prison for delinquent teens.

Morgue.

Fuck, I hope not. A few years back, Emma and I found half an animal carcass in the field behind one of our foster homes. Bloated. Covered in maggots. The smell of rotting flesh stuck with me for weeks, clinging to my skin like burned motor oil.

I tamp back a shudder.

Roger parks the car, tucks the cigar behind his ear, and peers in the rearview mirror, his glasses resting slightly askew on the edge of his nose. A roar fills my ears as every muscle tenses.

"Well then, shall we go inside?" he says, like we're not body rocking into a scene from *Hostel*. At our collective hesitation, he grins, and I'm sure my pulse has never spiked so fast. "I assure you, you're all safe."

That's exactly what I would expect a serial killer to say.

Irritation leaks into Nick's voice. "What kind of game are you playing here, Roger?"

Roger's response is the sound of the car door closing as he gets out. At the front of the building, he pauses, turns around. Moonlight shimmers on his face and I actually recoil—I could swear his eyes burn red. The image stays with me even as he slides inside the building.

"This is fucked up," I say.

Nick arches an eyebrow. "It's your fault we're here."

He's not wrong. Maybe I should have kept my mouth shut, but even with the heebie-jeebie vibes Roger was giving off, I never expected him to pack us into his Lincoln for a creepy-ass drive deep into the Mojave Desert.

I pull my cell out from the front pocket of my hoodie and check the screen. My heart sinks—no reception.

Nick laughs without humor. "Now you want to call the cops? A little late for that, princess."

"Ease off, Nick," Mat says. He twists in his seat. "Seriously. What can one old gringo do against the four of us? Aren't you curious what's in there?"

"A dead cat," I say.

Nick groans. "Mature."

I curl my fingers with thoughts of strangling him, but follow him out of the car and to the front of the building. My knees knock together like a busted driveshaft.

Chelsea slings her designer purse over her shoulder and points a finger at me. "If I die, it's on you."

Nick rolls his eyes and grunts out something indecipherable and probably insulting.

I hate how he gets under my skin. Screw giving him the benefit of the doubt. Now I'm just pissed. "Maybe you already know what's inside."

"Oh, for Christ's sake. Grow up." Nick shoves past me,

stalks to the door, and yanks on the handle. "What? Scared to see the dead bodies?"

"Not funny," Chelsea snaps.

Mat grins. "Haven't you seen *Saw*?"

"At least I'll leave a pretty corpse," Nick jokes.

The blood drains from my face. "I hate you all."

On the other side of the door, a dim lightbulb casts flickering shadows throughout the room. I take quick inventory—coatrack, small table, three chairs.

Roger.

I flinch. "Jesus. You scared the shit out of me."

"I'm afraid the lighting isn't the best," he says. "Follow me."

He enters numbers onto a keypad fixed to the wall—too fast for me to memorize the sequence—and an invisible door hisses open. I peer over Chelsea's shoulder into the faint light.

"We can turn around," I whisper.

She reaches back and squeezes my hand as the door behind us slams closed. "Actually, I'm not sure that's an option anymore."

Shattered fluorescent lighting tubes litter the hallways. An earthy scent masks the faint smell of bleach and gasoline. I'm sure this is the scariest place I've ever been, but I can't shake a sense of familiarity, a weird nostalgia that doesn't make sense.

My foot catches on a piece of uplifted flooring and I pitch forward.

Nick reaches for me. "Easy," he says. His thumb brushes

against the side of my hip, and an electric shock pulses through my veins.

He pulls away so fast my skin turns to ice. His hand slides over the tribal ink on his right bicep, as though to make sure he won't make the mistake of touching me again. Not like I wanted him to anyway.

I shift focus back to Roger.

There's a certain giddiness to him when he walks. I guess it's too much to hope we're walking into Wonka's chocolate factory. He pauses at a door and waits for us to surround him. We're like moths to a flame.

A glowing EXIT sign hovers over a metal staircase to the right that leaps up and down into darkness. An overhead bulb pulses and buzzes. I squint to read the faded signage on the wall, but the white letters are either scraped clear or coated with dust. Tiny spiders dance across my back.

Chelsea's finger brushes against my elbow. "So mysterious."

"Brilliant observation, Veronica Mars," I whisper.

Roger's eyes shimmer. If he's the kind of guy who gets off on murder, we're in such deep shit.

He punches in a six-digit code and the door swings open. A series of *tick-tick-ticks* echoes as fluorescent lights switch on in sequence. It takes a second for my eyes to adjust and then—

Nick stops dead. "Holy. Shit."

My eyes widen with disbelief.

Dozens, maybe hundreds of vehicles line row after row in

this makeshift parking lot. Even covered with a thin layer of dust, I can make out the models. Fuck me. I was wrong. This isn't a morgue—it's the place where muscle cars go to die.

A cluster of Camaros pull my attention. Behind them, an older Trans Am.

My saliva tastes like it's mixed with diesel fuel at the sight.

Five years, six months, fifteen days. That's the last time I saw my piece of shit father. He peeled out of the driveway in a rusted old TA, tires spinning black smoke, like he couldn't wait to get away from us, from me. Rumor has it I was conceived in that "Silver Bullet"—which is probably some twisted rationale for why I started boosting muscle cars in the first place.

But if there's one thing Dad did teach me, it's that you can't outrun the past.

"This," Roger says, sweeping his arm outward, "is the Trophy Case." A hint of something flashes across his face—sadness? Fear? He adjusts his fedora. "Once one of the most popular attractions in Vegas." He nudges his head. "Go ahead, look around."

Adrenaline surges up my spine.

Nick leans close, his breath feathering across my cheek. "That's a classic." I zero in on a black Trans Am, swallowing another memory of my father. A fiery red bird splashes across the hood. "Back in the day, the Pontiac's T-roof was about as close as you could get to a convertible. Looked good, but they leaked."

49

Jesus. It's like I've met my twin. Too bad his knowledge of cars doesn't quite excuse him from being a dick.

I brush my bangs out of my face. "But what's it doing in here?"

Nick shrugs. "Guess Roger's a . . . collector."

Sure, but we're in an abandoned warehouse deep in the desert—which doesn't make sense. Roger's art fills the mansion. He donates to public charities. For a guy who likes to show off, this goes against his character. "Something doesn't feel right."

Across from us, Chelsea and Mat weave through the row of Camaros. As Mat reaches toward the hood scoop on a '67, Roger stops him with a loud *tsk*. "You must not touch."

Nick points to another car, his eyes wide as hubcaps. "Whoa! That's a Pontiac GTO Judge." He actually grins when I check to make sure he isn't drooling, and much as I hate to admit it, it's cute. "Considered the first muscle car. Rare as shit."

"There's something familiar about it," I say.

Mat spins around and mimics playing air guitar. "Come on, you don't know?" I blink and he keeps going. "The original commercial for the Judge featured Paul Revere and the Raiders." His cheeks turn pink. "What? I like the classics. That sixty-second spot was considered one of the first ever rock music videos."

"I'm a little shocked you know that," Nick says. "But do you know who the car's named after?"

"What do you take me for?" Mat scoffs. "You think I never watched *Laugh-In* reruns?"

I tune out their banter and try to come to grips with what I'm seeing. Feeling. Whatever my reservations, Roger's Trophy Case is fierce.

"I'm sure you have questions," Roger says.

"Why'd you shut this place down?"

Chelsea lets out an obnoxious *whoop*! "Holy crap, you guys! Look at this." She fans herself. "It's a Lamborghini. A red freaking Lamborghini."

Mat bounds up the curved asphalt after her.

"I'd rather not go into the reasons right now," Roger says. Something over my shoulder catches his attention and he tenses. I look back to see Nick weaving his way through a row of Mustangs.

His mouth gapes. "Is this what I—?"

"A Shelby," Roger confirms.

There are actually four of them—one a dead ringer for the car in the movie *Gone in Sixty Seconds*. I'm not much of a pony girl, but I can appreciate that particular model. Clearly I'm not alone.

"Must be your favorite car."

"It's a Mustang, so obviously," Nick says, his eyes brightening.

I think back to our heated game of GTA. "Something you and Roger have in common."

His face falls. "I had one once."

"Crashed her?"

A muscle in his cheek twitches. "Stolen."

Tough break, but car thefts are a dime a dozen in this town. "Maybe you'll find another someday."

Nick runs his tongue over the top of his teeth. "Vicki was special."

The bitter edge to his voice is clear, so I drop the subject and lead the way up to the second tier of the warehouse. It's filled with older model Chargers, Challengers, a few muscle cars I don't recognize. My eyes land on a couple of Ferraris and a Lamborghini. Not as pretty as the older models—most cars aren't—but also, out of place.

Nick settles back into his comfort zone and spits out statistics with shotgun speed. He's like the Wikipedia of muscle cars, and it's kind of impressive. A kid in a candy store—like Roger, but way less creepy.

We pass a black and gray Charger. "They were known for their famous flip-out headlights," Nick says. "Dodge discontinued them in 1973 when the car went through rebranding."

He stops at a car I don't recognize. "The mighty Road Runner. This thing struck fear into the hearts of the Saturday night drag racing crowd. She was fast."

"Kind of a stupid name for a car," I tease.

"No shit, right?" He peers in through the driver's-side window. "The horn even *beep-beeps* like the cartoon bird."

At the DeLorean, he freezes. "*That* is an exact replica of the *Back to the Future* car."

"It's not a replica," Roger says.

It's almost adorable the way Nick gasps. Almost.

We catch up to Mat and Chelsea on the third floor. I don't know what I expected—*a gold-plated Rolls Royce?*—but I'm flush with disappointment. A dozen or so ordinary cars are parked in two neat rows. A Civic, two Corollas, even a minivan.

Chelsea raises an eyebrow. "Scraping the bottom of the barrel here, Rog."

He tenses. "They have their purpose."

I cough out a laugh. "What? Distraction from the real goods?"

But the smile dies when my eyes land on a midnight-blue RX-8. The right bumper is smashed in and a long scrape follows the length of the door. Mud cakes the wheel wells. My gut tells me this is the same RX I stole. The one that landed me in cuffs.

Bile rises and burns my esophagus.

I force calm even though everything within me writhes with rage. "Guess the joke's on me."

The fucking bastard set me up.

"Julia—"

The patronizing tone of his voice makes me snap. I whirl on him, my hands balled into fists. "You baited me!"

He jumps back as I lunge and I narrowly miss slamming

my knuckles into his nose. Nick grabs me around the waist and lifts me off the ground. I kick and scream at the air.

His breath whispers against my ear. "Easy, girl."

But I'm too far gone to listen. I squirm until I break free and shout. "Asshole!" I don't even know if it's directed at Roger or Nick.

Roger raises his hand in mock surrender. "I paid for the car so the owner wouldn't press charges," he says. "That's the truth. I had to store it somewhere. I'm sorry, I should have told you."

"Bullshit," I say. "You set me up. You set all of us up."

"I know how this looks—"

"Explain," Nick cuts in. "Now."

Roger rubs the back of his neck. "Maybe we should—"

"Explain," Mat repeats.

My body goes limp with relief. I'm fired up enough to do this alone, but having Nick and Mat at my side fuels my confidence.

"This collection is . . ."

I expect Roger to say something sentimental—important, valuable, noble.

"Incomplete," he says.

Cold realization washes over me as pieces of the puzzle start clicking into place. Roger doesn't have a soft spot for troubled teens. He has a use for them, and I have a sinking suspicion about why he's brought us here.

Chelsea furrows her brow. "What the hell could be missing?"

"Seven cars," Roger says, with a matter-of-factness that twists my guts into knots. Fuck me. I know I'm right. "And I must have them."

"Better our asses than yours, right?" I quip.

Chelsea gasps. "You can't possibly think that Roger—"

"Wants us to steal those cars for him?" I snort in disgust. "That's exactly his plan."

Any hope that I'm wrong disappears when his expression transforms into something cruel. "It's not like any of this is new to you. You're already criminals."

Son of a freaking bitch. Anger threads its way into my vocal cords, turning my voice into a high-pitched squeak of denial. "Are you a fucking lunatic?"

A web of emotion wraps around me so tight I can't even talk. Tears gather in the corners of my eyes. "Don't you guys see what Roger's doing?" I focus on Mat. "He set us up. All of us."

Chelsea shakes her head. "No, I—"

My patience snaps. "For fuck's sake, Chelsea, look around you!"

Roger claps his hands in some kind of kindergarten class-room management tactic. His voice rises. "Everyone calm down and listen to me."

"So you can keep lying to us?" I square my shoulders. "What could you possibly offer?"

Roger slides his glasses up against the bridge of his nose. "I have a proposal."

6

"A WHAT?" JESUS. NOW I'VE HEARD EVERYTHING.
I fold my arms across my chest. "Fuck you."

Chelsea grabs my wrist and yanks me toward her. "Jules,
stop!"

With my suspicions confirmed, I've speed-shifted from
fear to anger and Chelsea's pathetic attempts at Zen are only
adding fuel.

"Everyone calm down. Come with me," Roger says. He
leads us to the former break room and motions to a small
table. A dusty soda machine hums in the corner. "Sit. Take a
breath."

Not a chance. "I'll stand."

Mat flips around a chair to straddle it while Chelsea saun-
ters over to the soda machine. A Diet Coke *clunk-thunks* into
her palm. She flicks the tab and takes a long swig as she makes

her way over to a chair opposite Roger at the table. Gross. That shit's probably stale.

To my surprise, Nick inches closer. "Relax," he says through the corner of his mouth.

Easier said than done. One look at the RX in the corner and my pulse surges again.

"Is this where you threaten us?" I say, looking at Roger. Ignoring Chelsea's sharp intake of breath, I flare my nostrils and keep going. "Tell us that unless we steal those cars for you, we're back on the streets—or worse?"

I was joking about him being a sociopath before, but now I'm not so sure.

Chelsea taps her fingernails on the table. "Can we just listen to what he has to say before we overreact?"

"Overreact?" I say with a huff. "That's rich." I point at Mat. "You're a hacker, right? That's what you and Chelsea were talking about before with all that wind interference stuff." At his nod, I turn to Chelsea. "And your skill? Something to do with locks . . ."

She shrugs. "I might have broken into a few warehouses."

"Don't be so modest," Mat says. "You could probably win the Olympics of lock picking, *chica*."

Chelsea's eyes widen. "Wait, I could compete?"

Frustration gnaws away at me. A lock picker, a computer hacker, and a booster. Tight team, and I haven't even gotten to Nick. I jab him in the chest. "Let me guess, you're the muscle?"

57

His eyebrows arch. "Car thief," he says. He flicks his lip piercing with his tongue and smirks. "That's right, princess. You and I are the same. Except I don't come with my own street name . . ."

A cold sweat breaks out along the nape of my neck. I squeeze my eyes closed to block Nick's voice, silently begging him to shut up, to just shut the fuck up. But of course he doesn't and before I can interject, the word *Ghost* oozes from his lips like a contagious disease.

Mat grins. "Spooky."

"She's a fucking legend," Nick says. "What is it, Jules, forty cars?"

Again, forty-three, but who's counting?

Mat lets out a low whistle.

"Enough," Roger says. "Now that we've laid our cards on the table—"

I'm mad enough to blow a gasket. "Not all of us."

Roger leans forward and sets his clasped hands on the table. "Further to my proposition. The Trophy Case is missing seven cars. And I need them."

Mat shifts a little in his seat. "So buy them. It's not like you don't have the money."

Roger grimaces. "Unfortunately, these vehicles are not for sale."

Everyone's being so nonchalant, it makes my blood curdle. Don't they all see how fucked we are? Roger is a pillar of the community. A damn saint.

My patience snaps. "What's in it for us?" All eyes land on me and I shrug. I've had enough of the veiled kindness and underlying threats. We're just spinning our wheels here. "What? He's obviously got a plan."

"If you're successful in obtaining—"

"Stealing."

Roger glosses over it. "—all of the cars, then you may consider my home yours for as long as you wish."

"That's very generous of you," Chelsea says.

I shoot her a glare. "Are you kidding me?"

"Well, it is."

Mat silences my response with a look. "Let him finish."

"If you choose to move out, your basic needs—housing, education, et cetera—will be taken care of. Indefinitely." His eyes meet mine. "That includes Emma."

My throat clogs up like I'm guzzling motor oil. No way in hell he's dragging my sister into this.

"I know you're frustrated," Roger says to me.

"Try pissed."

He spreads his thumbs wide in acknowledgment. "Fine. But if you look at it as a business transaction . . ."

Chelsea picks at a piece of lint on her shirt and flicks it onto the floor. "Why not just hire a couple of thugs?"

"I'm afraid that route didn't pan out for me," he says. "And each of you was selected for a particular skill set."

Not to mention the convenient cover of housing a crew of

orphans. I can't hold back a snort of disgust. "Are we supposed to take that as a compliment?" My eyes flick back to the RX and my temper spikes. Good. Anger keeps me on my toes. I get stupid when I go soft. "News flash: Blackmailing us isn't cool. It's sick."

It's also kind of genius.

Roger scans each of our faces. "Do you all feel this way?" After a brief silence, he blows out a deep breath. "I see." He unhooks his fingers and lays his palms flat on the table. "I'm really not a bad man. Of course, you can reject my offer—without consequence."

I scoff. "Funny how you give us the illusion of choice."

The look on his face tells me I'm right. My skin prickles.

"True. If you refuse my proposal, I will simply kill you all and start over."

Roger starts laughing before I can get the gasp out. He slaps his palm against his chest, and chuckles. "I'm sorry. That was in poor taste." He wipes his eyes. "Of course no harm will come to any of you, regardless of your decision."

"But we'll be of no use to you," Mat says.

"When you turn eighteen, you'll be expected to move out, as per normal foster care arrangements."

Right. Except that none of this is normal.

"Once you've considered all of the factors, I'm sure you'll find my proposition intriguing," he says.

"What cars are on the list?" Nick says.

A sly smile tugs on the ends of Roger's mustache. "I'm

afraid that's classified information until you've agreed to the terms." He fixes his gaze on me. "I'm truly looking out for your best interests. Even Emma's. None of us would want anything to happen to little Ems. It's such a cruel world."

My temperature spikes. I lunge forward, fist clenched. "You hurt her and I swear . . ."

Nick grabs my wrist, spins me around. My body slams into his chest. I punch him once, twice, over and over. I can't stop. He wraps his arms tighter around me until my awkward struggle ends in a whimper of defeat.

There's no turning back from this—Roger has dead-ended us.

Nick runs his hand over the back of my head. I bury into him, soaking up the warmth, desperate for a split second of normalcy. Even in this terrifying moment of clarity, there's something about the way Nick holds me that feels so . . . right. I'm not ready to let go.

"We won't let anything happen to Ems."

"Dear God, no." Roger feigns shock. "My apologies if I gave you that impression."

The depth of Roger's scheming astonishes me. I shouldn't be surprised—I knew there was something off about him. But this level of maliciousness? I had no idea. I unwind from Nick's hold and wipe my eyes before turning around. The smug expression on Roger's face makes me want to vomit.

He stands, tucks his chair back under the table, and adjusts his fedora, his vest, straightens his glasses. "Such a delightful little girl."

"So, how would this work?" Chelsea says. "I mean, if we decide to do this, what happens next?"

Roger smiles. "Once you've all made a decision, I'll provide you with the necessary details and tools."

Mat leans back in his chair. "And if not all of us are in?"

"That's not ideal, but I suppose we could come to some sort of arrangement," Roger says. "However, I'd advise each of you to consider my offer carefully—and quickly. I'm not a patient man."

7

IT'S SQUID. MAYBE OCTOPUS. HELL IF I CAN TELL. Either way, it's not going in my mouth. If the stench alone doesn't make me gag, the texture will finish the job.

Nick's lips twist. "It doesn't bite."

I give him the evil side-eye and I push my plate forward. "Yeah, well, me either."

He shoves a forkful of the shit between his lips and makes a scene out of chewing. Up-*crunch*-down-*slurp*-up. Gag. A ball of vomit inches its way up my esophagus. Beside me, Emma pokes at her appetizer with a fork. I form a crooked smile of sympathy. "Not your thing either, huh?"

A flush of red creeps up the side of her neck. She drops her voice. "What is it?"

"Octopus," Roger says. He sits upright and slices off a piece of the meat for himself. My vomit ball swells, almost choking me now. "I would like for you to at least try it, please." My sister screws up her face with disgust. Roger isn't fazed. "It's a delicacy, Emma. Some people say it tastes just like chicken."

Sure, if chicken's made of rubber.

She leans forward and sniffs. "It smells funny."

Which is part of the reason I won't touch it. Fish, the odd shrimp—only if I'm desperate. I draw the line at tentacles. My taste buds are so far from adventurous, they're basically prudes.

Across from me, Chelsea dips a piece of octopus in a cream-colored sauce and stuffs it into her mouth. My breath tastes like bile. She chews-chews-chews for an eternity, swallows, and then opens wide to reveal a black beaded tongue piercing.

Emma is mesmerized.

Yeah, I get it, Chelsea is way cooler than me.

It bugs me, even though Emma's impression of her new foster sister should be the least of my concerns right now. We've got twenty-four hours to consider Roger's proposal and, after spending the day weighing the pros and cons, I'm no closer to a decision.

Roger *tsks* at Chelsea, then points his fork at my sister. "There is nothing wrong with widening your palette, young lady."

Ems and I gave up *widening our palettes* long before we hit the foster system. Even when Mom gave a shit, she was hardly a gourmet. Back then I was ballerina-waiflike thin. Agile and liftable, but pretty much a preteen walking dead. Guess it's not so hard to see how I transformed from ballerina into Ghost, though, since I was basically a skeleton.

Roger stops eating, sets his knife and fork on either side of his plate, and stares at Ems. Waiting. Her eyes flit nervously toward me, then back to the rubbery blob on her plate. Small hives dot behind her ear. "Do I have to?"

"Yes," Roger says. The softness of his tone masks expectation and underlying annoyance. "It is considered rude not to at least try what our chef has prepared."

Screw it.

I'd rather suffer Roger's wrath than watch my sister go into a full-on anxiety attack.

"Ems, you do *not* have to eat that," I say firmly.

"Course she doesn't," Mat says.

He shoves a piece of octopus in his mouth and my stomach lurches. His cheeks puff out and his eyes grow wide and bulgy with an exaggerated expression of mock disgust that sends Ems into a fit of giggles. By the time he swallows—his Adam's apple sliding up and down his throat—there's a piece of the shit on the end of Emma's fork, hovering in front of her lips.

"You can do it, homegirl," he says, encouraging.

Emma glows under the attention. She pinches the bridge of her nose, opens her mouth, and sinks her teeth into a speck of meat about the size of an ant. Even still, my stomach roils.

Emma swallows fast and shudders, her entire body vibrating

65

with disgust. "It does *not* taste like chicken." She sticks out her tongue and waves her hand back and forth with exaggeration. Her theatrics are met with a muted chorus of chuckles.

I hand her a glass of water. "Dramatic much?"

Truth is, it's nice to see her be a little kid again. I know it's partly my fault she's had to grow up so quickly.

"Drama must run in the family," Nick says.

I whip my head around to glare at him. I thought we'd made headway last night at the Trophy Case, but clearly Nick's reverted back to being an asshole. "What the fuck is that supposed to mean?"

"We do not swear at the table," Roger says.

My face explodes with heat. The air is thick, claustrophobic. I'm a volcano set to erupt, but I can't decide which way to shoot the lava—at Roger for pretending he's suddenly Dad of the Year, or Nick for rocketing straight back to the top of the dick-o-meter.

I toss my napkin onto the table and shove my chair back. My stomach rumbles like a turbocharged Mustang, but I've suddenly lost my appetite.

Nick raises one eyebrow. They're too bushy for his face and I'm almost pissed enough to say so.

"Little worked up over octopus, aren't you?" He flashes a wolfish grin before his teeth disappear into another piece of the grayish rubber. I'm tongue-tied with disgust.

"I don't appreciate being bullied into trying something I

know I won't like," I say, fending off a tidal wave of nausea. Damn, the stuff stinks.

"So you haven't tried it?" Nick says. He tugs on his lip ring with his top teeth while I pretend the motion isn't sexy as hell. It's more than the piercing. There's something about the way he challenges me that really revs my engine. Jesus. I probably need a full team of therapists to analyze that shit. "Seems to me you're just passing random judgment."

Smoke billows from my ears like my brain's spun a burnout. He can't be serious. "That's a little like the pot calling the kettle black, don't you think?"

Nick smirks. "Don't you mean white?'

"Uh, maybe we should change the subject," Chelsea says.

"Perfect," I say, shoving away my plate of octopus. "Just. Perfect."

The serving staff files in loaded up with trays of food. I'm sure I'll never get used to it, fancy dinners with real china and a personal waitstaff that tops up my water glass and passes the salt. But as one of them sets a plate of steaming roast beef in front of me, my veins fill with liquid relief. Fuck Nick and his pretention. I'm starving.

Roger tucks a linen napkin into the front of his button-up and lifts his fork and knife. "Did you find some new clothes at the mall, Emma?"

I freeze. The mall?

My sister stabs into a mountain of mashed potatoes that

erupt with butter and stuffs her face. "Sort of. Mr. Grasdal wasn't much help."

Roger takes a sip of red wine. "We don't talk with our mouths full at the table, young lady."

Dinner etiquette. This should be entertaining.

Ems swallows.

"You took the butler to the mall?" Chelsea sounds incredulous. "Next time, I'll go with you."

Emma brightens. "Can we still go in the limousine?"

"I'd rather take that sweet Camaro in the driveway," Mat says.

Roger's spine stiffens.

"It's a Chevelle," I say. "Nineteen-seventy."

"Seventy-one," Nick counters.

I turn my head to look at him. "Close enough. They're basically identical."

"Not quite. The grille's different on the seventy-one."

I roll my eyes. "Well, excuse me, Mr. Car Expert."

A smile plays on his lips. "Just think, I haven't even gotten into the changes under the hood. The improved fuel consumption, faster speed—"

"Go on. I'm mesmerized."

I'm mostly joking, but there is something hot about the way Nick knows cars. Not in a douchey way like Kevin. Scratch that, Kevin faked it. Nick may be a jerk, but he's not trying to be someone he's not. I can respect that.

"All right, cool it you two," Chelsea says. "I don't know

what you're both getting worked up over. It's just a car."

"A sweet car," Mat says under his breath. "How come it's in the driveway and not at—"

Roger cuts him off with a sharp look of warning. "It was my wife's, a gift on our twentieth wedding anniversary."

I trace the gold rim of my fancy dinner plate. "A car like that should be in the garage, at least. Want me to park it for you?"

Roger leans back in his chair. "The garage is off-limits." He pins me with a look that says he knows what I'm thinking. Interesting. I'm always up for a challenge. "It's my one rule. Break it, and there *will* be consequences."

Tough talk. Too bad I'm immune to Roger's thinly veiled threats.

I fold the thick duvet around my sister's body and pat it until she's tucked into a cotton cocoon. She wriggles free and bats away the strands of hair stuck to her forehead. "Jules, you're suffocating me."

"I'm protecting you from the monsters under the bed."

She rolls her eyes. "I'm not six."

No, my little sister is growing up fast. Too fast. I inch my way to the edge of the bed and study her face. Her skin is clear of the hives that alert me to when she's scared or on the verge of an anxiety attack.

"You're feeling okay?"

"I like it here," she says.

The simplicity of her words dig deep. Emma has suffered anxiety since our parents abandoned us. None of our fosters took it seriously, even though they were part of the problem.

Stability.

The doctors tell me that's the cure.

I tap the tip of her button nose. "You just have a crush on Mat."

Her eyes widen. "I do not!" But then her dimples become craters as a slow smile creeps across her face. Something about that grin makes my heart hurt—it's when she most looks like our mother. I hate that her happiness brings out a memory of someone I despise so much.

"Okay," she concedes, "he *is* cute."

"And old."

She burrows deeper under the covers. "Not too old for you."

"I definitely do not have a crush on Mat."

"Because you like Nick."

My breath hitches. "Emma!"

She's obviously off base. Nick is obnoxious and pompous and completely unpredictable. A total dick. His attitude toward me changes so fast I could get whiplash if I let myself dwell on it. Which, of course, I don't.

"He's totally not my type."

She smirks. "You've made questionable choices before."

I want to believe she's only talking about my ex-boyfriends, but there's an edge to her voice that warns of something else. I look away.

Discarded clothes cover her floor like mini landmines. The towels are bunched into the corner next to an empty laundry hamper. I count three empty soda cans and two bags of chips. If I close my eyes, I can almost believe this is a normal family environment.

"You've got everything you want here," I say.

Her voice clogs up. "Not everything."

I'm surprised to see she's almost in tears.

The fissures in my heart spider-web like a cracked windshield in the cold. Emma's crush on Mat, her awe of Chelsea, even hinting of something between me and Nick—they're all symptoms of something much more tangible and raw. A desperate need to belong.

"Julia, you won't go into the garage, right?"

I lick my lips, stalling.

She squeezes my wrist. "Promise me you won't."

Emma's not trying to be mean, but her words are a clear reminder that she somehow knows I'm responsible for us bouncing from one bad foster home to the next.

Stability.

Family.

I want that too.

But how do I tell her this isn't the right place?

I can't. Not without spilling the whole truth. Which leaves

us at a standstill, because I won't let her see that side of me. And so for now, she'll go on believing that this can work. And why wouldn't she? Piece by strategic piece, Roger has given my sister the illusion that we *can* be a family. Dysfunctional as it may be.

What Emma doesn't realize, what she may never know, is that the bastard is in a far better position to tear us apart.

8

CHELSEA STRETCHES ACROSS MY BED ON HER STOMACH, ankles crossed as she thumbs through a magazine. It's not her normal *Vogue*, but something on surveillance with tech gadgets I know nothing about.

"Let's do it."

The rest of us stare at her and she shrugs. "It'll be fun. Unless we get caught, obviously. But we won't."

Fun. The word settles on my tongue like bad breath. I consider launching into a monologue about morality, but let's face it, I'm no poster child, and that's not really what's holding me back.

Mat whistles low. "Lot of expensive chrome in that warehouse. We're not talking Ford Escorts and RX-8s." At my wide-eyed expression, he adds, "With respect, Ghost."

The nickname still makes me squirm. Moving into the

mansion was supposed to exorcise that part of my past. In light of Roger's proposition, a resurrection seems imminent.

My heart flutters with a mix of fear and adrenaline.

"I'm not sure we've got the chops to pull off this kind of boost," Nick says. He stands in the doorway, arms crossed, like fully entering my room will concede some kind of truce. "We're not talking low-hanging fruit here."

At least that's something Nick and I can agree on.

"Beyond my skill set," I admit.

Morals, fear, and fresh starts aside, I don't have a clue what we're up against. A simple Google search of rare and expensive muscle cars coughed up a hundred or more candidates, and I wouldn't bet our odds on any of them.

"Individually, maybe," Chelsea says. She bounces her gaze between me and Nick. "But how many cars could you have stolen if you'd had access to a lock-picker or a hacker?"

At least double.

"We're talking top-level security here," Nick says. "No disrespect, Chelsea, but when it comes down to it, we're all amateurs."

Mat snorts. "Speak for yourself, *cabrón*. I've cracked some tough databases."

Chelsea snaps her fingers. "So that's how you passed algebra."

I slide down onto the floor, using the bed frame as a backrest. My enormous walk-in closet overflows with shit I'll never wear, and the duffel bag stuffed with my basic necessities is still half-packed. No matter what I told Vanessa, Ems and I aren't staying here—this is just a pit stop.

Nick paces like a caged tiger. "I'm out of the life now."

I offer a weak smile. "Me too." Or so I thought.

I'm wavering and that sucks. I can't stop thinking about Emma and how being here, even for this short time, has tempered her anxiety. Roger's proposition means a chance of normal for Ems.

Stability.

I owe her that.

"You've got your sister to think about," Nick says. "Makes sense you'd give it some serious thought. But what's in it for me? I can survive on the streets."

For a brief, startling few seconds, his ice-blue eyes lock on mine and I see it—unease. A small shred of vulnerability.

Tension radiates off him in waves. "There's no way we can pull this off," he says.

"Definitely not without the right tools," Mat says. "I'd need scanners, rerouters, access to a Tor networking site." He acknowledges my blank stare with a grimace. "Sorry. Tor is software that allows me to post anonymously."

"Got it," I say.

"And computers." He pumps his eyebrows. "Two good ones for sure. Maybe three."

Chelsea sits upright on the edge of the bed, setting the magazine on her lap. I crane my neck to look at her as she

75

pulls a pillow to her chest. "So we make a shopping list."

Irritation leaks into my voice. "Not everything gets solved with a Gold Card."

She doesn't take the bait. "I can think of some sweet lock-picking doodads that would come in handy—bump or specially cut keys, a torsion wrench, a few picks—standard tools. Roger will spring for the good stuff." She winks at Nick. "Bet you and Jules could think of some things that would help you bring your A game."

Nick scowls. "I'm never off it." He rubs his hand behind his neck, causing his biceps to inadvertently flex. His muscles tighten and he acts all tough, but there's a hint of resignation in his sigh. "I could probably come up with a few things."

He glances my way for confirmation, but I'm tongue-tied with indecision. I can't believe we're even considering this.

"I'm obviously in the wrong room."

My head snaps to the bedroom door at the sound of Emma's voice. My guts twist. I scramble to my feet. "You're supposed to be asleep. Are we too loud?"

She groans. "Definitely not. It's too *quiet* here."

"I know exactly what you mean," Chelsea says.

Doubtful. Emma is used to drifting off to the sounds of screaming, bickering, and the constant drone of police sirens.

"Music?" Mat says.

"I don't have any songs on my iPod yet," Emma says.

Nick holds up a finger. "Hang tight."

Seconds later, he returns with an iPod and a set of new headphones. He hands them to Emma with a sheepish grin. "Can't guarantee there's anything you'll like on there, but it will cut the silence."

My stomach flips. "Uh . . ."

"No worries, Jules," he says, shoving his hands into his jeans pockets. "It's all age appropriate."

Actually, it's jazz.

I pull out the earbud and hand it to Ems. She snuggles into the blankets and pulls a stuffed bear close to her chest. "Happy, Mommy?"

Embarrassed, I duck my head. "It's my job to check for curses and stuff."

It shouldn't be, but it's the role I've held for the past four years, and I take it seriously.

"You think I've never heard swearing before?"

Of course she has—and not just from our parents and foster parents and probably even me. That doesn't make it right. We're supposed to be taking steps forward, but so far, being at Roger's is like jumping into a time machine. Backward.

She plugs in one earbud and hands me the other. "Listen."

I shift closer. A soulful saxophone solo cuts through the melody of piano and trombone while a sultry female sings about a boy. Her voice tugs on my heartstrings. It's not at all what I'd expect from Nick, but I guess even he can surprise me.

Music soothes the savage beast.

"Bet you could do a solo to this," Ems whispers.

I yank out the earbud. "I'm done with ballet."

Her expression softens. "I meant for me."

The longing in her voice tears me up inside. Without Roger's help—his money—I can't afford to send her to dance lessons. "So much pressure," I murmur, thinking back to aching muscles and swollen feet.

"You did it."

"I quit."

Emma sighs. "Because you had to. I know you loved it."

Loved. Past tense. Dance is tainted now, part of the past I'm desperate to forget. Uncomfortable with the way the mood's shifted, I try to lighten things up. "You don't want to copy me, anyway."

"I want to be you."

Tears spring to my eyes and I swat them away with enough force to cause a bruise. Jesus. I'm an emotional basket case. "Tell me you like it here."

She scrunches up her nose. "I already told you I did. You're not planning something, are you? Because it kind of looked like you guys were planning something."

There's a hint of panic in her tone, a sign I should back off. But I'm about to make one of the biggest decisions of my life. I need to be sure before I cross that line. "Are you sure Roger doesn't scare you?"

Mischief dances in the hazel flecks of her eyes. "Come to

think of it, that vest is kind of terrifying." She shakes her head. "I'm kidding. He's a bit . . . awkward, that's all."

Conniving is a better word choice.

Emma puts her hand on my cheek. "I know it's hard for you to trust. But we can't change the past, Jules. This is the closest we've had to . . . normal."

I'm shocked at how old she sounds as she spits back the words I've heard echoed by our social worker. This should be me comforting her, not the other way around. I pull her hand away and hold it in mine. Her palms fill with sweat.

She yawns. "Thanks for tucking me in, Mom."

A dull ache spreads across my chest and I wonder if when she teases me, it reminds her of the parents she doesn't have. As her eyes close and her breathing slows, I realize she's right—we can't go back.

Emma's future depends on me and I know exactly how to get her everything her heart wants.

Hushed whispers float down the hall. I can make out enough words to know the conversation has shifted from *should we?* to creating a list of the tools we'll need to pull off the job.

Seven cars.

It's one hell of a heist.

Everyone stares at me when I enter the room, as though I've somehow leveraged myself into a leadership position. I'm uncomfortable in the role.

"I'm in," Chelsea says.

Mat gives me a thumbs-up.

I swallow hard and turn to Nick. "You?"

"We're backed into a corner," he says, jaw tense. "We could go to the cops but . . ."

No one would believe us.

I tilt my head back and close my eyes. Swallow the lump of indecision that's stuck at the base of my throat. "I'll do it," I say. There's a murmur of relief. "With conditions." If there's one thing botching my last boost taught me, it's to never go in blind. "First, we need a list of nonnegotiable supplies."

Chelsea tears out a page from the magazine. "Done." She's written our list of "demands" in blue ink next to images of complex technogadgets. "What other conditions?"

I blow out a breath. "Before I commit, we're going to need to see the list of those cars."

"We're in."

Roger looks up from his magazine. "Wonderful."

Disgust ripples down my spine. "If you agree to the conditions. . . ." I wait a beat before continuing. "For starters, we've listed some tools we'll need."

Mat hands over Chelsea's scribbles.

Roger scans the paper, his eyebrow lifting as he nears the end. "You have expensive taste."

"Pocket change for you," Nick says.

Roger doesn't bother acknowledging the comment. "Will there be anything else?"

I hold out my hand. "Yeah, the list of cars."

9

THE LIST IS RIDICULOUS. "WHAT THE HELL IS A MAKO Shark?" I ask.

"It's a concept Corvette," Nick says. "Only two were actually made—sweet as the car looked, it didn't quite meet Chevy's expectations."

"Well, it's a dumb name," I mutter.

Nick's face hovers over my shoulder. "You've got to be shitting me." He points to the third car down—a 1968 ZL1 Camaro. "That's one of the fastest and most collectible muscle cars ever made. We'd never find it in Vegas."

Roger adjusts his glasses. "Reggie Jackson sold the car at an auction for $290,000. The buyer was local."

"Can't be that collectible, then," I say.

Nick's cheek muscle twitches. "Or, the buyer got a steal."

"Jackson's a baseball legend," Mat says. "So it's not like he needed the cash. Might not have known what he had."

"He knew," Nick says. He flicks a finger at the fourth car on the list. "Hardtop or convertible?"

Roger purses his lips. "Convertible."

Nick laughs. "Impossible. They only made two hundred and ninety-six convertible Coronet R/Ts. That's a seriously collectible car."

I raise an eyebrow. "More so than the Camaro?"

Ignoring the question, Nick runs his thumb over another of the cars, a '68 Cosma Ray Corvette. "Jesus, Roger. This is a Barris." He rubs the back of his neck. "*George Barris* worked on this."

"I'm aware."

I nudge a little closer to Nick. "Now I'm impressed."

A goofy look crosses his face. "You know who he is? Man, he did some of the best restoration work in the business." His voice lifts. "He worked on the original Batmobile."

That's one fact I actually knew, but mainly because my former foster dad used to watch Barris's TV show. And okay, I've been known to geek out from time to time.

The thing is, I get cars. The sound. The vibration. There's something about the roar of an engine dropping into gear that makes me feel . . . free. No responsibilities. No guilt. Just me and the machine, whether I'm racing, stealing, or gawking from the sidelines.

My gut tells me Nick can relate.

He sucks in a breath. "These last two are impossible."

An Aston Martin DBS—formerly driven by James Bond—and a 1967 Shelby GT500. In parentheses, Roger has written: "(previously owned by Jim Morrison)." Guess that explains the Doors poster in the games room.

Chelsea nibbles on her fingernail. "Why are they more difficult?"

Solid question. Sin City car theft may be steadily on the rise, but the vehicles on Roger's list are a far cry from Civics and Silverados. None of them are sitting ducks.

Nick runs his hand through his hair. A strand falls over his left eye and I resist the knee-jerk urge to brush it away. "They've both been missing for years," he says.

My mouth goes dry. "And you expect us to find them?"

Roger looks up from his magazine, and my skin prickles. "I'm confident you'll figure it out."

At least someone is.

"You've got at least four Shelbys in the warehouse," Nick says.

"This one's different."

"The Aston Martin doesn't fit," I say, a little rattled by the finality of Roger's tone. "The other six are muscle cars—"

Nick shakes his head. "Almost. Corvettes aren't considered real muscle."

A continuing debate among car enthusiasts.

"Still . . ." I turn to Roger. "The Bondmobile isn't really your type."

"Your opinion isn't necessary."

Nick fidgets. "It would take us *years* to boost the muscle on this list, and that's assuming we can find them all." He snags the paper from my fingers and thrusts it at Mat. "Think you can track them down?"

Mat studies the list. "Given some serious time . . . ?"

Roger snaps the magazine shut and stands, empty tumbler in hand. "You've got seven weeks."

My heart flutters. I'm not sure if I want to faint or laugh. He's got to be joking.

Chelsea's eyes widen. "Seven cars in seven weeks. Is that even—doable? I'd need a lot longer to crack the security systems." She glances at Nick for confirmation. "I mean, they'd have sophisticated locks, right?"

A cold sweat breaks out along the nape of my neck. "You're asking the impossible."

"I certainly hope not. You've agreed to the terms."

My instincts flare. "Why the rush?"

"Because I can."

A dangerous anger curls up my spine. The answer's too simple, too calculated. Roger's hiding something. "You're arrogant. And that's a cop-out."

"Perhaps."

With a stiff nod, Roger leaves the room. My mouth hangs open in shock.

"Asshole," Nick mutters.

Another thing we agree on. "Epic understatement."

I slide next to Mat and reread Roger's list. Maybe we can handle the Super Bee, the Camaro, at least one of the Corvettes. The Coronet is possible with the right tools. But the Aston Martin and the Shelby? Those cars aren't rare—they're mythical.

Mat flops down in Roger's chair and kicks his legs up onto the coffee table. "Guys, we're not seriously considering this, right?" When no one replies, his jaw drops. "You're all *loco*."

Nick grunts.

I lean against the fireplace and tuck my hands behind my back. The stone is warm, somehow soothing. I know what the right thing to do here is—pack our bags, turn Roger in, suffer the consequences.

"There's got to be more to this." I chew on the inside of my cheek. "Maybe we can find some kind of leverage."

Chelsea raises one perfectly plucked brow. "He's already offered eternal life support—what more do we want?"

"Money."

All eyes land on me.

"Look, nothing is guaranteed. Paperwork means squat. Even if we can boost these cars, Roger might still send us out on our asses. And then what?" I revert back to familiar logic, my basic needs. "Cash would provide some stability."

"I don't think that means what you think it means," Mat says.

Chelsea leans forward. "How much are we talking?"

I hadn't gotten there yet. "Ten grand?"

"Not enough." She leans back and folds her arms across her chest. "I need a paid pass into Harvard."

My head spins so fast I get whiplash. "Come again?"

I don't mean to sound skeptical, but I can tell by Chelsea's expression it's too late. She's pissed. "When I left, my parents took everything away from me—my trust fund, my inheritance. I graduate next year with no hope of affording college."

"Scholarship?" Mat says gently.

Chelsea rolls her eyes. "Please. My grades have been on a downward spiral since my parents kicked me out. Even if I nailed senior year, most scholarships don't apply for kids who move out. The only way I'm getting into an Ivy League school is if someone influential buys me in."

"Why would Roger have any say at Harvard?"

Her eyes search my face. "You know nothing about him, do you?" My hackles raise, but before I can eke out a response she shakes her head. "Roger donates a crap ton of money to Harvard every year."

"So if he gets you in, you'll do it?"

Chelsea nods.

Great, but she's only one quarter of the puzzle. "How about you, Mat?"

He shakes his head. "I think I'm out. Now that we've had a look at these cars . . . too much risk, not enough payoff."

My pulse quickens. "We can't do this without you."

Fuck, I'm not even convinced we can *with* him.

He gives me an apologetic half smile. "Someday I'll track down my parents and when I do, I've got to be better than a thug."

"Mat was adopted," Chelsea cuts in. "He's been looking for his biological family ever since he left the jerk that raised him—I'd want answers too."

I can tell by Mat's strained expression that this is important to him. It's a cheap bargaining chip, but I'm borderline desperate. "What if Roger could help?"

Hope creeps across his face. "I'm listening."

"He's got connections. Money. Unlimited resources." The words spill out with increasing speed. "With all of that at your fingertips, you'd be set. Right?"

A tiny spark ignites in his eyes. "Getting into adoption records is tougher than cracking the FBI database. Maybe with Roger's help . . . Couldn't hurt to ask."

Relief drains from every muscle. Two down—one hard-ass left.

"If we're going after a unicorn, Roger has to make it worth my while," Nick says. "I want him to cough up some cash."

"How much?"

"One hundred thousand dollars."

I blow out a breath. "Steep."

Nick snarls. "For a guy like Roger? That's nothing."

"Agreed," Mat says. "I've tapped enough DMV databases to recognize these are pretty high-end boosts. I can't even wrap my head around how we'll get our hands on Morrison's ride."

"No way Roger will go for this," Chelsea says. "It's too complicated."

Maybe. But Roger isn't a simple man. My gut says he'll agree to our terms—because beneath the veiled threats and tough-guy bravado, there's an undercurrent of something else. *Desperation.*

And if there's one thing I know a little about, it's that.

I find Roger in the dining room snacking on oysters and cheese. I don't know what's more disgusting, the smell or watching him stuff one of those slimy things in his mouth. I gag a little out loud.

He cocks his head and motions for me to sit. Jesus, there's even a piece of seafood caught in his mustache. I think I'm about to be sick.

"How do you eat that shit?" I find a chair far enough away that the oyster smell doesn't ignite my gag reflex. "Never mind. I don't want to know. We'd like to further negotiate the terms."

Roger runs his tongue over the top of his teeth. They shimmer like they're coated in oyster oil. Nausea coils in my stomach.

"I wasn't aware I'd left an opening for further negotiations." He cups his hands on the table, fingers interlaced. It's the first time I've noticed the thin gold band around his skeletal ring finger. "However, you have my attention. Continue."

Cocky SOB.

I quickly outline the terms. The money stuff doesn't bother him, but he hesitates when I get to Mat's request. He dabs his lips with a napkin. A red letter M is monogrammed into the linen. "And for yourself?"

"The deal for my sister's lifetime support stands. She wants to dance, so that's got to be a part of it too."

"Done."

My shoulders sag with relief.

"I'm still waiting to hear your terms. What do you want."

Good question, and I've run out of stall tactics. I think about ballet and dance and going back to the hot lights and the stage. My toes curl into the floor until they cramp. "I'm too old for—" Roger's face lights up with interest. I pull back. "Same deal as Nick. I want a hundred grand for the Shelby."

Maybe I don't know how I'll spend it, but it's enough to get me and Ems out of here. Start over. Settle down. Tears prick my eyes and I bat them away before Roger can further prey on my vulnerability.

He folds his napkin into a perfect square and sets it on the table. I hold my breath with anticipation. He pushes his chair back, stands, and extends a hand. "I accept these terms."

My entire body hums and a fuzzy sensation floods my head, making it hard to focus. I should be celebrating my win, but the truth is, I have a sinking feeling I've just sold my soul to the devil.

10

I COVER MY MOUTH TO TRAP THE SNORT OF LAUGHTER. "*What* is on your lip?"

"*Pour quoi?*" Nick twirls one end of his fake mustache. "Does it not give me ze illusion of sophistication?"

I roll my eyes at his botched French accent. "Yeah, porn stars are super sophisticated. Jesus. That thing doesn't even look real."

To be honest, I'm making a bigger joke out of it than necessary, probably to cover up the mash-up of emotions that have been churning my guts since we agreed to take Roger's deal. Maybe it's how Nick copes too. Because after playing dress-up in this costume store for more than an hour, all I've found is a pair of gloves—and Nick's surprising sense of humor. Now that we've stopped sniping at each other, I'm stunned by how smoothly his laugh slides under my skin.

Across the store, Chelsea and my sister use their overflowing shopping carts as bumper cars, and last I checked, Mat was in the suit aisle working his Latino charm on a blond salesgirl.

Being left alone with Nick should put me on edge, but it's like something has shifted between us. He's different. Softer. Like he gets we're all in this together. Or maybe I'm imagining a difference to quell my rising panic. Seven cars. Seven weeks.

We must be fucking nuts.

I try on an absurd pair of heels while Nick thumbs through a rack behind me. The aisles at the back of the store are packed tighter together, making me hyper aware of our closeness. We both turn and end up face-to-face.

Like that's not awkward.

Nick waggles his eyebrows and the left side of his mustache breaks loose, snagging on his lip piercing.

A ridiculous grin splits my face. "Oh my God. I can't even . . ." I stand on tiptoes to adjust the mustache. My balance shifts and I teeter forward, almost falling into Nick. He grabs my elbows to steady me. We're close. Too close. The heat from his breath pulses across my neck.

Suddenly I feel exposed.

"Um . . ."

We both shift a little to the left, which only wedges us closer. I've got nowhere to go but into his chest. His solid. Muscular. Chest. The tips of winged tattoos show through the tight T-shirt that stretches across his broad shoulders.

"Mustache can't look that bad." Startled by his voice, I look up and he winks. "You fell for it—literally."

"Dream on."

I try to push away, but my knees buckle a little. His eyes sweep across my neck, my chest, settle on my lips. My pulse goes from zero to sixty. I swallow hard as he closes the gap between us, the scent of his peppermint breath drawing me in.

"Jules?"

His voice is smooth, like a fine-tuned Camaro. I drink it up. "Yes."

"Yes?"

Jesus, YES! My brain protests with the force of an air raid siren that I should back the hell up. Our lives are too complicated, too unstable. Nick doesn't even like me. But the glint in his eye tells me something different.

A strangled groan escapes my lips. I'm an idiot to think I could be immune to this.

"So, yes to the mustache, then?"

I blink so hard my eyes hurt. "You were asking for an opinion about the fucking mustache?" I punch him in the shoulder and take a step back.

His eyes twinkle with mischief. "What did you think I meant?"

My stomach bottoms out. Fuck. I really am an idiot.

"Guys, is this not the best ha . . . ?" Chelsea's voice trails off. "Oh crap."

93

I spin around so that Nick won't see the disappointment and confusion on my face, and work up a smile for Chelsea. A newsboy cap sits askew atop her red curls. She looks freaking amazing.

"Now that's how you pull off a costume accessory," I say, directing the comment at Nick without turning around. There's an edge to my voice that borders on pissed and I know I'm mad at myself for letting my guard down, even a little.

Chelsea offers a lopsided grin. "Found one for you too."

"Please, no."

She reaches for my hand. "Come *on*."

I let her lead me away, grateful for the out. We find Emma at the front of the store, twirling in front of a mirror with both hands pressed against a hat far too big for her head.

Chelsea leans in. "Sorry if I interrupted something back there."

Just me being stupid.

I shake my head fast. Too fast. And I'm careful not to meet her eyes. "All good."

Emma waves at me in the reflection. "Isn't this hat *purrrrfect*?"

Fitting question, since it looks like it's made of cat fur. I wrinkle my nose. "Looks hairy."

We've explained away this whole excursion under the guise of foster sibling bonding, each taking turns to hang out with Emma while the others power shop for accessories that will help build our alter egos. The disguises will only mask so much. A heist of this magnitude will take more than fancy gadgets and stick-on facial hair.

"Well, I think it's gorgeous," Chelsea drawls. She sidles up next to Emma to model a new wig. She's speed-shifted from fiery redhead to ditzy blonde and the result is a bit jarring.

"Not you at all."

She clucks her tongue into the side of her cheek. "And *that* is why it's perfect. The whole point of dressing up is so you don't look like yourself, right?"

Mat peeks around the corner wearing a pair of oversize white sunglasses, a black hoodie, and baggy jeans. *"Buenas tardes, chicas."*

Good afternoon, indeed.

Emma claps her hand over her mouth. "You look ridiculous."

He lowers the glasses and winks, sending her into a fit of childlike giggles. Moments like this are heady reminders of what's at stake.

Chelsea shoves me into a dressing room. "You need to start trying stuff on, STAT. If anyone needs a disguise, Ghost, it's you."

My expression must register shock, because Chelsea laughs as she pulls the door closed. "I'll be right outside. Holler if you need sizing."

Costume pieces fill the room—fancy dresses and short

skirts that would barely cover my ass, feather boas, pseudo-designer purses, and heels so high my feet scream in protest at the sight of them. Chelsea must think we're boosting cars at a drag show or something, because this certainly isn't standard car theft attire.

"I don't hear movement," she singsongs. "I'll dress you myself if I have to."

Suddenly motivated, I lift one of the boas and wrap it around my neck. Pretend to strike a pose. My pale face glows in the reflection, almost disappearing under the overhead lights. I shift position. "Can't I just throw my hoodie over my head?"

I get that Chelsea wants to do the whole bling-bling thing, but dressing up is for the stage. I gave up the spotlight when I left dance. Now I'm more old school—black sweatshirt, dark jeans, and a reliable pair of shoes with sturdy heels that won't snap if I trip over a damn pothole. I like to call it Hoodlum Chic.

"Relax, Jules." Chelsea tosses another item over the dressing room door. "Try this sexy number on next."

Twenty hot and sweaty minutes later, I end up with a couple of wigs, sunglasses, a pair of heels I'm more likely to use as a weapon, and a black cocktail dress with a V-neck that swoops almost to my belly button. Twice on the way to the cash register I try to put it back, but Chelsea won't let me. "A girl can never have too many little black dresses."

"And yet, I've managed to survive all these years without one."

She rolls her eyes. "You'll thank me someday."

I wouldn't bet on it.

We meet up with Nick and Emma at the front register. He hands the teller fifty bucks and she gives him a small bag. Emma's eyes grow huge when he hands the bag to her.

My eyes bounce between them. Casually I say, "Whatcha got there, Ems?"

She reaches in and pulls out a pair of pink satin slippers. They're not official ballet, but the sentiment couldn't be more real. My insides explode and the ice palace around my heart suffers a warning crack.

"Wow, that's"—my throat constricts—"really thoughtful."

Ems beams. "Right? He's totally a keeper."

My insides blush. Nick quickly glances away and rubs the top of my sister's head with obvious affection. I'm stunned by how fast my pulse picks up speed.

"She kind of hinted about being a dancer," he says, looking a bit sheepish. "And then she picked up those slipper things. Squealed loud enough to wake the dead." He shrugs. "Seemed important to her."

To me, too. Seeing those pers in Emma's hand takes me back to when I started ballet. I was all gangly arms and legs, clumsy as hell. Ms. Griffin guided and molded me through hours of strict discipline and tough love.

My toes inadvertently flex and my calves stretch.

A dull ache moves into my chest.

I miss it—the rhythm, the routine.

"You didn't have to do that," I say.

"If I thought I had to, I wouldn't have."

Emma spots Mat and starts running toward him, waving her new shoes like checkered flags.

Appropriate. Because with this unexpected gesture, Nick has lodged a solid win—with both of us.

Emma straps on a helmet and climbs into the red go-kart at Pole Position Raceway. The number two is painted on the side of the door. Her hands grip the steering wheel with steely determination, eyes ahead.

An overhead whistle blares.

She pumps the gas pedal and shoots forward, narrowly missing the car in front of her.

"Not so fast!" I yell over the music that blares through the indoor speakers.

"It's go-karts," Chelsea says. "Hitting the other drivers is part of the fun."

She's right, but the second Emma rounds the first corner, disappearing from sight, my nerves become elastic thin. When I finally spot her again, the air leaks from my lips like a deflated balloon.

"Kid can drive," Chelsea says. "That's how I learned. My dad took me to the track every weekend until I decided shopping and cheerleading were way more fun than doing circles in a car that tops out at ten miles an hour."

My voice goes quiet. "Why did you do it? I mean . . . you had everything. Why give it up?"

"Attention mostly."

I can't help it. A tidal wave of resentment washes over me. Emma and I never had much, but we would have given it all up for a fraction of the stability Chelsea took for granted.

"That makes me sound like a brat, doesn't it?"

"Yes." My lips press into a firm line as I struggle for composure.

"You don't know my life, Jules." She shakes her head. "Forget it. I don't expect you to understand."

Emma whirls around the track again, calling out my name. I look over and wave. Distracted, Emma crashes into the back end of another car and pitches forward. The seatbelt snaps her back in place.

I spot Nick and Mat weaving their way through the crowded tables, trays loaded up with burgers, fries, and milkshakes. I'm grateful for the distraction. Something tells me Chelsea and I will never see eye-to-eye.

Nick plops one of the trays in front of me. "Double cheese, no pickles, onions, or tomatoes." He pauses. "So basically, just ketchup."

Mat puts his hand to his forehead and scans the track. "Ems still driving?"

"Nothing's getting her away from that car," Chelsea says.

"Not even this chocolate raspberry shake?"

I laugh. "Not even that."

Which is probably a good thing, since we're about to start planning our first boost—the 1970 Dodge Super Bee 426 Hemi Fastback.

"Say that five times fast," Chelsea says.

Mat searches for a picture of the car on his phone and turns the screen so Chelsea and I can take a better look. It's an aggressive beast—long body, short back end. A black stripe wraps around the tail.

Mat zooms in on the logo, a cartoon bumblebee with wheels wearing a helmet and goggles.

"Dodge only made a limited number of this model, less than one hundred," Nick says. "The old Hemi engines weren't known for running cool or getting good mileage."

Chelsea squints at the image with a frown. "It's ugly."

Nick chokes on his milkshake. "Blasphemy." He grabs Mat's phone and starts scrolling through pictures in an attempt to find the car's best angle. Finally, he gives up. "Wait until you see it up close. You'll change your mind."

Mat pulls up a YouTube video of an idling Super Bee. Even over the buzzing background noise of the go-karts, the Dodge engine lets out a roar.

I cringe. "Holy shit, that's loud."

That's the thing about muscle cars. They don't slide out of

garages and warehouses—they charge like a bull, sputtering up a smoke show in their wake. That rumble might as well be a catcall to the cops.

Nick bites into his burger. Cheese gushes out the side and splats onto the tray. "Let's call this one Janice."

Chelsea tilts her head. "Excuse me? We're naming the cars?"

"It's code," I say. "That way, if we're discussing them, no one listening on the waves knows what we're talking about."

"Okaayyy." She still looks skeptical. "Do they need to be girl names?"

"Traditionally," Mat says. "And these *are* muscle cars. . . ." Chelsea and I shoot him twin glares. He holds up his hand. "All right, all right. *Lo siento.* I'm cool to switch it up. Nick?"

"That would be the safest," he says.

Chelsea taps her bottom lip. "This looks like a Jack to me."

"Jack?" I open the notes application in my cell phone and type the name next to the Super Bee. "Good. How about the Mako Shark?"

"José."

Chelsea arches an eyebrow at Mat. "Jack and José? Sounds like the start to a very good party."

Nick lifts his milkshake and tilts the cup so the straw points at me. Pink ice cream oozes down the side. "The Camaro has to be Reggie."

After the previous owner, of course. I type it in.

101

A high-pitched squeal from the track pulls my focus. Emma's hands strangle the steering wheel as it goes back and forth, trying to wriggle her way out of a cramped corner. The determination on her face is scary—and familiar.

"She's like a mini you," Nick says.

My hackles raise. "Don't you ever fucking say that."

The last thing I want is Emma following in *my* footsteps.

Nick's eyes go wide before it seems to sink in, and he puts his hand over my wrist. "Shit, Jules. I meant it as a compliment."

I turn back to the list, embarrassed at my outburst. "All good," I mumble.

"Okay then," Chelsea says, always good at shifting moods. "Let's go with Adam for the Coronet. Sexy name for a sexy car."

"You may want to revisit that," Mat says. He Google searches an image and flips the screen around to show us. Chelsea scowls. "Gross."

"Yeah, it's pretty much the ugly duckling of the muscle car world," Nick says. "They tried to pretty it up by making it available in all kinds of colors—Sublime, Banana, Hemi-Orange . . ."

"Please, God, tell me Roger wants Banana," Mat says.

I shake my head. "Plum Crazy Purple."

He rolls his eyes. "Figures. The guy's nuts."

"Moving on to the Cosma Ray," I say, before Chelsea can ask to rename the Coronet now that she realizes it's not worthy of her rock star crush's namesake. "It's one of Barris's. How about George?"

Mat gives me a thumbs-up. "Nice one."

"James for the Aston Martin," Nick says. "As in James . . . Bond."

"Someone woke up on the right side of the bed," Chelsea says, nudging Nick's shoulder.

A heaviness settles in my chest as I stare at the last car on the list—the 1967 Shelby GT500, previously owned by Jim Morrison, lead singer of The Doors. Naming the car is one thing, that's the easy part—but it means nothing if we can't track it down.

"The obvious choice is Jim," I say.

Chelsea's eyes light up. "Jack, José, Jim—talk about a few good men!"

"According to the legend, Morrison didn't even like the car," Nick says. "It was a gift from his record label. There's a couple of versions of the story, but the gist of it is that he crashed the Shelby on the way to a gig. Instead of calling the cops, he hitched a cab ride to his show. A couple of hours later he came back for the car—gonzo. No one's seen it since."

The reality of the situation sets in. "Guys, there's no way we can pull this off."

Mat finishes off his shake and tosses the cup into a garbage can. "You're underestimating my mad tracking skills, Jules."

I muster an apologetic smile but doubt lingers in the pit of my stomach. The car's been MIA for more than two decades—and we've got seven weeks to track it down. There is nothing good about those odds.

"Since that's the most important car, I vote for a female name," Chelsea says.

Nick and I exchange knowing glances before simultaneously blurting out, "Eleanor."

It's the name of the famous Shelby from the movie *Gone In 60 Seconds*. It shouldn't surprise me that Nick and I would be in sync, but it kind of does.

He smiles. It's a beautiful smile. The kind that burrows its way under my skin and sucker-punches me right in the chest.

Mat crumples his empty burger wrapper into a ball and fires it at the garbage can. It circles the rim and plops in.

"Luck," Nick quips.

"Skill, *cabrón*."

He grabs a laptop from his messenger bag and flips open the screen.

Chelsea shuffles closer to him. "Whatcha doin'?"

His fingers fly across the keyboard. "Research. This place is close enough to the Strip that I can log into the public Wi-Fi. It's one of the few spots around with a fiber connection that gives me enough gigabyte speed to . . ."

He glances up, notices that we're staring at him with confusion, and chuckles. "Forget it. All you need to know is that I'm tracking down our first target."

Emma's voice carries over the racetrack. "Jules! Nick! Come race with me."

"Not a chance," I call back.

"Afraid you'll lose?" Nick taunts. His eyes get that mischievous glint that causes my stomach to flutter.

"Whoa," Chelsea says, joining in on the teasing. "You're not going to take that, are you?"

"Jesus, Jules, you look scared," Mat adds. "You're as white as a gh—"

"For fuck's sake, you guys." I'm trying hard not to laugh. "Enough with the stupid ghost cracks."

Nick shrugs. "Sorry, Jules. You're just so . . . transparent."

I shove my tray of untouched food aside and stand. "You prepared to put a wager on this challenge, hotshot?"

"Race you to the starting line." Nick grins, then darts away.

I take off after him, pushing my way through the crowd of people gathered around the entrance. People file out from their go-karts. I catch sight of Emma and wave her over.

Her face is flushed.

"Is Nick coming too?"

I glance over to find him already strapped into the number three car. Emma reclaims the two. Across the track, I find the empty number one and jump inside. Fasten the helmet.

A jolt from behind nudges the car forward.

"You're too late, Barker," I say, without even looking back at Nick. An unfamiliar warmth unfurls inside me, and a smile creeps into the corners of my mouth—I'm surprised at how easy, how comfortable this all is. "See the number on this car? Read it and weep, my friend."

He idles up next to me and winks. "Hey, Ghost . . . watch me disappear."

11

A GIANT FLAT-SCREEN LOWERS FROM THE CEILING IN the games room. Nick hits the lights while an oversize picture of a blue and black Super Bee rocks into focus. I refer to the list on my phone: This is Jack.

Chelsea screws up her face. No question she'd be happier stealing Rolls Royces and Audis—which is just another reminder she's out of her element. All the gadgets in the world can't net us those high-end rides.

Mat grabs a cue from the rack next to the pool table and uses it like a pointer stick, tapping the screen. "Ladies, meet Jack." Using a remote clicker, he flicks through a series of photographs while providing voice-over commentary in a low, game-show-host tone. "True, he's not the most handsome guy on the lot, but he makes up for it in power and speed."

Nick clears his throat. "Not compared to today's hot rods,

but he can still push zero to sixty in just over five seconds—with the right driver."

Our eyes lock in silent challenge.

"It's a four speed," I say. "Manual transmission." Nick lifts an eyebrow and I shrug, feigning nonchalance. Truth is, I've done some of my own research. "I know how to work a stick."

Mat shakes his hand. "Aychiwawa." Turning back to the screen, he points to the front of the car. "This beauty right here is called a looped bumper—often referred to as the car's bumble bee wings."

"Aw, now you're just showing off," Chelsea says. Mat ducks to avoid a piece of popcorn she lobs at him. "Okay, I'm sold on Jack's profile pic. Tell me how to get this stud muffin home."

My neck tightens and I roll it from side to side.

Mat clicks through to the next picture. "Well, you're in luck because your guy is here"—he nudges his chin toward an enlarged image of a modest clay house with a well-manicured front yard—"at the home of Grant Danvers, an entrepreneur by day, showgirl ogler by night."

Chelsea's mouth gapes. "You found that out by logging into the DMV?"

"This is the age of social media, *chica*," he says. "Instagram, Snapchat, Twitter—Danvers is fully connected."

To emphasize the point, he forwards to a screenshot of a Facebook profile and a recent status update.

"'Show me the titties,'" I read aloud. "Classy."

Chelsea grunts. "God. He's not even good-looking."

"Where's this loser live?" Nick says.

"East Flamingo Road." Mat splits the screen—a map of Vegas on one side, the Danvers house on the other. "He keeps the car in the driveway—which, as you can see, is surrounded by some serious fencing."

Thick, yes, but not impenetrable.

"Unfortunately," Mat says, side-eyeing Chelsea, "I couldn't zoom in close enough to figure out the lock system on the gate."

I chew on my lower lip. "Nick and I can focus on that when we scout the car."

Chelsea hops off her stool and stoops to grab a six-pack of Coke from the mini-fridge. "Can we talk about getting diet soda down here?"

Nick rolls his eyes. "Tell it to Sugar Daddy Roger."

She scowls at him, then hands each of us a can before wiggling back onto her seat. "I don't get what we're waiting for. Scouting or whatever. Let's just go get it."

I crack open the Coke and take a long swig. The bubbles tickle my esophagus. "Too risky." I wipe the corner of my lip with the heel of my hand. "We need to establish Danvers's routine—we already know he frequents the Strip. How often?"

Mat scrolls through his cell phone. "According to Twitter, three nights a week."

"Gross," Chelsea says.

"We also don't know if the car runs," Nick adds.

I raise my soda in mock toast. "That too." After a pause, I add, "Or whether it can be hot-wired."

Chelsea swivels toward me. "Can't they all?"

"Most of the older cars, yes," I say carefully. "Unless it's been modified or the security's upgraded. Most people who have a true appreciation for hot rods tend not to mess too much with them, though."

On cue, Mat clicks back to the first image of the car and enlarges the frame. "Paint looks original."

Clearly I'm not the only one who's done some research.

"Assuming the interior's the same, we're golden," Nick says.

"A quick trip through Danvers's enlightening Instagram feed tells me he's more interested in the ladies than Jack." Mat grins. "I'll spare you the photographic proof."

"Why hold back now?" Nick says, winking.

I deflect a pang of misguided jealousy and blow out a breath to refocus. Lots of factors, limited time. "Flamingo Road is just off the Strip, right?"

"It's a long street." Nick moves closer to the map. "East runs right between the Bellagio and Caesars Palace."

I gather my hair in a ponytail and curl it up into an easy bun. The motion draws Nick's attention and suddenly I'm aware of his eyes on my exposed neck. My voice catches a little. "That explains the extra security."

The streets on either side of Las Vegas Boulevard (famously

known as the Strip) can be rough—littered with pawn shops, tattoo parlors, twenty-four-hour wedding chapels, and run-down motels. Not to mention drunks, tweakers, and drunk tweakers.

I glance over at Nick. "You up for a drive?"

He chugs the rest of his drink and shrugs into his leather jacket. "Can't think of a better way to spend a hot Tuesday night."

Nick's motorcycle might be on its last wheels. The rear fender's bent, the chrome polish is scratched, and the body is so chipped, the black finish looks marbled under the floodlights in front of Roger's house. A small patch of oil marks the pavement beneath the engine.

He fastens his helmet and shifts forward in the seat. The leather jacket tightens across his shoulders and back.

Heat flushes up the side of my neck. "Bike needs some work," I say, faking indifference. Truth is, I'm terrified of anything on two wheels. I don't even know the last time I rode a bicycle. Not like I'd admit that to Nick. Or anyone. In my experience, copping to any kind of vulnerability just makes you weak. "No car we can borrow?"

His expression darkens. "Someone stole mine, remember?"

Right. Vicki.

He cranks the ignition key. There's a soft tick, but the engine doesn't turn over. He tenses. Tries again. The motor sputters and then peters out.

"Maybe we could take one of Roger's?"

Nick smirks. "Sure, let's borrow the RX."

Low blow, but the point drives home.

Nick reaches under the gas tank and tugs out a couple of wires. He twists them together in a motion that is all too familiar. This time when he turns the key, the engine *click-click-clicks* and then roars to life. "Huh. Guess we take the bike after all," he says.

The scent of gasoline and exhaust curls under my nose. I can't help it—my stomach flutters. The sound, the smell—they're a damn turn-on, heightened by Nick's hot-guy-bad-boy vibe. Jesus. I need to give my head a shake.

His gaze flickers across my face with impatience. "You plan on running alongside, or you getting on?"

My vocal cords jam up. "On . . . ?"

"The bike." When I hesitate, he moans. "Aw, shit. Don't tell me you're a motorcycle virgin?"

I bristle. "So what if I am?"

He grabs the spare helmet hanging off the handlebar, wedges it onto my head, and fastens the chin strap. A smile plays on his lips. The second his skin touches mine, the fuel intake to my brain burns real low. His scent is a musky mix of engine oil and exhaust. I take in an illicit breath.

"Get on," he says.

The bike rides double but there's no backrest, so I climb on and snake my arms under his jacket and around his waist.

I slide back as far as I can, but my thighs still rub against the back of his. The bike purrs beneath us.

"Listen up," he says, all serious. "When I lean, you lean with me. That's important." A fist of fear punches me in the gut. "Riding is a balancing act, so you need to move *with* the bike."

Which sucks, because all of a sudden I've developed a serious case of mock rigor mortis.

Nick knocks the kickstand out with his foot. The bike jolts. I hang on with the force of a vise-grip.

"Relax," he says. "I won't bite—this time."

I gnash my teeth and hang on, terrified.

He twists the throttle. The bike lurches forward. I collide into him and nervous sweat fills my palms. *Breathe.*

I've street-raced in the back alleys, speed-shifted from second to fourth, and cornered thirty miles an hour over the posted limit. I once gunned down the highway at a '78 Firebird's ungoverned top speed. But this? This scares the shit out of me.

Nick pulls onto the freeway. Wind whips through my hair as the sprawling mansions alongside the road pass in a blur. Adrenaline hammers my bloodstream, morphing anxiety into thrill.

Nick zips through traffic and we lean left. Right. Our movements are synchronized like ballet dancers who've partnered their whole lives. My limbs turn lucid, the grip around his waist slack. The situation hovers between dangerous and deadly, but somehow I feel *safe*. Even as the dotted lines on the hot asphalt become one continuous streak of white.

In the distance, the tall hotels glimmer and thousands of neon lights line the Strip. Nick takes a sharp corner and the bike wobbles. He gets back control, but not before I scream.

He chuckles so hard his body shakes.

At the corner of Las Vegas Boulevard and Flamingo Road, Nick takes a right and throttles down. My thighs tremble, pulsing with the vibrations from the bike's steady hum. He pulls up to a curb and cuts the engine.

My heart races like we're still going fast.

I'm desperate for Nick to say something, to tell me I did good, or that he's impressed. Anything. Instead, he nudges his chin toward a house across the street. "That's Danvers's place. Time to get to work."

I zoom up on the front of the bungalow, adjusting the telephoto lens on the camera for maximum range. Then close in on Jack.

The Vegas nightlife clamors in the background, punctuated by the throaty growl of a few passing motorcycles and muscle cars. That bodes well. If we can get through the security gate, the Super Bee's "bumble rumble" will just . . . blend in.

"The zoom isn't much good in this light," I say. "We need to get closer."

Dusk settles over Sin City, darkening the sky. The towering pillar of the eleven-hundred-foot-tall Stratosphere hotel peers over the horizon. On the other end of the Strip, the Luxor pyramid light beam extends into the brilliant sunset.

We slide off the bike in silence, gather our things. Nick tucks his hands into his pockets and looks left, right, left again. I half-run to catch up to his long stride as he crosses the street. The designer camera bag slaps against my hip. He moves with purpose, tension. I can't hold back. "Is this your gearing-up-for-a-boost face or are you just in another mood?"

"Forget it."

I stop in the middle of the sidewalk. "Look, I get you don't like me but—"

Nick turns around. "I never said that."

"Your silence speaks volumes." I hitch the camera strap farther up my shoulder and start walking again. "But we're stuck together—for at least the next seven weeks—and I can't keep doing this hate-me-like-me-tolerate-me-despise-me bullshit. I've got enough to worry about without adding your moods to the mix."

He shoves his hands in his pocket. "I just hate this area."

Finally. "The Strip?"

He nods.

"Because of the gambling?"

More than two hundred thousand slot machines churn twenty-four hours a day—and it's not enough to accommodate

115

the forty-some million annual visitors. Just five percent of them say they come here to gamble—eighty-seven percent leave with only the shirts on their back. Probably says a lot about willpower.

Nick's face flickers with annoyance.

I let out an exasperated sigh. "Come on. Give me something here."

He stops in the middle of the sidewalk. "Fine. You want my story? It's really short—a damn cliché. My old man lost it all on the slots—our house, the business. Even my fucking car."

I blink. "I thought someone stole Vicki."

The second the words are out I want to reel them back in. After weeks of waiting for him to open up, I ask about his car. Jesus. I'm an ass.

He stares at me a little too long. "Dad bought me that car for my thirteenth birthday—a '69 Boss. Just a skeleton. Candy Apple Red."

"Sweet car."

Few Mustangs make my radar—there's one on every Vegas street corner—but the Boss nets good coin on the black market. "I stole one like that before—"

He cuts me off. "Dad knew that car meant everything to me. I spent hours in the shop trying to piece her back together. Didn't take long before I ran out of cash."

"You started boosting for parts?"

The muscle in the side of his cheek pulses. "No. To pay off my dad's gambling debts and take care of my little brother."

My mouth forms a soft *oh*.

His hands ball into fists at his side. "Dad sold my car anyway."

"That's fucked up," I whisper.

"I tried to get her back. Spent two months doing basic recon." He chuckles without humor. "Had big plans to pick up my brother and get us both out of this shithole city."

My stomach sinks. "And that's when someone took her. Ouch."

Nick grabs the back of his neck. "Funny. I have a few other choice words for the person who pulled off that boost."

Holding a grudge takes effort—even when you don't even know who to be mad at. No wonder Nick has a giant chip on his shoulder.

His eyes soften under the orange and yellow neon lights from the nearby hotel and gambling hall. A warm glow partially covers his face, shading in the dark circles under his eyes. He looks tired. Pained.

I reach for his arm. "Where is your brother now?"

He winces, and I can't tell if it's from my touch or the question. "In the system, somewhere in Nevada—somewhere far from Vegas."

"You don't know?"

He yanks his arm away and scowls. "Keeping together wasn't an option for us," he says. "First time I had a run-in with the law, my foster parents kicked me out. They agreed to keep Chase if I left quietly and didn't turn them in to the state for collecting money for me. Chase was doing good—going to school, staying out of trouble." He kicks at a loose pebble on the pavement. "They'd probably still be getting checks from the government if Roger hadn't picked me up."

My thoughts turn to Emma. "You didn't ask Roger if Chase could move in?"

"And uproot him again? Not a chance. Roger was just supposed to be a temporary fix, anyway," he says. "A place to stay until the heat died off."

"You get caught midgrab?"

It's almost eerie how parallel our stories have become and I wonder if it's enough to finally ease the tension between us. My gut tells me there's more to this.

"A couple of months ago I tracked Vicki down—again. Started plotting a boost." He lowers his chin. "But I also took a couple of jobs that went bad. Really bad. Roger picked me up before social services could get involved. If they'd found out about Chase . . ."

We pause at the house next to Danvers's and Nick glances over his shoulder. Light traffic flows back and forth. "Roger fixed it so Chase was safe, and got me away from Riley."

"Is that your dad's name?"

"My dad's a useless SOB, but he's not dangerous. At least not to anyone other than his bank account. He'd have pawned his dentures if it wasn't illegal," he says. "Riley's my old boss. Runs a ring of car thieves on the south side."

The name twigs a vague memory.

"After each boost I kept saying, *This is it, Barker, you're going legit after this,* but it's never as simple as that." Holy hell, can I relate. "Once you enter the land of the illegal, someone always owns you. That was Riley, for me."

I pull the loose ends of my hair back and roll them under my fingers. "Is Riley the reason you knew about me?"

Nick flinches. "I keep in touch with a few of the guys from his crew—they heard you got pinched." He clears his throat. "Then you strutted in with that white hair . . ."

I'm grateful it's dark enough that he can't see my blush. "So you've got something against my hair? Or my rep?"

Nick stiffens. "Much as I've enjoyed this walk down memory lane, we've got shit to do. Let's get what we came for and get out of here."

It should be enough that I've peeled away another layer of Nick's body armor, but disappointment clouds the victory. I focus on the car, our mission.

Mat's pictures of the Super Bee don't do Jack justice. Chelsea may not be impressed, but I'd take him home in a heartbeat. Polished chrome, freshly waxed paint—superficial restoration, if any at all. I note the clean tires. "Doesn't look like Danvers drives it much."

"He wouldn't in this heat," Nick says. "Those old fuel pumps can't hack these temperatures. The gas gets so hot it can boil and the car surges from fuel starvation. Not exactly a show stopper."

119

"It's amazing what your brain retains," I say with a shy smile.

"I'm more than just a pretty face, you know."

He takes my hand, and I stare at our interlocked fingers as sweat beads between my shoulder blades. I know it's just part of the charade—a young couple out for a walk—but my insides twist.

Nick mistakes the tremble of my hand for nerves. "Relax, doll. We're just out taking some pictures. Nothing illegal in that."

Yet.

I flick on my Bluetooth and with a free hand, adjust the mic. Mat's voice crackles through the line. "*Buenas noches*, kiddos. What's happening?"

"Just getting acquainted with Jack," I say. "Dude's got game."

"No friends?"

He means Danvers. My eyes scan the house windows—curtains closed, lights out. *Show me the titties,* I remember. "Nah, Jack's buddies dipped."

Nick slips a small digital camera from the front pocket of his leather jacket and tucks it into his palm. The gadget looks like a regular point and shoot, but Mat says the macro lens will zoom in on the finer details Chelsea needs to figure out the locking device.

Nick drops my hand and starts snapping pics while Mat

fires off a list of required angles and a few bonus shots that include random images of the property.

"There's a sign in his front window," I say. "Think it's a security company."

Mat chuckles. "It's just for show. I hacked into their client list. The guy hasn't paid his bill in over a year, so they cut him off."

Excellent.

Nick slides the camera back into his pocket and does up the zipper. Gives me the nod, as if to say, *We're good to go.*

Taking the cue, I speak into the Bluetooth. "All done here. We'll just say bye to Jack and—"

Nick spins me into his arms. He pulls me against chest and whispers low in my ear. "Police." His heart thumps. Or maybe it's mine—ours. I'm so jacked up, it's hard to tell.

Headlights creep toward us in slow motion.

One of Nick's hands moves to my waist, the other to the back of my neck. He tilts my head up and our eyes connect. I shift my gaze to his lips.

Everything else fades into the background.

My head lifts toward his and he answers with a downward tilt toward mine. My eyes close. His breath is hot. I stand on tiptoes, closing the distance between us. Fuck it. I don't care if it's fake, I'm kissing him.

Our lips brush—

"Jules."

His voice is a sharp whisper.

Shhhh. No talking.

"Jules?"

My eyes open. I blink, disoriented and confused. A flush of embarrassment crawls up my neck.

A smile plays in the corner of Nick's mouth. He jerks his head back. "They're gone. Let's roll."

12

The List
Jack—1970 Dodge Super Bee 426
José—1965 Corvette Mako Shark II
Reggie—1968 Chevy ZL1 Camaro
Adam—1970 Dodge Hemi Coronet R/T
George—1968 Corvette Cosma Ray
James—1964 Aston Martin DBS
Eleanor—1967 Mustang Shelby GT500

CHELSEA'S VIOLET WIG GLOWS LAVENDER UNDER THE dim streetlight. She tugs her hoodie up and pulls three small metal objects from the back pocket of her severely baggy jeans. For the first time since we met, I see a bit of the street kid behind the glamour—even if it's just a front.

She hands me something that looks like an Allen key, and

clenches another item between her lips as her hands wrap around the lock.

"Where'd you learn how to do this?"

"I'm self-taught." Chelsea taps the side of her head. "It's just problem solving. I look at a lock the way you probably look at a car—you study it, assess it, figure out how to beat it."

"Or you Google search it," I quip. "Seriously though—you're good."

She grins. "But not great. I still got caught." Her fingers work on the lock. "Check this: There I am, a pick between my teeth and a nail file in my hand, and suddenly . . . cops everywhere. You'd think I was pulling an *Oceans Eleven* the way they swarmed on that warehouse."

"Must have been some decent shit inside."

"Beats me. I never got that far." She snorts. "But, girl, the lock system was *suhweet*. I was so hyped up, I didn't think about things like security cameras." Her cheeks flush. "Rookie move, I know."

"No judgment here," I say, throwing my hands up. "Questionable judgment landed me in cuffs too."

"It's for the best," she mumbles.

My skin bristles. "How can you say that? I get that your parents weren't perfect, but don't you miss them?" Ems and I struck out with ours, and my heart sometimes aches with the loss of what should have been. "Unless I'm missing something, they didn't beat or abandon you. You'd rather live in foster care?"

"Maybe the system isn't so bad."

I huff with disbelief. "We've clearly not hung out in the same foster circles."

She looks sheepish and I get the sense there's more to her story than she's letting on, but I'm too riled up to ask.

"Fourth and counting," I say, holding up a hand. "First up, the Joneses—we couldn't keep up with them, or their stupid rules. Round two, old Mrs. Potts and her creepy Hansel and Gretel cabin. The Millers were the worst though."

She runs her tongue along her bottom lip. "We're not as different as you think."

"You can't think we're the same?"

She shrugs. "I'm just saying, we've all given up a lot. We do what we have to, to survive."

The simplicity of her words sets me on edge. Ems and I didn't leave our parents. They left us. We didn't have a choice. But Chelsea wouldn't get that—technically, she's not a throwaway. "If you want to walk a mile in my shoes, you'll need to lose those pretentious heels."

Her eyes spark and I can tell she's pissed. Okay, maybe I'm acting out, but I can't help it. This hits too close to home.

"Keep an eye out," she says.

I press my back against the fence so I've got a clear view of the street. It's two in the morning and Danvers has been home for three hours. At one, he peered out his front window, flicked off the lights. That's the last we've seen of him.

"Fuck." Chelsea spits the small tool into her palm and shakes her head. "Stupid piece of shit—"

I blink in shock. She went from supermodel to truck driver in less than two seconds. Maybe she's madder than I realized.

"Wrong equipment?" I cut in, nervous.

She tilts her head back. "Please." Then gets back to work. "I broke a fucking nail."

The tension between us lightens. "Aw, Muffin."

Her middle finger shoots up, giving me a close-up of her torn nail. It's painted blue and black, the same color as the Super Bee.

After a series of soft clinks and a string of muttered curses, the lock disengages with a loud *clunk*. Chelsea freezes. My eyes flit from the street to the house to the yard and back. At my all clear, she lifts the lock off the gate and tucks it into the front pocket of her hoodie.

"You're up."

And like an eclipse, Chelsea slips into the shadows as Nick appears under the light. I'm jittery and the pressure on my chest is torturous, but he puts a steadying hand on my shoulder and my nerves settle. "Ready?"

I shake my hands, bounce a little on my feet to loosen up. My arms stretch upward. I twist my hips. Unfurl my fingers. Lean deep.

Nick flicks his tongue across his lip piercing. "Interesting ritual."

"What? You don't have some kind of routine?"

He winks. "Sure. I just like a little privacy."

Shit. I can't believe he just made me blush.

The gate creaks under the weight of our hands. We pause, listen. Keep moving forward. It's not just Danvers I'm worried about. He lives on a corner lot, and even though the surrounding homes are dark and still, my senses are on high alert. I don't like surprises.

Surprise!—the neighbor dog needs to take a piss.

Surprise!—nosy Nettie next door has insomnia.

Mat's voice crackles through the Bluetooth. "Clear on our end."

"Copy that," I say.

We stoop low and slink toward the Super Bee. Nick caresses the front bumper as I dip beside the driver's-side door. A countdown begins in the back of my head. *Sixty seconds.* That's how long it should take to pull off this boost.

I pull on the handle and the car door clicks open. Nick and I stare at each other through the windows in surprise. Holy shit, it's not even locked.

I wedge the door open and slide onto the bench seat. The vinyl is cool against my thighs. Nick pops open the passenger door and stands guard. I clench a small flashlight between my teeth and duck my head under the steering wheel, looking for the wires.

Forty-one, Mississippi.

My fingers find the opening under the dash and fumble around. Something grazes my thumb, but it's not what I'm looking for. *Thirty, Mississippi.* The fluttering in my stomach picks up speed.

Focus.

Nick leans down and pops his head through the passenger door. I'm sure the same countdown is running through his mind. "You got this?"

My hands shake. The flashlight beam hovers over the ignition.

Twenty, Mississippi.

There's not enough time to hot-wire this car. I dig around in the front of my hoodie and pull out a screwdriver. Nick and I exchange a look before he nods. It's our only option. I jam the Phillips into the ignition and twist.

The car sputters to life. I pump the gas.

Adrenaline surges through me.

Nick slides into the car and pulls the door closed, his face flush. "Keep the fuel going," he says. "More gas."

In the rearview, a plume of smoke floats out the back end. I scan the dash—half a tank, less than twenty thousand miles on the tack. Jesus, this car's hardly been driven.

Ten, Mississippi.

We're almost home free.

Mat's voice blasts into the Bluetooth. "Lights on, far end of the house. I repeat, lights on."

I turn to Nick, wild-eyed. "Danvers is awake."

"Let's go."

I slam the car into reverse and step on the gas. Jack jerks, sputters, and threatens to stall out. Fuck. I throw it into neutral.

Nick's voice rises a full octave. "You have to engage the clutch!"

No shit. His words jumble around in my brain. I try again, but the gear sticks. I can't get it into reverse. My head pounds as I'm reeled back in time. Kevin. The RX-8. No . . .

I manhandle the gearshift.

Hit the gas.

The car lurches forward and my heart rams into my rib cage. Nick's head slams into the dash.

"Fuck, Jules, I thought you knew how to drive a stick."

I'm scared, but more than that I'm pissed. My voice trembles. "Lay off. I'm not used to the clutch." *This* clutch. The car's vintage, and every stick is different. Nick knows that.

He slides closer. "I'll drive."

I look up and see headlights in my rearview just as Chelsea's panic-stricken voice blasts through my earpiece. "Cops, you guys. Cops!"

I'm paralyzed, drowning in déjà vu.

Nick smacks the top of the dashboard and I jolt hard enough to make my neck snap. "Make a decision, Jules."

The smart thing would be to let Nick drive, but my pride overpowers logic. I square my shoulders, ram the gearshift back, and stomp on the gas. The engine roars. Tires spin. A cloud of exhaust billows out the back end and the scent of burned rubber fills the air.

Nick slaps the dashboard again, once, twice. "Reverse!" he shouts.

The ghost of Kevin mocks me.

Fuck him.

Fuck Nick.

I dig my heel into the clutch, quick-shift down, up, and to the left. The gear pops into place.

A siren wails in the distance.

Nick loses his shit. "The gas, Jules!"

The car bolts backward. I crank the wheel and hit the break, spinning us into a one-eighty so I'm facing forward. Nick grips the door handle so tight the hair on his knuckles stands at attention. "Go, Jules! Go!"

My foot hits the gas pedal like it's weighted down with bricks, and the car bucks through the gate and onto the road so fast I'm sure we'll catch air. I yank the steering wheel left. The tires squeal against the asphalt. In the rearview, I catch sight of Danvers in his boxers running from his front door. His fists shake like some kind of cartoon character.

I shift to third and take a hard right. Sirens grow louder, but I can't tell from where. Nick twists around in his seat.

"Two cars." His teeth gnash against his lip piercing. "Maybe three blocks back, gaining fast."

My stomach sinks when I realize I'm leading us into another high-speed chase. A series of shimmering faces move across the windshield—Vanessa, her mouth turned down in disappointment; my sister, her eyes brimming with confusion and tears; Kevin, his lips curled up in an I-told-you-so smirk.

Nick pulls out his cell and puts it on speaker. "Mat, we need a route out of here. Fast."

"Cutting the street cams and pulling GPS now."

"I won't blame you if you want to jump," I say to Nick. It's my fault the cops are on us. I lost track of the count, couldn't get the car into reverse.

"Don't be an idiot."

I stare straight to mask my relief. But that's when I notice the red traffic light at the intersection ahead. A quick glance in my rearview tells me the cops aren't far behind. If I can hit the interstate before they catch up, we might have a shot.

"Five fifteen should be coming up quick," Mat says. "Take the off-ramp to the right."

I step on the gas. We punch through the light, leaving behind a stream of extended tire squeals and angry car horns. I crank the wheel right and we bounce onto the off-ramp.

Nick pitches forward. "Shocks could use some work."

I round the corner so fast two wheels lift. It's probably no more than an inch, but my stomach leaps with a split second of fear. The tires slam back onto the pavement and I merge into traffic.

Nick lets out a whoop. "You did it, Jules. You lost them!"

He reaches over and squeezes my knee. His touch is unexpected. Electric.

When I glance over he smiles, a lazy grin that makes my insides explode and my chest bloom with pride. I take the car into fourth and roll down the windows, allowing the Vegas heat to blow through my hair.

Nick pulls away and grabs his cell. Speaks into it like he's on a walkie-talkie. "Everybody to the Trophy Case. We've got Jack and we're bringing him home." His voice fades over the steady thump of my heartbeat. "I repeat, Jack is coming home."

Behind us, the neon lights of the Strip disappear. A low humming vibration starts in my chest. I flick on the radio. Jim Morrison growls through the speakers about a "Moonlight Drive."

I glance up at the overhead moon and grin.

Chelsea and Mat wait at the corner of I-95 and Kyle Canyon Road. Mat fist-bumps me through our respective windows, and Chelsea leans over the dash to give me a thumbs-up.

The air hums with excitement and relief, but as the adrenaline rush weakens, I'm starting to crash. "Roger know we're coming?"

"He's already there," Chelsea says.

Figures.

This should be the easy part—drop off the car, cross Jack

off the list, start planning the second grab. But my heart rattles in my rib cage like a window shutter in a tornado.

Nick picks up on my unease. "Home stretch."

I can't risk looking at him, because the emotions I've stuffed in the back of my conscious come rushing to the front. At some point we'll do a post mortem on this boost and all the things that went wrong—we narrowly missed getting caught and it's because I couldn't get the car in reverse. I need to own that.

We roll up the windows and I turn on to the gravel. Flick on the high beams. The Super Bee sputters like it wants to go fast. As the awkward silence stretches between us, I focus on the road, on not beating myself up over the mistakes. It was our first boost together—no one expects perfection.

Maybe I do.

"You did good back there," Nick finally says.

I duck my head forward so that my hair hides the side of my face. My cheeks catch fire. "You're a bad liar."

His hand inches toward my leg, then pulls back before making contact. A hollow ache forms in my chest.

"We'll take this one car at a time," Nick says. He's not angry or gruff, but some of the tenderness is gone.

Up ahead, Roger's car idles outside the gates of the Trophy Case. He barely acknowledges us as we slide through and drive around to the back of the building. Pebbles crunch under the car's wide tires.

133

A giant bay door creaks open and Roger waves us inside.

I inch forward, waiting for further instruction.

Roger circles the car, hands clasped together and pushed tight against his chest.

"He's so . . ."

"Touched," Nick says, making me laugh.

Roger runs his finger along the hood, the side of the door, across the back. I shift, becoming more uncomfortable by the second.

"If he starts masturbating, I'm out of here," Nick says.

I gag. "Thanks for that."

Roger motions for me to roll down the window. Engine noise ricochets off the concrete walls.

"Park it over there," he says, pointing to an empty stall in a row of similar-style cars. "Make sure you back it in."

My fingers tense on the wheel.

"I'll do it," Nick says.

Screw pride. I jump out of the car and stand next to Chelsea and Mat. The three of us watch in silence while Nick eases Jack into position. Roger stands ramrod straight, his hands balled into fists at his sides, arms trembling. He's like a fucking kid.

Nick hops out of the car and taps the hood. "Nice-looking car, Rog."

Roger stiffens. "Indeed."

He yanks a handkerchief from the front of his vest and

crouches to get a better look at the bumper. Buffs out a speck of dirt.

"Car wash might be faster," I say.

When Roger doesn't answer, Mat loudly clears his throat. "If that's everything . . ."

Roger swivels his head and stares long enough to give me the heebie-jeebies. Finally, he pulls an envelope out of an inside vest pocket and counts out some cash. I don't know what I expected—check, IOU, whatever—but at the sight of all that money, my pulse starts to purr.

"Consider this a signing bonus," he says, handing off a stack of bills to the others. At me, he pauses. My mouth goes dry. "Good work, Ghost."

The nickname lands hard.

I squeeze the money so tight, I'm sure my thumb will pop right through the center of the bills.

Mat tosses his money on the floor. "This wasn't the deal."

"These things take time, Matias."

Anger leaks into Mat's voice. "I suggest you work faster."

13

I SPOT MAT HUNKERED DOWN AT A COMPUTER TERMINAL tucked into the back corner of the public library. The place is massive, but aside from the couple copping a feel on the second level, Mat pretty much has the place to himself. Even the librarian's too engrossed in a book to notice I've smuggled in two cans of soda and a tube of Pringles.

Mat glances up before my ass hits the empty chair next to him.

I nudge my chin. "Check out Romeo and Juliet up there."

The guy's hand is up the back of the girl's shirt, and she's grabbing his ass. I'm not one for PDA, but I guess Shakespeare really turns some chicks on.

"Tragic," Mat drawls.

He's tucked into the reference section at the back wall with a wide view of the place. Through the bank of windows along the west wall, palm trees sway in a light breeze. Sunlight streams through the glass.

To our left, a mix of nonfiction books fills an end cap display, including a thick compendium of muscle cars. An angry-looking '69 Mustang Boss leaps from the glossy cover.

I set a can of soda next to Mat and pop open the chips. The pungent scent of vinegar makes my nose twitch.

Mat reaches for his Coke, eyes on the screen. *"Gracias."*

"De nada."

He gives me the side-eye. "You're catching on, *muñeca.*"

Yeah, except I haven't figured that one out yet and I'm too stubborn to ask. I think it's the equivalent of "doll face," but the bulk of my Spanish is translated from insults and swears.

I point to the screen. "Getting anywhere?"

Mat pushes back his chair, snaps open his soda, and hits the enter key. "You're just in time to see this thing go live."

This thing is a new trawling program Mat's created, designed to scour the Internet based on specific search parameters. With less than six weeks left to boost the remaining cars on Roger's list, the Darknet is our best shot at tracking down the Aston Martin and the Shelby. "You think this will work?"

He shrugs. "Got a better plan?"

Solid question.

I pull a spiral-bound notebook out of my school bag and flip open to the middle. I've documented everything we know about the last two cars, sorted into columns: James and Eleanor.

Mat takes a swig of his drink and wipes his hands on his jeans. He shuffles his chair, fingers hovering over the keyboard. "Let's plug in some data. Start with the Shelby. Color?"

I skim my notes. "Nightmist Blue."

"One word?"

Fuck if I know. Mat types it in twice—one word, then as two—along with various other key words: Jim Morrison, The Doors, 1967 Shelby GT500, and so on.

I frown. "You call that discreet?"

"Trust me."

He doesn't know me well enough to recognize that's a big ask. But if anyone's going to knock down my walls, Mat's got the best chance. He's got this calming vibe about him, like I could tell him anything. Well, almost.

Mat hits enter and the computer screen goes black. Slowly, a series of green lines scroll from top to bottom, picking up speed until they become continuous streams of neon gibberish. Every few seconds, a soft *ping* whispers through the speakers.

"What's happening?"

Pride seeps into his voice. "The program runs an initial filter, sorting through the information we've entered. It spits out anything unreliable or irrelevant and will eventually compile a list of sources that will require more checking."

"You programmed this yourself?"

His dimples widen. "And you thought I was the weakest link."

I punch him lightly in the arm and he pretend rubs it like I've hurt him. My chest fills with uncharacteristic warmth.

"But really, how'd you do that?"

He crunches down on a chip. "You want an instruction manual?"

"Seriously, dude. You're not nervous about getting caught?"

He pauses, scopes out the room with exaggerated left and right head turns.

Okay, I get the picture. Even the lovebirds sucking face in the Shakespeare aisle have vanished.

His attention turns back to the information scrolling across the screen.

I start counting the *pings*. Five, six . . . ten . . . "Sounds like we're getting results."

Mat runs a hand through his hair. "I haven't quite worked out all of the bugs, so it's a bit hit or miss."

I can tell it kills him to admit it. We're halfway through the second week of our deadline and still haven't landed a single clue that will give us the GPS on the missing Bond car or Jim Morrison's lost Shelby. Without those two marks, this whole heist is a bust.

Best not to go down that negative path.

I snag the muscle car book off the shelf and start flipping pages. The chapters are broken into profiles of famous car collectors—some sultan dude, Jay Leno, Clive Cussler, a bunch of other rich guys. They all own warehouses filled with high-end vehicles—Land Rovers, BMWs and shit—but a couple of Mustangs catch my eye, including a gunmetal gray Shelby.

"How many of these cars were even made?" I say with a groan. "There's, like, three of them in Roger's collection alone."

"Ask Nick. He's your trivia expert," Mat says. And then, "Unless you guys aren't talking this hour."

At his knowing smirk, a blush rides up the side of my neck. Is everyone in on it? "Ain't that the truth?"

The librarian angles her body so she faces us. I shift the soda cans and chip container out of view. "Why use the *public* library?"

Thanks to Roger, Mat has three laptops at the mansion, not to mention an assortment of top-notch gadgetry that virtually secures his spot as the biggest tech geek in the universe.

"I'm tapped into the library's IP," he says. "I've blocked the address, but I don't trust the trawler to fully stay under the radar. Like I said, I've been working on it a while, but this run is a test. If something flags, the IP leads here—not to Roger's house."

A tinny beep makes him jump. He types something onto the screen. Waits.

"What's happening?"

"Absolutely nothing." He slumps in his seat. "The trawler didn't work."

My intestines twist. I rest my hand on his forearm. "We've got time. . . ."

But we both know that's a lie.

His bicep twitches. "The more time I waste with this shit, the longer it takes to find my family."

"What a mess." I breathe out. "How'd you end up here, Mat?"

"You mean instead of in juvey with the rest of the other Latino hoodlums?" It's not quite what I meant, but he chuckles. "You're not the first to ask. My last bust got me into Roger's Wonderland, but not before the cops threw my skinny ass behind bars. I spent an hour with some moron coming off a crack high." He circles his finger around his ear. "Batshit crazy. Next thing I know, I'm being dragged out of the cell by some dickhead telling me it's my 'lucky day.' Roger bailed me out."

"You lived on the street before that?"

"Couch hopping mostly. Picked up odd jobs here and there to earn my keep." At my extended silence, his eyes darken. I'm shocked by the change in his demeanor—different, hard. "You think I didn't try to make an honest go of it?"

"No, I . . ." My voice trails off. Hell, I don't know what I think.

"I got a job at a body shop, but I'm no Nick." A shadow falls across his face. "And it's not like I've got any Latino brothers to lean on. No family business to work for. My *familia* dumped me. I haven't figured out how to make peace with that."

A sudden need to protect him sparks a fire in my stomach. "Why bother trying to find them? They don't fucking deserve you."

His smile is sad. "Do you know what the stats are on Hispanic adoption in this country?"

I shake my head.

"Low. And before you go blaming the government, that's not the issue," he says. "There are fewer Latino kids up for adoption—it's rare. I need to know *why*. Why didn't my parents want me?" His expression hardens. "I deserve to know at least that much."

A fist squeezes my heart. "I'm sorry."

The corners of his eyes crinkle. "Don't be. We've all got our shit. Done things we're not proud of." He tosses some things into his knapsack and fake grins. "But we're screwed if I can't fix this program."

I look away, afraid he'll see the doubt that's graffitied across my face. "You'll get it. Is there anything I can do?"

"Sure," he says, nudging me with his shoulder. "Pray for *un milagro*."

Mat's right—to pull off this boost is going to take one hell of a miracle.

14

The List

~~Jack-1970 Dodge Super Bee 426~~

José-1965 Corvette Mako Shark II

Reggie-1968 Chevy ZL1 Camaro

Adam-1970 Dodge Hemi Coronet R/T

George-1968 Corvette Cosma Ray

James-1964 Aston Martin DBS

Eleanor-1967 Mustang Shelby GT500

NICK CLEARLY ISN'T FIRING ON ALL PISTONS.

Either that or he's actually crazy enough to believe we can pull off what he's proposed—two boosts in one night.

Using more traditional tracking methods—like hacking into the DMV and tapping car collector chat rooms—Mat has tracked down José and Reggie, the Mako Shark and the '68 Camaro.

Geography isn't the problem.

"Just hear me out," Nick says. He worries his lip ring with his teeth. "We start with José. After we're in, Jules and I make the boost, while you"—he points to Mat—"and Chelsea head over to Reggie's. We'll meet you there, make that grab, and then follow you two to the Trophy Case."

"You want to use a stolen car to boost another car—on the same night?" My jaw unhinges. "Are you a moron?"

The room goes silent. Anxiety builds in my chest like a volcano itching to blow. I flop into the oversize chair at the end of my bed and start working through the logistics.

It's impossible. Unless . . .

"What if we split up? Chelsea and Nick take one, Mat and I the other . . . ?"

Smaller teams decrease the risks, the potential for mistakes. Alone is better. That's where I'm most comfortable—calling my own shots, owning the consequences. *Not* having to lean on someone else. I guess working with Mat is the next best thing.

"I don't like it," Chelsea says. "What if we run into unexpected security—something we need Mat for? Or maybe you guys hit a lock Mat can't pick? You and Nick have the same job, basically, but Mat and I can't double for each other."

Still sounds like a bad idea. "Then convince me we need to do both in one night."

"I could use the extra time." All eyes land on Mat. He spreads his hands wide, palms up. "I might have a lead on the

Aston Martin, but Eleanor? She's like a damn ghost." He shoots me a wry grin and my cheeks go hot. "If we can pull off a twofer, it would buy me an extra week."

I can't completely shake my sinking feeling about it, but Mat's logic is something I can get behind. "What kind of security are we looking at, Chelsea?"

She tosses her tablet onto the bed and calls up an album of photographs. I lean over the chair to get a better view. "This is where we'll find José. The garage door has a five-digit PIN which Mat has decoded using a simple—"

"Phishing scheme," he says. His mouth curls into a crooked smile. "Turns out José's daddy enjoys playing online poker. I hacked into his profile and sent him a couple of"—he uses his fingers to make air quotes—"*important e-mails* to draw out the information I need. From there, I logged into his mail server. Found out the guy won almost ten grand on a full house not too long ago—nines and aces."

"He's also a volunteer firefighter," Chelsea says. "Mat figured nine-one-one would be part of the PIN."

Mat clucks his tongue. "Nine-nine-nine-one-one, to be exact." He holds up a rectangular device. "This is a remote PIN pad, which I've already precoded. Nick and I skipped out this morning and tested my theory. The garage opened. There's a gate, but the lock is fairly standard."

Okay, so I'm impressed. "Cameras?"

Mat winks at me. "I hacked the server and downloaded

twenty seconds of footage from last Wednesday. I'll disable the feed and set the canned film to loop."

"Looks like you're off the hook on this one, Chelsea," I tease.

"Don't worry, I'll earn my keep at Reggie's house." She points to a second set of images. "If Mat cuts the alarm, I can pick the lock at the first gate here." Her piercing knocks against her teeth. "But that's only the first line of defense. It's a hike up the driveway—which is lined with cameras and two roving spotlights—to a second gate. That lock has a Chubb detector on it."

Nick snorts. "I doubt that means what I think."

Chelsea rolls her eyes. "Easy, perv. It's a type of level tumbler lock with an integral security feature. The second it detects tampering, it relocks itself."

My neck muscles tighten.

"I'll just have to figure out how to avoid triggering the automatic jamming mechanism," she adds quickly.

I turn to Nick. "You're sure we can hot-wire these?"

He folds his arms across his chest and leans against my dresser. "Not the Mako Shark," he says. "Even though the car proved unstable at high speeds—the nose is too low, the fenders too high—Chevy installed a sophisticated anti-theft system that we can't bypass. Not in this time frame."

"Quit trying to impress her and tell her what we found."

Nick flushes. "We zoomed in on the garage with Mat's

binoculars . . . and the key for the 'Vette is hanging on a peg-board."

I cough. "So José's almost in the bag. Tell me more about Reggie."

He runs his hand over his face. "If Chelsea can get us in there, we should have no problem hot-wiring the Camaro. The trick will be getting it down the driveway without waking the owner. It's a long downhill, and this thing sounds like a jet plane taking off."

"Didn't you say this Camaro was the fastest and most collectible muscle car ever made?"

"All things being equal."

I grunt. "Guess we'll find out what she can do on a quarter mile."

"How far's a quarter mile?"

The sound of Emma's voice startles me. I slap my hand against my chest. "You've got to quit scaring me like that."

Emma smirks. "Maybe if you invited me I wouldn't have to sneak up on you."

Nick reaches down and rubs the top of her head. "We're having adult talk."

I bite my lip to stop from laughing. That tactic so isn't going to work on my sister. Her eyes narrow into thin slits. "Legal age in Vegas is twenty-one. Besides, I know you're talking about race cars. I like racing."

Nick makes a face. "I've seen you drive."

She crosses her arms. "Do you forget I beat you?" She spins around and points to me. "And you. Of course, you two were so busy trying to show each other up that my win was overshadowed."

My voice cracks. "Emma!"

Nick doesn't flinch. "Are you saying I owe you a victory lap?"

"I'll take a ten-second car."

My jaw drops. "Oh my God. You've been watching too many *Fast and the Furious* movies."

"There's no such thing," she says.

Chelsea pumps the heel of her hand upward. "Hell yeah, sister. That Vin Diesel . . ."

I shoot her a look. "Okay, okay. Now that we're all impressed with your racing skills, what's up, Ems?"

She lowers her eyes. "Can you spot me on the barre?"

My first instinct is to blow her off, until I realize how long it's been since we've spent time together. I've been so wrapped up in planning these boosts, I've almost forgotten the whole reason I took on the gig. One look at the ballet slippers dangling from her fingertips and a fresh wave of guilt floods through me.

"Just what this house needs, another diva," Mat says. His dimples widen with his grin.

Emma's face brightens. "Someday, I hope."

I stand and brush off my jeans, my thoughts conflicted.

I'm happy Emma still wants to dance, that she's not too old to chase the dream. But being in that room—my reflection bouncing off the wall of mirrors—is a stark reminder of everything I've lost. The life I can't have.

For Emma's sake, I shake it off. "I think you were born a diva," I tease. At the door, I turn back to the others. "I'll be back after I teach this kid how to pirouette."

Emma bends into a perfect plié. Straight lines, impressive balance. I admit, I'm surprised. "Whoa, Ems, you've been practicing hard."

Her cheeks turn pink. "Trying to." She turns her head toward the wall of mirrors. "I know Roger built this room for you. . . ."

I shrug off discomfort, trying not to let her words affect me. "I don't mind sharing."

"Especially since you're never here."

There's an edge to her voice that makes me wary. No way she could know the real reason I haven't been at the mansion as much, but I don't like her guessing, either. Emma's insecurities always threaten to rise to the surface when she's in the dark.

Emma lifts her leg onto the barre and stretches. "Why don't you take me with you?" She bends forward, hand on her calf. "Like when you and Mat went to the library—you could have asked me to come too."

The accusation threads into my bloodstream and quickens my pulse. "You put a tracker on me or something?"

"I hear stuff," she says, and refocuses on her stretch.

"Because you eavesdrop." Our eyes meet and I'm startled to see tears. A knot forms in my stomach. "That wasn't nice. . . ."

She shakes her head. "It's the truth."

"You know you can ask me anything, right?"

I'm struck by how healthy she looks—thin but strong, her once gangly arms filling out with the kind of tone that will help her with dance. She pulls her leg down and shrugs.

The motion stings. Even with seven years between us, she's always been my best friend, the one person I could count on and trust. I thought she felt the same.

"Why don't you like Roger?"

I sigh. "He's just different." The right words jumble around in my mouth like marbles. I can't lie to her—Ems and I don't do that, at least not outright. But telling her the truth isn't an option either. "I need more time to get to know him."

Emma looks thoughtful. "He's good to me."

That should be enough. Could have been if I didn't know there was more to the story.

"And sometimes I feel special. Important. Like royalty."

I laugh. "That's good, right?"

"Yeah, but I want *you* to feel taken care of."

I snort. "Don't need to be cared for." Though a tiny part of me wonders if I do.

Why does it have to be so hard?

I reach forward and take her into my arms, run my fingers through her hair. It's been years since she let me touch her like this; lately she's been in that awkward preteen stage where too much affection isn't cool.

"I miss Mom," she whispers.

Tears gather in the corners of my eyes as I fight to control the emotions. I want to tell her that our mother's not worth missing, that I'm doing the best that I can, that we don't need our parents, or anyone but each other. But I can't get the words out, because the truth of it is, I miss her too.

Emma breaks away and stands on her tiptoes to smooth away the tears running down my face. She kisses my forehead, like I used to do when she was upset. How did our roles get so reversed? "Everything's going to be okay, Julia. . . ."

I can't help but wonder if she believed me then any more than I do her now.

Chelsea's frustration fires through my Bluetooth earpiece like a series of short shotgun blasts. "Shit. Piss. Fuck."

I'm not quite used to her alter ego, the rough and tough lock picker with a mouth like a truck driver jacked up on adrenaline. No wonder I don't trust people—is anyone who they seem anymore?

"This lock is being a real bitch."

"And José was supposed to be an easy date," I mutter.

I watch Chelsea and Nick from across the street, keeping an eye on the windows in the house for any sign of movement. We're already thirty seconds into this boost and not even through the first gate.

"Should we be worried?"

Mat slouches down farther in the passenger seat of the Civic, another of Roger's loaner cars. His laptop rests on his knees.

Annoyance chips away at me. "Hey. I'm serious."

His voice drops to a whisper. "She'll get it."

His laptop *pings*. I peer over the front seat for a closer look. Even dimmed, the screen's too bright and I squint to make out what the trawling program has dredged up. "James?"

"I wish."

Movement across the street catches my attention.

"See," he says. "Told you she'd get it."

Chelsea swings open the gate. Nick sprints to the front of the garage. A motion sensor light freezes him midstep.

"Shit. Forgot to disable that." Mat clicks on his Bluetooth. "You're good, Nick. There's no alarm. I'm looping the security footage now." Under his breath, he mutters, "I hope."

"You can't mess with me like that."

Mat raises an eyebrow before entering the code into the remote PIN pad. The garage door slides open and Nick slips inside. My eyes flit from the front door to the garage, back to the house.

Sixty seconds.

Chelsea jogs across the street and hops into the driver's seat. She slams her head against the backrest. "Holy crap, I totally thought I was going to blow that." She fist-bumps Mat and then twists around to me. "You good to go?"

"We've got this."

I wish I felt more confident, or knew how Nick was doing. He should be done by now.

His voice cuts through the tension. "The key's not here. It was right fuc—" He breathes out a sigh. "Never mind. Got it. Jules, be ready."

On cue, I pop open the door. "See you at Reggie's house."

"Drive slow," Chelsea says. "Don't draw attention to yourselves."

I'm learning that Chelsea's panic sometimes turns her into a bit of a know-it-all. "Got it."

I hit the street just as Nick backs out of the garage. The winged Corvette door lifts with a soft hiss. The car's distinct coloring stands out under the streetlight—deep blue body paint that fades to gray. Easy to see how it was inspired by the sleek mako shark.

"Much nicer up close," I say, hopping into the seat. The door lowers and I buckle up. My eyes land on the shifter and I realize the Mako's an automatic. "Or not," I say. "What good is a sports car if you can't shift it into gear?"

Nick pulls out onto the street and makes a slow left turn. "That's not my only problem with this thing."

I roll down the window to listen to the engine noise. Obviously the car's a collectible, but I guess I understand why it's not always recognized as a muscle car. It's missing that earthy rumble, that angry growl that tells everyone to back off. Without it, my pulse is steady. Like we haven't just stolen an expensive concept car, but are cruising urban Las Vegas in a Pontiac Sunfire.

"Chelsea wanted to remind us not to attract any attention."

He snorts. "This car's a gawker magnet."

The point is driven home at the first set of lights. We pull up next to a black sedan. The driver rolls down his tinted window. Heavy bass thumps into the street. "Nice car."

I pretend not to notice.

The music fades. "Hey, I said . . . nice wheels."

I muster a weak smile and look over. Jesus. It's like the guy stepped straight out of the downtown Mob Museum. Gray and white pinstripe suit, tilted gangster hat, cigar hanging from his lips—he's a wannabe Al Capone. My creeper radar shifts into overdrive.

"Thanks," I say loudly, nodding with enthusiasm. My smile is as fake as his toupee. To Nick I say, "We have a fan."

I press my back into the seat and Nick leans forward. His jaw tightens. "Shit."

The hair on the back of my neck stands on end. "You know this guy?"

"Something like that."

The light turns green. I expect Nick to hit the gas and get us out of here, but he pulls in behind the sedan instead. His pained expression tells me we're not hitting up the 7-Eleven for a Slurpee.

15

MY LUNGS FILL WITH AIR. "WHAT'S GOING ON?"

Nick grips the steering wheel so tight his biceps flex. He stares ahead, his jaw like chiseled stone. "I'll handle it."

What does that mean? Handle what?

He pulls into a parking lot and cuts the engine, leaving the keys dangling in the ignition. The Al Capone guy gets out of the sedan and leans up against the door, lights a cigar. White smoke drifts into the streetlight. It's all so damned cliché.

I'm struck with realization. "That's Riley, isn't it?"

Nick stretches across me and locks the passenger door. His hand brushes against my hip, stays there a little too long. "Roll up the window and stay here," he says under his breath. "Keep your eyes open."

Right. Eyes open.

What the hell am I looking for?

156

Across the parking lot, a drunken bride and her tattooed groom spill out of the small wedding chapel that's wedged between a pawnshop and a twenty-four-hour liquor store. A burly guy on a Harley raises an oversize beer can and gives me a toothless grin.

Nick gets out of the car.

He's not even gone two seconds when my heartbeat picks up speed. I drop open the glove box looking for something—anything—I could use as a weapon, but all I find is a busted pair of Ray-Bans and a couple of poker chips.

The two fist-bump like old friends.

"Shit, Riley, thought you were never getting out," Nick says.

The seconds tick by with agonizing slowness. The longer we loiter in public view, the stronger our chances of getting caught. I should slide over into the driver's side, fire up the engine, and peel out of the parking lot. Nick's a big boy—he can handle himself.

I rub my hands over my face to rebalance my equilibrium. As if I could leave him behind.

A high-pitched squeal pulls my focus left. The bride now lies on the pavement with her wedding gown up around her thighs. Her groom hovers over her, hand outstretched like he wants to help, but they're both doubled over in laughter.

Probably drunk.

Riley's low chuckle reverberates through the window and sinks into my gut. "Fuckers let me out." He blows out a puff of smoke and nudges his head toward the car. "Yours?"

Nick rubs the back of his neck. His T-shirt slides up enough to reveal the taut V where his stomach and pelvis meet. I can't help it—my eyes are drawn there. A bead of sweat trickles between my shoulder blades.

He glances over at the 'Vette likes it's no big deal. "Just a junker I'm working on for a friend."

My concern blooms into anger. Guys like Riley don't fall for BS like that.

Riley cranes his neck to get a better view. "That your friend?"

The dude on the Harley gives me thumbs-up as he passes, the *rumble-spit-rumble* of his engine drowning out Nick's response. Tension steams like an overheating radiator.

Riley takes another drag, then flicks the cigar onto the pavement and stomps out the glowing end with the heel of his shoe. "I'd hate to think you were back to boosting, Nicky—for someone else."

Oh man. We are so screwed.

Nick shoves his hands in his pockets. "Just some small-time shit here and there." He kicks at the pavement and a pebble pings off the Mako Shark's hubcap. "You still running the same crew?"

"Your spot's vacant." Riley gives Nick a Cheshire Cat grin. "Yeah, I know, you're out. It's okay to keep your options open though—you wouldn't be the first to come back."

As if on cue, the passenger window of the sedan rolls down

and a hand reaches out to wave. My stomach flips end-over-end like it's catching air. There's something eerily familiar about it—the oversize ring on the index finger, the black sleeve of a weathered leather coat . . .

My heart jams on the brakes.

No. It can't be . . .

Nick's face splits into a grin. "Shit. How's it going, Kev?"

Fuck me, it is.

My smarmy ex climbs out of the car and right back into my life. Sunken eyes, scraggly hair. I choke on a gag and slink lower in the seat. He locks arms with Nick in a far-too-brotherly handshake.

Realization guts me—Kevin and Nick *know* each other.

Boosted cars together.

Heat circles my neck like a noose. I gather my hair into a ponytail and tuck it under my hoodie. Sink farther down in the seat.

Not subtle enough. Kevin spots me.

He sticks his hands into the pockets of his ripped jeans and ducks low, peering through the Corvette's front window. One heel lifts off the ground. His beady eyes zero in on me while his lips curl into a sneer of disbelief.

"Well, holy shit." He swaggers toward me and revulsion pools on the tip of my tongue. I can't believe I ever had sex with this loser. He touches his lips, acts coy. "I never thought I'd see you again."

"I'm not that lucky."

He laughs like I'm joking. "Seriously, girlfriend, I heard you got pinched."

"No thanks to you, dickhead."

Nick tilts his head with confusion. "You two know each other?"

"Jules and I go way back."

My face goes hot with embarrassment.

"She's with me now," Nick says. He sounds so sincere I almost believe it.

"All good, bro." Kevin double-thumps the 'Vette's hood with his palms. "I'm done with her anyway. Gotta admit, I'm surprised to see you together. You know who she is, right?"

Nick's hands ball into fists by his sides. His jaw jerks. "It was good seeing you again, Kev."

From the corner of my eye, I notice Riley. He cocks his head to the side, another cigar pressed between his lips. Locks his hard stare on me. Smoke floats across his face. I'm rooted to the passenger seat, my hand on the door handle, prepared to bolt. Riley stares me down like a panther ready to pounce. He tips his cigar at me and takes another puff.

"You're like King of Holding Grudges," Kevin says. He raises a bushy eyebrow. "And I know how much that car meant to you."

"Like I said, we should be going."

"Yeah, I thought so," Kevin says with a wide grin that shows off the gaps in his teeth.

A shiver runs up my spine. Air should start flowing again, but it's like the world is closing in around me. Why would Kevin think Nick had a grudge against me? What car?

Kevin backs away from the Corvette, hands up in mock surrender.

Nick climbs into the car and turns over the ignition.

"What the fuck, Nick? Why did you pull over?"

"You think he wouldn't have chased us down?" he says out of the corner of his mouth. "Riley's not the kind of guy you want to dick around with."

"We could have outrun him."

"That would have been subtle."

I fold my arms across my chest. He's right, but I'm still pissed.

Nick puts the car in gear and drives up alongside the sedan. Kevin rolls down the window and gives us the two-finger salute. I think about flipping him off, but Nick's caution raises my own red flags. I'm in no position to instigate a fight I can't finish.

"Maybe we'll see you around sometime," Nick says.

God, I hope not. But like I said, I'm never that lucky.

Kevin winks. "Count on it. Oh hey, Jules . . . say hi to your little sister for me, will ya? Cute kid. Hate to see anything happen to her."

Blood rushes through my veins so fast I'm sure one of them will pop. "You stay the fuck away—"

Nick rolls up my window before I can get the rest of the threat out. He peels out of the parking lot, leaving a rooster tail of black smoke in his wake.

I smack my hands on the dash. "Asshole!"

"It's over," Nick says. "We won't ever see them again."

"How can you be so sure?" My fear boils over into anger. "He *threatened* Emma."

Nick flinches. "It's just talk."

"If that were true, you wouldn't have pulled over."

Nick avoids my gaze and I know I'm right. I slump back in the seat and close my eyes. It's too much to process. "Shit. What are the chances?"

"It's a small city," Nick says. "Not a lot of major players. You two were bound to meet sometime."

It's not what I meant, but my explanation is cut off by Chelsea's panic-stricken voice in the Bluetooth. "Guys? Where the hell are you?"

"We hit a bit of trouble," I say, side-eying Nick. "We're clear now."

"Don't be so sure," Chelsea says.

My stomach flinches with unease. "We're a few blocks out. Be there in eight, maybe ten minutes."

"Good," Chelsea says. "Because we've got a serious fucking problem."

162

16

The List

~~Jack-1970 Dodge Super Bee 426~~

~~José-1965 Corvette Mako Shark II~~

Reggie-1968 Chevy ZL1 Camaro

Adam-1970 Dodge Hemi Coronet R/T

George-1968 Corvette Cosma Ray

James- 1964 Aston Martin DBS

Eleanor-1967 Mustang Shelby GT500

JOSÉ MAY BE A LONER, BUT REGGIE LIKES TO PARTY.

The prize Camaro is hidden in a garage next to a sprawling bungalow tucked between a cluster of tall trees that barely muffle the sound of music thumping from outdoor speakers. An occasional squeal followed by raucous laughter punctuates the heavy beat.

More than a dozen vehicles line the edge of a long, gravel driveway.

Chelsea chews on her bottom lip. "We got good news and bad news."

The bad's a no-brainer. Even if we get to the garage undetected, we run the risk of being seen. It's like trying to sprint a marathon in high heels.

"Someone want to tell me how this isn't *all* bad?" Nick says.

Mat adjusts his Red Sox ball cap so the visor rides lower on his forehead. He shoves his hands in his pockets. "I ran a scanning program and it looks like the security grid is shut down."

"Okay . . ." Nick says.

"So the complicated lock Chelsea hasn't figured out yet won't be a problem."

My mouth goes dry. "Well, that's a relief."

"But there's a bigger issue," Chelsea says. "A couple of the cars are parked—"

"In front of the garage," I finish.

Shit.

"At least two," Mat says.

The ground vibrates as the music from the party shifts to rap. At least the Camaro's engine noise won't be a concern. "What kinds of cars?"

Chelsea pulls out a camera and focuses on the front of the house. "We figured you'd ask, so we took a peek. Zoomed in on these."

The Toyota Camry is the fourth most boosted car in the U.S. I can hot-wire that one with my eyes closed. But the second vehicle is newer. Fancier. Some kind of BMW. Which is impossible to steal without a special key fob.

"Maybe we should pull the plug on this," I say. "Cops might already be looking for José. We should get him home."

Mat taps the side of his head. "I've been listening to the scanners. Lots of boosts going down tonight, but nothing about the 'Vette yet."

Nick studies the photo. "Depending on where Reggie is in the garage, I might be able to squeeze him out, but we definitely need to move the Camry."

I tap the screen. "The tires on the BMW are pointing slightly to the left. What if you and Mat push the Beamer? I think you'd get two, three feet before the wheels turned in toward the trees, which would give us some extra room."

"Smart thinking," he says.

Chelsea shakes her head. "So now we've gone from boosting two cars tonight to four? Great. What the hell am I supposed to do?"

I squeeze her shoulder. "Make sure we don't get caught."

"Jeez, why didn't I think of that?" She slings her backpack over her shoulder. "How about I get you in the garage?"

"Or do that," I say.

With the plan set, Chelsea and I slink up one side of the driveway, while Mat and Nick take the other. As my feet navigate the steep slope, I note the potholes, any potential obstacles. With the Camaro's low front end, a fast getaway might not be an option.

The music grows louder on our approach. Voices carry from around the side of the house. With any luck, the party will stay contained in the backyard.

At the Camry, I fish around in my pack for a Slim Jim to pop the lock.

Nick and Mat move into position behind the Beamer.

"You call those muscles?" Nick harsh whispers to Mat. "Time to hit the weights, bro."

"El tuyo," Mat says.

Nick grunts. "Yeah, up yours too."

The car nudges forward.

I get to work popping the lock on the Toyota. Wedge open the door. As soon as my ass hits the seat, I start unscrewing the panels on the steering column. My internal clock is already out of whack.

The panel pops off and I fish around for the nest of wires, careful not to do too much damage. The Camry isn't part of the bigger picture; it's a necessary casualty, though I doubt the owner will see it that way.

My breathing steadies, heartbeat regulates. I'm on familiar ground here.

Chelsea's champagne voice bubbles into my earpiece and for the first time, I don't flinch. I think I'm getting used to her being in my head. "BMW's out of the way," she says.

I'm up.

I twist the wires together. The engine fires up and in one fluid motion, I cut the automatic lights, sit up in the seat, and shift the car from neutral to first. Press a little on the gas. The Camry crawls forward.

Nick waves me to the other side of the driveway. I ease the Camry out of the way, turn off the car, and yank the e-brake.

Two down.

Chelsea's already at work on the garage door.

"Find me a drill," she whispers.

I root around in her bag to dig out the small cordless drill and a selection of bits. She chooses the smallest and sticks it into the center of the doorknob. The drill bites into the metal with a soft whir.

"Bigger."

I choose the next size up.

Sweat beads across my forehead. When she starts drilling again, I glance around, nervous some drunk might come out of the house and catch us. The music blares in the background. I smell campfire smoke and a hint of chlorine.

When the center of the lock finally pops out, Chelsea drops it like it's on fire. "Motherfucker, that's hot."

We push open the door and I shine a flashlight into the room. A beam of light lands on the car. Jesus. It's emerald green with black detailing on the hood scoop and along the side panels. The polished chrome rims sparkle.

Reggie is breathtaking.

Chelsea whistles low. "Looks like we know who the real stud in this group of seven is."

"It actually hurts to steal this car," I say, deflecting the seed of guilt before it can take root. To pull this off, I need to stay focused. "Dude's going to be shattered."

Chelsea heads for the door. "Meet you at the bottom of the hill."

I barely hear her slip away as I get to work. The music from the party fades into the background. I focus on the tasks, grinding through the motions of finding and prepping the wires. My fingers tremble.

This is my first official boost from this heist without Nick.

It feels good.

Like I've got back some control.

I coil the wires and the engine engages with a roar. Tools clatter on the shelves. The garage door rattles. My whole body vibrates with the power. I fumble around in the glove box and grab the remote garage door opener. Hit the button.

My pulse skyrockets.

I buckle in and put the car in gear.

The headlights flick on. I look up—

And freeze.

A blond girl in a black bikini stands in the light, her mouth wide with shock, eyes the size of twin moons. Panicked, I rev the engine. She dodges out of the way as I stomp on the gas.

The tires spin a burnout and black smoke fills the back of the garage.

Reggie bucks forward and hits the gravel hard. Rocks spray in all directions. I shift to second and the back end swings out before the tires grab.

I'm so going to die.

I angle the car between the vehicles in the narrow driveway, praying I don't hit a big rock or something that will pitch the car sideways. By the time I clear the last of the cars, I'm in third.

"Take a sharp left at the pavement," Chelsea shouts in my earpiece.

The car vibrates. Every bump, every rock, sends a shockwave through to my arms. My fingers go numb.

At the bottom of the driveway, I crank the wheel. The back tires spin, jolting the car left. I regain control and let out a high-pitched whoop. Reggie's a bucking bull and I totally just nailed this rodeo.

Up ahead, Nick pulls onto the road in the 'Vette and we race along the Boulder Highway.

His low voice worms in through the Bluetooth, curls right under my skin. "Think you'll be able to keep up?"

I smile at the challenge.

On the first corner, I pull out alongside Nick and slip into fourth gear. "You know why they call me the Ghost, right?" Our eyes connect through the glass that separates us, and I can

see the surprise. I feel it too. I'm slowly sliding into my skin—
even if it comes with its own nickname.

"Because of your haunting personality?"

I stifle a laugh. "Nope. It's because I can disappear."

With a wink, I stomp on the gas.

17

The List

~~Jack-1970 Dodge Super Bee 426~~
~~José-1965 Corvette Mako Shark II~~
~~Reggie-1968 Chevy ZL1 Camaro~~
Adam-1970 Dodge Hemi Coronet R/T
George-1968 Corvette Cosma Ray
James-1964 Aston Martin DBS
Eleanor-1967 Mustang Shelby GT500

CHELSEA CHEWS ON ONE FINGERNAIL, PAUSES TO inspect the chipped polish, nibbles again. The action goes against her near-perfect nature, which is my first clue something's off.

Four days have passed since we delivered José and Reggie. With the Coronet literally in our sights—we're across the street

171

from the house—I thought we were in good shape. How naive.

She focuses on the iPad screen, her eyebrows knit with concern.

The silence is killing me. "What's up?"

Her eyes dim, and I get it.

Adam's place is buttoned up tighter than the infamous Bellagio vault. Thick fencing surrounds the property, which is locked by a keypad Mat can't crack the password on. None of the number and letter combinations are working.

He pounds at the keyboard with determination.

Nick shakes his head. "All this for a fucking Coronet?"

It's not the best-looking car on the list, but the fact that it makes the list at all means it's more than just a *fucking Coronet*. The owner obviously agrees. "What are our options?"

Mat shoves his laptop up onto the dash. "More time?"

"We don't have it," Nick says.

I scan the surrounding landscape. It's a rich part of town, on a cul-de-sac peppered with enormous homes. Streetlights and small bushes line the streets—not enough coverage for anything significant. We're out in the open, which adds another layer of complexity.

Time for plan B.

"What if we wait for the car to leave?" I say. "Boost it from another location. It's clunky, but maybe more feasible than this?"

Nick's reflection shimmers in the car window. His eyebrows furrow. "It's a stretch."

He's not wrong. For all we know, the Coronet's parked in the driveway because it doesn't run. And that five-car garage is bound to house more expensive cars.

"Wait, it could work," Mat says. He snatches his laptop off the dash and rests it on his knees like a security blanket. "Let's look at our intel on the guy. Dominic Harris. Not much for social media." He looks up from the screen. "Normally that would bug me—everyone's on something these days—but he's older, so it fits. Divorced."

"That's a start," I say. "He on any dating sites?"

"One," Mat says. "His tastes run young and blond."

"Good luck picking anyone up in that hideous purple thing," Chelsea says.

Plum Crazy. The hoops Mat jumped through to find this car almost justify the name. Hours of weeding through data, sorting through fake leads and dead ends. There's no time to track down another purple Coronet.

"It's Friday," I say. "With any luck, he'll have a date."

"Or, we end up staking out the place all weekend," Nick says. "Waste of fucking time."

My skin bristles. "Unless you've got a better idea, this is the plan. Let's give it till Sunday."

His eyes darken. "And if we're no further ahead?"

"We talk to Roger," Mat says.

"And say what? That we can't do it?" Chelsea shakes her head. "No way, José." She pivots toward Nick. "Jules has the right idea. We'll tag team it, take some of the pressure off. Mat and I will take first shift. You and Jules go get some rest. If something happens, we'll let you know."

I chew on the inside of my cheek. "You're positive this is the only local Coronet?"

"They only made two hundred and ninety-six hardtop R/Ts," Nick says. "It's damn lucky Mat found this one."

"What if we skip to the Cosma Ray?" My voice lifts with hope. "It's not like we have to follow any order, right?"

I recognize the issue before Mat even responds.

"I've got a couple of leads on George, but nothing solid," he says. "Still working on James and Eleanor, though. These last three are a bitch. I've made some modifications to the trawler, but it will take some time to sift through the data."

I pat Mat's shoulder. "You're doing great, Mat. We'll try this. In the meantime, maybe we'll run across another Adam. Keep looking?"

"Got it, Ghost."

I'm too wired to relax.

I pass by Emma's room and peer inside. She's down at the pool, but something about being in her space gives me comfort. The ballet slippers Nick bought for her at the costume shop rest on the bed. I can't stop staring at them.

As I sit on the edge of the mattress, I pick up one of the shoes. Emma's feet are small for her age, a size three or something. The satin brushes against my fingertips, drawing out the memories I've struggled to forget.

Tchaikovsky flutes, violins, and triangles ding in my subconscious. I used to be good. Better than good. Talented enough to be Clara in *The Nutcracker*.

My heart picks up speed as I remember blistered toes and crippling tendinitis, fighting through the pain because I knew the practice, the determination, would culminate in one magical performance that would make my parents proud.

Emotion chokes me.

I can almost see them sitting in the front row. Proudly occupying those same two seats at every performance. Tears sting my eyes. Dad used to bring me roses—white to match the color of my hair—with a fiery red carnation in the center. The heart of the passion, he called it.

Mom never brought flowers after he left.

And eventually, she just stopped coming entirely.

I swipe at my tears with the back of my hand. Jesus, when did everything get so fucked up?

My chest fills with sadness, and still, this nostalgia leads me downstairs to the ballet barre in the basement. I pause at the games room to watch Nick work out his aggression with a loud round of Need for Speed. I consider joining him, but it's not the physical release I crave.

I flick on the lights in the fitness room. Open the door to my secret ballet studio. My heart pounds with indecision. It's been years since I've touched the barre.

The soft theater lights glow, like a beacon drawing me home.

I touch the smooth surface of the barre with tentative fingers. Kick off my shoes and remove my socks. My reluctance begins to fade, replaced with the anticipation and adrenaline rush I've come to associate with boosting cars.

My leg swings up onto the barre. I point my toe, bending into a deep stretch. Muscle memory kicks in and fire erupts along my calf. I flex in. Out. Point long and lean. I extend one arm outward and catch a glimpse of my reflection in the mirror. There's almost nothing of the former dancer left.

Fresh tears brim in the corners of my eyes. The destruction didn't happen at once. I transformed slowly, my legs and limbs growing heavier, moving from light and airy to something . . .

Dark and dangerous.

The dance steps once meant to impress an audience—my parents—became the foundation for a new set of skills. Stealth. Agility. Focus. Fundamental components of dance now adapted for something far less noble.

I switch legs, lengthening my spine and twisting my hips outward. The knots in my muscles begin to unwind. *You've got this.* I unzip my hoodie and toss it on the floor a few feet away. My pale arms look like sticks in the mirror. I've lost so much definition.

Moving away from the barre, I take hesitant steps across the floor, mimicking an old routine I'd once practiced until the veins in my arms swelled and my toes jammed. I jump lightly, performing the simple chase, then bravely take the transitional step, drawing one leg up, toes pointed to touch the back of my knee. The French names of the moves float into my mind, Ms. Griffin's voice calling out each move: *passé, retiré, pas de bourrée . . . Julia, point your toes more, chest up, arms back.* I pretend I'm light as air, but it's obvious I'm out of practice. My movements are clunky, out of sync.

A song plays in my subconscious. I hum the melody from memory, forcing my body to keep rhythm. My feet glide across the floor and I plant myself in fifth position before spinning into an awkward pirouette. I'm wobbly at best. My eyes lock on a spot against the wall and I try again, turning once, twice, a third time before I lose balance.

Fear seeps out of me with my sweat.

I spin faster, one turn after another, over and over until I forget where I am, forget that I'm not a real dancer anymore. I imagine myself onstage with glitter-dusted cheeks and the heavy scent of hairspray lingering in an atmosphere ripe with nervous energy. My limbs loosen up, my feet become stronger, lighter, less awkward.

I bend my arms and focus on the wall, finding my center—as long as I have my focal point, I won't become disoriented.

Jesus. If only life worked like that.

I move from fifth to fourth position, slide into the turn. My legs ache but I keep pushing, forcing one pirouette after another. I spin so fast everything goes blurry and dark.

I can't stop. I turn and turn and—

My legs give out. I crumble fast, slamming my ass onto the hard floor.

"Christ, Jules, are you okay?"

Embarrassment flushes up the side of my neck at the sound of Nick's voice. He hovers over me, his chiseled jaw set with worry. I ignore his outstretched hand and push myself into a sitting position to massage the cramped muscle in my calf, alternating pointing my toes to stretch them out. "Just a little out of practice."

He rubs the back of his neck. "I'd forgotten you were a dancer."

"Yeah, well, I'm not."

There's an extended beat of silence while I try to figure out how to stand without making more of an ass of myself. "What are you doing here?"

He arches an eyebrow. I try to pretend it's not sexy as hell, but the soft expression on his face is almost my undoing. I hate that he pities me. "Watching." His expression softens. "That was . . . beautiful."

The word hits hard. I deflect the compliment, not knowing where to stuff it, and look away. "Creeper."

"Worth every minute." He reaches out his hand again, a

smile playing on his lips. "Chelsea called. They've got a line on the car." He pauses as I struggle to get up. "For Christ's sake, would you let me help you?"

"Fine."

His fingers curl around my wrist to pull me upright. I vault upward and, unable to keep my balance, topple into him. My chest smashes against his, sending vibrations along my skin. I'm sure he can feel my pulse through the thin material of our shirts.

My breath hitches.

His hands press against my lower back, steadying me.

I try to break free, but he holds me in place. "It's okay to be vulnerable," he says.

"You mean weak?"

"Powerful," he says.

I duck my chin, but there's a blanket of hair to mask my burning cheeks.

"I've never seen anything like that," he says. My eyes drop to his lips, like if I don't watch them moving, none of what he says is real.

I shrug away discomfort. "I'm out of practice."

"Easy to know where Emma gets her love of dance," he says. "She wants to *be* you."

"I was just messing around," I say, suddenly desperate to change the topic. Now that I'm finished, my muscles have begun to tense up. I've already forgotten the sense of freedom ballet used to bring. Standing here with Nick, his hands still holding my wrists, I am trapped.

Everything about this place cages me in. I pull away from Nick and start gathering my things off the floor. Slide into my hoodie. "The car . . ."

Nick blinks at the change of topic, but recovers quickly. "You should go get ready. Looks like you've got a date."

My stomach bottoms out. "With?"

"Dominic Harris," he says. "The owner of the Coronet. Mat intercepted an e-mail exchange—tonight, your name is Cherry." His eyes glint with mischief. "And Chelsea says to wear the black dress."

My throat constricts.

"She said you'd know which one."

I hate makeup—the texture, the smell, the way it feels on my face. Unfortunately, it loves the girl in the mirror. Her eyes are striking, her hair almost silver under the muted light.

A flicker of unease dances across her pupils, and that's when it hits home. The girl *is* me. An unfamiliar emotion crops up, and I blink to stop from crying. It took twenty minutes to apply this eyeliner. I'm not smudging it.

"You look so pretty," Emma says.

She sits next to me at the dressing table, thumbing through makeup I've barely used—shimmering eye shadows in metal golds and coppers, ruby lipsticks, and smoky eyeliner. Some of the containers haven't even been opened.

"Almost as pretty as Chelsea?"

She tilts her head with way too much awareness and my stomach knots, knowing I've played my insecurity card.

"Prettier," she says, and it doesn't even matter that she's kind of mocking me. The words strike all the right chords. "Nick will love it."

I pause mid–lipstick application. "It's not a date."

She folds her arms across her chest. "Whatever you say."

"We're just all going out together."

She reaches across the dressing table to grab me a Kleenex, which I use to dab my lips. "Then why can't I come with you?"

I don't have a valid answer, and with each question, my guilt continues to mount. Emma and I don't keep secrets. Not from each other.

Nick knocks on the bedroom door. "Jules? You ready? We have to get going."

"One sec," I call back, and then to Emma. "The Strip isn't the place for a little girl."

A flash of annoyance crosses her face. "I'm not a kid, Jules. I'm ten and a half." I laugh, but one look at her expression and it's clear she doesn't find it funny. "I know a lot more than you think. . . ."

"What are you talking about?"

She crosses her arms again. "Like, that there's more to your date tonight than you'll admit." I open my mouth to protest and she shushes me with a wag of her finger. "And I'm not talking about Nick."

The choker around my neck feels like it's closing in. "What has Roger said to you?"

"Nothing!" Her eyes gloss over like she's about to burst into tears. "I'm not stupid. I know it's your fault we keep getting kicked out of foster homes. You think I don't know you almost went to jail?"

I feel the color drain from my face and my stomach flips end over end. "How could you—?"

"It doesn't matter." Emma puts her hand on my arm and rubs the inside of my wrist, her small fingers tracing the outline of the tattoo bearing her name. "I know you'd do anything for me. But you don't have to do . . . that . . . anymore. We have everything we need."

My world feels like it's crumbling in, Emma's words demolishing the facade I've carefully crafted. I press my hand against my chest, positive my heart has stopped beating all together.

Emma's cheeks flush with something not quite anger, not embarrassment. . . .

Disappointment.

Pain crawls across my chest. I did this. Knocked myself off the pedestal Emma had me on. I knew I couldn't stay there, but I didn't expect the fall to hurt so much.

Nick knocks with more insistence. "I told Chelsea an hour, Jules. Let's go."

I press my lips against the top of Emma's head. I've justified my actions for so long, pretending Emma would never find out, that her image of me would never shatter. Her confession tonight changes everything. "This conversation isn't over."

"You need to go," she says softly.

We stand together at the mirror and she wraps her arms around the side of my waist. The black dress clings to my hips, and the plunging neckline forms a sharp V of cleavage.

My cheeks flush with panic.

I should change into something else. Something less revealing, something more . . . me. How can I possibly go out like this?

"I was wrong," Emma says. "You don't look pretty—you're gorgeous."

I'm rendered speechless.

Nick thumps again and Ems rolls her eyes. "All right, all right. She's coming." She flings open the door and pokes him in the chest. "You. Take care of my sister."

I slip into my heels and hobble my way across the carpet. My feet already hurt and we haven't even left the house. As I go to grab my purse, I catch Nick leaning down to whisper something in my sister's ear. She swats his arm and runs away.

Nick shakes his head. "What the hell was that all ab—?" His Adam's apple bobs. "Jesus."

I scrape the top layer of red lipstick off my bottom lip with my teeth.

"I . . ."

His words trail off again.

I could help him out, change the tone of the moment, make him laugh, but I kind of love that he's tongue-tied.

He rubs his hand across his stubbled jaw and mutters something under his breath. "Come on."

He grabs my hand and I almost trip with the force of him yanking me out the door. Once steady, I blow out a deep breath. "Go slow," I say. "I need to get used to these heels."

His eyes go from soft to hard, and he looks like he might devour me in one bite. "Fuck going slow. If we don't get out of here fast, I can't guarantee I'll keep my hands to myself."

18

The List
~~Jack-1970 Dodge Super Bee 426~~
~~José-1965 Corvette Mako Shark II~~
~~Reggie-1968 Chevy ZL1 Camaro~~
Adam-1970 Dodge Hemi Coronet R/T
George-1968 Corvette Cosma Ray
James-1964 Aston Martin DBS
Eleanor-1967 Mustang Shelby GT500

THE FOUR OF US SIT IN THE BELLAGIO LOBBY, HASHING out the plan. The place is distracting, dazzling, all polished marble and gold trim. Truth is, I stick out like a homeless person at the ballet—except this time the satin slipper is on the other foot.

I feel everyone's eyes on me—most of all Nick's. He sits

so close I'm practically on his lap, and he tenses every time some guy gives me elevator eyes on his way to the casino.

"A very cute valet just parked Dominic's car," Chelsea says, grinning. Her plain black dress pants and white blouse are ideal for blending in with the rest of the waitstaff at the hotel restaurant.

"The parking garage is a vault," Mat says. "You either need your ticket or an employee key card to get inside."

My stomach drops like a busted tranny. "That explains why I'm dressed like a prostitute."

Nick whispers in my ear. "Don't say that. You're stunning."

The compliment sucker-punches me. There's nowhere to look, so I stare at the ceiling. Hundreds of blown-glass flowers hover overhead. In a city known for gaudy neon lights and sparkles, the Bellagio is still one of the classiest hotels.

Not the most expensive on the Strip, but of course, Hollywood has trumped up its notoriety. Ironic, maybe, that we're about to boost a car here, where George Clooney and his ridiculously cute costars pulled off one of the biggest casino heists in film.

"We could try bribing the valet," Nick says.

I lean forward and tuck a strand of Chelsea's hair back up into her wig—she's gone from fiery redhead to no-nonsense brunette. "We don't have enough cash."

Mat glances at his watch. "No time for another plan, *amigos*. We're less than fifteen minutes from go time."

He's already laid the groundwork. After logging into Dominic's e-mail, he sent Cherry Moony—like that isn't a fake name—a revised time for this evening's date. It gives me about forty-five minutes with Dominic before his real date shows up.

Nick leans in close. "You ready?"

I swallow and nod.

Mat goes over the plan again. I'll distract the maître d' with my nonexistent cleavage, while Chelsea slips in behind, disguised as one of the staff. When I'm hooked up with Dominic—provided he doesn't catch on quick that I'm not the girl he's been chatting up online—Chelsea will sneak in close enough to pick his pocket, score the valet ticket, and hand it off to Nick. I'll excuse myself from the date. Nick will grab the car. We'll all ride off into the sunset.

"Piece of cake, right?" I say.

Nick helps me to my feet, squeezes my hand, and sends me off with Chelsea. I hobble toward the restaurant, my heels *click-click-clicking* on the patterned marble floor.

"In retrospect, we probably should have avoided spikes," Chelsea says. "You walk like there's one up your ass." She pauses outside one of the storefront windows and I lean on her to take some of the weight off my feet.

"I suck at being a girl."

Chelsea arches an eyebrow. "I doubt Nick is complaining." At my stunned expression, she laughs. "Hey, no judgment here.

If you've got it . . ." Her eyes scan the length of me, pausing at the open V of my gown. "Flaunt it."

I fold my arms across my chest, feeling naked. My skin is goose-pimpled under the heavy AC. "Can we just get this over with?"

We pass a few more high-end stores and a candy shop with a fountain that bubbles over with chocolate. The price tag on a small box of truffles in the display window reads fifteen hundred dollars.

"Jesus. Who buys that?"

Chelsea grimaces. "I have." Somehow I'm not surprised. She pauses outside the front of the restaurant and shrugs. "Chocolate is serious, dude." She puts both hands on my shoulders and squeezes. "Don't fuck up."

Then she kisses me on the cheek, spins me around, and slaps my ass.

My heart rumbles like I'm behind the wheel of a drag racer as I head for the maître d'.

"Good evening, Miss," he says, acknowledging me with a gentle bow. "Do you have a reservation this evening?"

I work hard on pulling my lips into a smile. "Mr. Harris is expecting me."

He looks me up and down, clearly judging. "Follow me, please."

We weave to the back of the room, to a small cluster of candlelit tables tucked away from the busiest part of the restaurant. It's as if someone's flicked a dimmer switch and ordered insta-romance.

I recognize Dom immediately. His bald head shines under the overhead chandelier. His dark blazer covers a crisp white shirt, the first two buttons undone far enough to suggest confidence. At least I look the part.

He looks up from the menu and smiles.

My creeper radar is either busted or there's sincerity behind those kind brown eyes. He stands and holds out his hand. I almost relax.

"You must be Cherry."

Fuck. Do I look like a Cherry?

"And you're Dominic."

He comes around the table to pull out my chair. The last guy that did anything chivalrous was my dad, and that was long before I started dating. I sit, even though my knees tremble.

Dominic is huge—tall, muscular. He obviously works out.

"I don't understand why you won't post a profile picture." He leans in and whispers, "You're stunning."

Heat burns my cheeks. That's the second time tonight someone's used that word to describe me. It doesn't fit at all.

He settles into his seat and unfolds a napkin. The tables on either side of us are empty, and we're tucked behind a marble pillar that's wrapped in vines and large silk flowers. Enough privacy for two people to have an awkward conversation.

Except I realize there's literally *nothing* for us to talk about.

"I hope you like champagne," he says.

An open bottle of it sits in the middle of the table, and there's an empty flute in front of me. I wring my hands together under the table. "That would be lovely."

Lovely? Good Lord.

He pours each of us a glass. The bubbles trapped within the crystal flute mesmerize me. I marvel at how they fight to get to the surface, only to explode. My nerves float to the base of my throat. This was a such a stupid idea. I can't pull it off.

"Did you have trouble finding parking?"

The question catches me off guard. "The valet service here is quite good." I take a sip of the champagne.

Dominic leans back into his chair. "I can tell you're nervous. Don't be." He reaches into his inside pocket and pulls out a wallet. "Maybe we should just get this out of the way. Then we can both enjoy the evening."

I pause midsip, too stunned to speak. I'm so not that girl—I don't even think I can pretend to be *that* girl, a girl who can be bought—and I'm working up the courage to say something when he fishes out his license and hands it over.

"Dominic Harris," he says, and gives me a goofy grin. "Forty-three, just like I said."

The tension swooshes from my chest like a deflating tire. "Nice mug shot."

"I never understood why they don't let us smile in these pictures." He shrugs out of his suit jacket, stands, and drapes it over the edge of his chair. The white edge of his valet ticket pokes out from the breast pocket. "Instead, they make us pose like we're Jeffrey Dahmer or something."

His cheeks turn red.

"Smooth, Dom," he says. "First rule of dating? Don't talk about serial killers."

I actually laugh. "I don't think I have anything to worry about."

"Appreciate that." He lifts his glass and tilts it toward me. "Your turn."

I blink, trying to process, and then realize he's waiting for me to confirm my identity. Obviously I can't give him my ID. I'm terrible at flirting and just the idea of it makes me sick. "It's not polite to ask a lady her age."

He mock salutes. "Touché." We clink flutes and he adds, "To mystery, then."

Ugh. If only he knew.

"So, tell me about yourself." He unfolds the linen napkin and sets it on his lap. I do the same. "Something I haven't read in your profile."

Right, my profile.

I recall some of the things Cherry has told Dominic about herself—she's a school librarian and loves to garden. Oh, and she has cats. I know nothing of those things.

I tilt my head like I'm trying to be coy, but actually I'm scoping out the room for Chelsea. A blond waitress passes us on her way to deliver food to another couple. The tangy scent of pasta sauce trickles by. "You first," I say.

His jaw jerks and I think he might be annoyed. His recovery is smooth. "Well, you already know I love cars. . . ."

Bingo. I pounce. "Collector?"

He flushes. "I'm afraid my collection is fairly lacking. The Coronet in my profile is the only semi-rare vehicle in my garage—the rest are expensive, but fairly common."

I zero in on Adam. "Forgive me, but that's a Dodge, correct?"

He beams, clearly pleased. "Yes. I'm afraid it's not much of a looker though, when compared to other muscle cars of its era. Dodge did try and give it a makeover in the seventies."

Five optional high-end impact colors.

"Mine is Plum Crazy Purple."

I cover my mouth. "No!"

He shakes his head, laughing. "It is. I can show you later—I brought it tonight." Dominic tops up my champagne and I force myself not to take a sip. I need to stay focused, on point.

"Four-speed?"

Again, he looks impressed. "You know how to drive a stick?" He leans across the table. "Only twenty percent of drivers can."

"I can a little." The lie jams up under my tongue. I wash it down with champagne. "Perhaps you could teach me?"

"My Coronet's a little tricky," he says.

Out of the corner of my eye, I see Chelsea weaving her way toward us. Relief fills my entire body. I don't know how much longer I can keep up this charade.

"You have to speed-shift from first to third because second gear sticks," he goes on. "Makes the car stall, which, as you can imagine, is a little embarrassing. If the engine cuts out—"

"She can be hard to start again," I finish. *Shit.* I've got to get this information to Nick.

Chelsea approaches the table. "Water?"

"Please," Dominic says. His eyes crinkle when he smiles.

The observation affects me. I get what's at stake here, but I like Dom. He's kind and down to earth, and utterly oblivious to what's going on. My heart trips over guilt. I've morphed from simple car thief to master manipulator and it doesn't sit right, especially now that my sister knows. Has always known.

Chelsea pours me some water and then pivots toward Dom. The movement is so slight, I almost miss it. She reaches for his glass, fills it, and shifts the container to her right hand. Her left slides into his pocket to retrieve the valet stub. She tucks it into her pants before we can even thank her for the water.

"We're ready for our waitress," Dominic says. And to me, "Would you find it imposing if I ordered for you?"

"Please do—just no seafood."

Dom grins. "Did you know that more than sixty thousand pounds of shrimp are consumed daily in Las Vegas?"

I screw up my face. "That's disgusting." But then I laugh, realizing I might have come off too harshly. I have to get out of there before nerves give me away. "Would you excuse me? I need to use the restroom."

We stand in unison. There's an awkward split second as I realize I'm actually saying good-bye and a part of me is kind of sad. "Thank you."

He tilts his head in question. "For?"

I force a smile. "I'm already having a nice evening."

Without waiting for his reply, I turn and walk to the front of the restaurant, my eyes straight ahead, focusing on not tripping, on not falling.

On not crying.

Outside the door, I slip off my heels and sprint, barefoot, toward the lobby, shoes dangling in my right hand. I fumble in my purse with the other and grab my phone, dial Nick's number. He doesn't answer. I try Chelsea.

She answers on the first ring. "You did it!"

"I need you to get a hold of Nick."

"He's getting the car."

My heart sinks. "Adam has a sticky second gear. If Nick doesn't know that, he could stall . . . flood the gas."

"The valet is bringing the car out now," she says, a little

194

breathless. "I'll let Nick know. He'll meet you on the north side of the hotel—Flamingo Road."

I hang up and walk quickly to the doors. The Vegas heat blasts me as I step out of the air-conditioning and slip on my heels. I snake through the crowd of people watching the dancing water show at the front of the hotel. Turn left.

A gold-covered mime watches me pass. Some guy in a poorly fitted Spider-Man suit tries to cajole me into getting my picture taken with him. I keep my head down, careful not to make eye contact. I can't stop thinking about Dom.

Hundreds of flyers featuring naked women litter the pavement. The air stinks like stale beer, overpriced hot dogs, and weed. At the corner of Flamingo Road, "Darth Vader" quips, "Hey, babe, who's *your* daddy?"

Nick pulls up in the Coronet and taps the horn.

A homeless guy with a sign begging for cash gives me the thumbs-up. "Rad car, man."

Nick pushes open the door and I jump in. I exhale a breath I'm sure I've been holding since I left the restaurant. He turns left onto Las Vegas Boulevard, trapped behind a tourist bus and a Lamborghini.

"Thanks for the heads-up about second gear."

"No problems?"

"Nah, my Mustang had a tricky second gear too. Just needed to jiggle the—"

"Gearshift to the left," I finish.

He goes silent and everything starts clicking into place. I can't believe I've missed all the clues—Nick's animosity toward me, Kevin's vague comments. Red Mustang. Tricky second gear. Fuck me. *I* stole Vicki. It's *me* he's holding a grudge against, the reason for the chip on his shoulder.

A cavern opens inside my chest and fills with guilt.

"Nick, I—"

"Bad traffic," he cuts in.

My mouth drops open, but one look at his expression and I know the conversation is closed. We've worked so hard to tear down some of the walls between us. If I push now, will I force them back up again? I slump against the seat. Maybe now's not the right time, but this isn't the last of this; I'll find some way to make it right.

Music hums through the street. People walk arm-in-arm holding giant mixed drinks or tall beer cans, a drunken walk from casino to casino. The massive billboards are alive with pulsing lights.

"We'll head left on Sahara," Nick says, nudging his chin toward the upcoming Circus Circus hotel. I shiver at the giant image of a clown, lit up by more than fifteen thousand bulbs. I can't even imagine the electricity bill. "Chelsea and Mat will meet us at the Trophy Case."

Another reality sinks in.

We've got four and a half weeks to boost the remaining three cars on Roger's list. Maybe it's the champagne, or the magic of the Strip, but for the first time, I actually feel like we might pull it off.

If only my relief didn't take a backseat to a much more dominant emotion—remorse.

A strange sound gurgles from the back of Roger's throat.

Mat raises his eyebrows with amusement. I get it. I've always said our foster dad wasn't firing on all cylinders. This is a whole new level of creepy.

Roger rubs his hands together. "Perfect. Yes, yes. Just perfect."

Nick backs the Coronet into its designated slot, gets out of the car, and flips Roger the keys. Roger's too slow to catch them and they hit the pavement with a clatter. He bends to pick them up, beady eyes trained on Nick. "Do *not* do that again."

Mat mutters under his breath, "Creep."

This time that word hits the mark. Roger has begun petting the Coronet. His hand slides along the hood, along the doors. He leans in so close I expect him to lick the paint.

"I can't even watch this," Chelsea whispers.

Me either. My eyes land on the last stall in the row of Corvettes. Reserved for Barris's Cosma Ray. My insides twist into knots. Compared to this next boost, everything before it has been a piece of cake.

But it's time to step up to our A game—Mat has found George, and in just under two weeks, shit's about to get real.

19

I STAND NEXT TO ROGER AT THE DINING ROOM WINDOW that overlooks the pool. Rope lighting pulses in an alternating pattern of red, white, and blue, projecting star shapes onto the patio below.

In the distance, Las Vegas Boulevard flickers with neon signs and an endless blur of streaming traffic. Something about the juxtaposition makes my skin prickle. The illusion of safety is just another of Roger's tricked-out mirages.

"Further negotiation?" His upper lip curls. "You're beginning to try my patience, Julia."

I don't have a choice.

In the scene below, my sister emerges from behind a cluster of bushes beside the pool. Her sparkling gold bathing suit flashes as she half runs, half walks across the deck. A quick glance over her shoulder. Wide eyes. She cups her hand over her mouth.

That's when I see Nick poke his head out from behind a rosebush. His swim trunks ride low on his hips, broad chest puffed out as he monster-walks with fake menace looking for my sister. My stomach flutters. The fact that he's down there playing with her when I know he has issues with me only strengthens my resolve to make things right between us.

"I need you to get Nick's car back—the Mustang."

It's not just to assuage my guilt about stealing Vicki. Things changed last night. Boosting cars—I get why I'm doing that—but what we did to Dominic . . . I don't like the person I'm becoming. Have become.

Below, Mat joins in on the poolside action. Emma is the hide-and-seek Jedi, but I suspect the boys will give her some competition. At the sight of them all together, the threads around my heart begin to unravel. I turn away from the window, overcome with emotion. "Can you do it?"

Roger swirls the amber liquid in his glass and takes a long swig. The scent of whiskey oozes from his pores. Is he drunk? His voice turns sharp. "If I do this favor, what do I get in return?"

I've got nothing more to offer than what I've promised. He already has my soul. "Once you have your cars, you'll have everything you want."

His eyes gloss over and the pain in them does something strange to my heart.

"I'm afraid some things aren't so easily obtained."

There's an awkward beat of silence as I realize that in some ways, we're not that different. Beneath that shallow exterior he tries to pass off as body armor lurks a broken man who's lost his wife, his family. I know a little something about that.

"That's true," I say, cautious. "Which is why when something *is* easy, we should do the right thing. Don't you agree?"

Roger moves from the window to the wooden hutch, pulls an open bottle of Scotch off the shelf, and refills his glass. He gulps the whole thing back in one mouthful and then tops up the tumbler with the last of what's in the bottle.

"There's no guarantee I can find the car," he says.

Ignoring the snap of annoyance in his tone, I wet my lips and say, "I can ask Mat to track it down." I know without question he would.

He raises his glass in mock toast. "Then steal it yourself."

I shake my head. "It's got to be legal."

Otherwise, it's an empty gesture. I don't expect Roger to understand, but getting Vicki back isn't just about earning Nick's forgiveness. I don't know what's next for me. I just know it won't be . . . this.

Roger sits at the end of the dining room table, swirling his drink. Ice cubes *clink-clink-clink* against the glass.

"My wife and I built that pool for our children," Roger says. "Of course, that was before we learned we couldn't have any. We considered adoption, but then . . ."

She died.

The air between us thickens.

"Watching Emma play outside has been good for me—to see a child using what we . . ." Roger looks away.

"I'm sorry."

He seems surprised by the words, and I guess I don't blame him. We haven't exactly hit it off. But with Emma, we've found some common ground. Maybe I should be more worried about that than I am.

I pull up a chair beside him and lean forward, my hands interlaced on the table. "It's important. Not just to Nick, but to me as well. I need you to buy it back."

Roger flinches as though I've touched a nerve. "And if it's not for sale?"

"It will be," I say. "Everyone has a price."

20

The List

Jack-1970 Dodge Super Bee 426

José-1965 Corvette Mako Shark II

Reggie-1968 Chevy ZL1 Camaro

Adam-1970 Dodge Hemi Coronet R/T

George-1968 Corvette Cosma Ray

James-1964 Aston Martin DBS

Eleanor-1967 Mustang Shelby GT500

NICK PROPS HIS ARM ON THE OPEN WINDOW AND lightly taps the roof of the truck. His other hand steers. An uncharacteristic smile plays on his lips.

In the backseat of the crew cab, Mat and Chelsea flop against opposite windows, zonked out. Drool slides down the corner of Mat's mouth. I flip around to take a picture. Yep, clearly slobber.

Nick's grin widens. "Harsh."

"Payback." The cargo trailer hitched to the truck bounces as we hit a pothole. "I don't get how they can sleep through this racket anyway. Truck could use some shocks."

"Keeps me awake," he says, winking.

Well, that and the fact that he's been mainlining coffee since we left the mansion almost two hours ago. The sun's only now just about to hit the horizon. It's early. Way too fucking early. But if we're going to make a clean grab on the Cosma Ray, we need to be in Hollywood before the crowds squeeze us out.

Hollywood.

My stomach twists. A road trip should make me happy, but my nerves are frayed. We're just a few hours away from our toughest boost yet.

I fire up the iPad and pull up the blueprints of the Petersen Automotive Museum. Mat hacked the security, giving us a solid view of the exits, security cameras, and hidden corridors. The place is like a massive chrome labyrinth.

Based on the schematics, I think I've pinpointed where the travelling Barris exhibit will land—and with it, the Cosma Ray (aka George).

He's not bad on the eyes, but that's the extent of my intel. "Give me the skinny on George."

Nick leans forward to dial down Jim Morrison's voice. The radio's busted, there's no iPod hookup, and this CD is the only thing I could find in the glove box. We're kicking it old school.

"Typical Stingray body," Nick says. "Think Mako Shark, but with modifications."

I scrunch up my nose. The thing I remember most about that boost is the unfortunate run-in with my ex. I call up a couple of images of the Barris car on the tablet. Sharp peaked nose. Retractable headlights.

"Corvettes do nothing for me."

Nick chuckles. "Yeah, they're more of a midlife crisis car." He nudges his chin toward the iPad. "Unless it's a Barris. The paint job alone on that car ate up more than two hundred man hours."

I enlarge the picture. "Dude, it's, like, two-tone orange."

He swerves to avoid another pothole and the back end of the trailer slides out. I grip the armrest until the truck evens out.

"Peach, actually. Apricot pearl, platinum, and tangerine metalflake, blended over a white underbase."

"I love it when you talk dirty to me."

Nick's cheeks go pink. "George was built to be shown off, not driven."

A common theme with most of the vehicles in Barris's traveling road show. I don't get it. Sure, they're nice to look at, but without that rumble of the motor or the sweet scent of gasoline flowing through the fuel pipe, what's the point?

"The Cosma Ray is some of Barris's best work," Nick says.

"It won a bunch of awards, including the Grand National Sweepstakes."

I cup my hand over my mouth in mock surprise. "No!"

A flash of annoyance flickers across his face. "Barris is the reason I even got into cars. I modeled Vicki's modifications after work I'd seen him do on a Mustang."

I dig my teeth into my bottom lip, weighing the pros and cons of continuing this discussion. I don't trust myself not to tell him about the conversation I had with Roger. "Is Vicki an old girlfriend?"

"Jealous?"

Like hell I'd admit it. "Isn't that how most guys name their cars? That or after their—"

"Mother." There's a subtle shift in his tone that lets me know he's uncomfortable. "Victoria was my mom."

"Can I ask?"

"Lung cancer," Nick says. "She was stage four before we even knew she was sick."

"Shit."

He glances over and raises his eyebrow.

"I didn't mean to be insensitive, it's just . . ." My throat closes. "That's got to be hard."

"I didn't have much time to think about it back then." He swerves to avoid a random garbage bag in the middle of the highway. "I figure she knew for a while and tried to get things in order for me and Chase. Didn't quite work out that way. When she died, it hit Chase hard. My father too."

"That when he started gambling?"

I'm no expert on addiction, but I know loss makes people do stupid things. Mom turned to booze when Dad left, then numbed her pain with drugs. Things escalated fast.

"My father was a lying piece of shit before Mom got sick. Her dying just made him . . . shittier." He lifts his fingers off the steering wheel, flexes, tightens his grip. "In the beginning, I almost didn't mind when he hit up the casinos, because every once in a while, he'd strike it lucky. Win enough to put food in the fridge and pay for Chase's school."

He strums the steering wheel with his thumb, like a nervous twitch. "His luck ran out. I hooked up with Riley to pick up the slack. But the more I made, the more Dad gambled away. Eventually, we lost the garage, the house."

"Your dad was a mechanic?"

"One of the best, back in the day. Learned a lot from him about restoration work. A lot about Barris, too."

I twirl a strand of hair between my fingertips. "Is that what you'll do with the money Roger gives you? Become a mechanic?"

A hint of a smile ghosts his lips. "A hundred Gs won't get me back the garage, but yeah, it's a start."

We lapse into silence.

"Get some rest, Jules," he says. "We've got a long day ahead."

He turns up the stereo to another Doors classic. Something about the lyrics rings with sincerity: *The time to hesitate is through.*

With the chorus of "Light My Fire" echoing in the background, my eyelids grow heavy.

The *thunk* of the truck door slamming jolts me awake. I wipe my mouth with the back of my hand, sit up, and scope out the surroundings. A lineup of vehicles stretches in front and as far back as I can see.

It's either a traffic jam or . . .

My stomach clenches.

Roadblock?

"What's happening?" Mat's voice is groggy with sleep.

I curl my feet under my butt for added height. The domed metal top of the Petersen Automotive Museum shines like a grounded UFO in the distance. We're so close.

Chelsea sits up. "Where's Nick?" She rubs her eyes and smooths out a few wayward strands of hair. "Wow. That's quite a look I'm rocking."

"Lucky for you we're not going to a fashion show," Mat teases.

Chelsea punches him in the arm.

"Nick can't have gone too far." I bite off a piece of hangnail from my thumb, drawing blood. "It's pretty backed-up, though. Think it's cops?"

Mat yawns. "Maybe, but it won't be about us. Even if the Nevada police have started piecing things together, we're in California now. No jurisdiction."

Chelsea leans forward. "That's probably the lineup to get into the place. Didn't it just reopen?"

The truck door swings wide and Nick hops in. "Welcome to the land of the living," he says, all smiles. "Got tired of talking to myself."

"So you conjured up a few strangers to shoot the shit with?"

Nick flashes me a grin. "What's wrong? Miss me?"

My cheeks go hot. "You wish."

Chelsea sticks her finger down her throat and fake gags.

"The bad news is that we're stuck in this line for a bit—crowd control." Nick puts the truck in gear. "By the time we get inside the building, we're looking at late afternoon."

Mat groans. "Got any good news?"

Nick's whole face lights up and it does something funny to my stomach. "Barris's team brought the Batmobile!"

I curl my fingers into fists, dying to rip the wig off my head. It's itchy as hell.

But the museum is rigged with more than four hundred security cameras—there are eyes everywhere. Last thing we need is for someone to catch my ghost locks on film. So instead, I'm an insta-blonde, Chelsea's rocking the brunette, and Mat has contained his wild curls under a Seahawks baseball cap. He's full-on geek.

I catch another look at Nick in my peripheral and almost burst into laughs. A fake mustache presses up against his upper lip. As good-looking as Nick is, not even he can pull that thing off.

He drapes an arm around my shoulder. "You still hate ze mustache?"

"Creeper." My pulse quickens at his touch. "It doesn't even match that stubble on your chin. What is that anyway? Some kind of messed-up superstition? Like athletes that don't shave until after the play-offs?"

He leans in close. "Admit it, it's hot."

Okay, he's not all wrong. Wall-to-wall body heat has rendered the AC in the museum useless. Everything sticks to me—my T-shirt, my hair. Real and the fake. It's gross.

I shift to avoid the eyes on a roving security camera, and scratch just under the wig with one finger. Instant relief.

Nick points to a black and gold convertible that rotates on a pedestal. "That's a 1913 Mercer Type 35J Raceabout," he says, voice low. "Pretty much the Superman of the car industry."

"And yet, no cape."

"Doesn't need one. With the flick of a lever, this thing could drop its fenders, running boards, and lighting equipment in a matter of minutes, and be ready to fly around the track."

I squint to read the spec sheet. "But at a top speed of

seventy miles an hour, not *quite* faster than a speeding bullet."

"You have no appreciation for the classics." He puffs out his chest like a superhero. "I'm just going to leap over this crowd for a picture."

"Don't mind me. I'll just stand around and keep watch."

Or rather, assess who is watching us. There are three cameras in this section of the museum alone. Alarmed fences surround most of the cars, and DO NOT TOUCH signs warn of strict consequences for delinquents. Something tells me we're not the only rule breakers in the joint.

I slide over to the corner of the room and engage my Bluetooth. "Dude, the security in this place is insane."

"*Sí.* I've got seven in the exotic cars showroom. Chelsea is currently taking selfies with a Ferrari."

"Of course she is. Have you found the Barris exhibit yet?"

"Other side of the Mustang showroom," Mat says. "Meet you there?"

I flag Nick over. "Sure, I'll just make a quick pit stop for a paper towel."

Nick raises an eyebrow. "What for?"

I grab his hand. "To mop up your drool when you see where we're going."

A picture of the Cosma Ray features prominently on the banner that stretches across the entrance to the Barris exhibit. The line is about fifty people deep. I stand on tiptoes to peer over the crowd, but there's no point. The showroom is jam-packed with gawkers.

Nick waves me over. "Check this out."

It's the tenth time I've heard this since we hit up the Mustang exhibit more than half an hour ago. He's a kid in a candy store, drooling over every make and model like a salivating English Mastiff. Every few minutes he checks in to show off a picture or fire off a statistic. No, I had *no idea* that the first Mustang was unveiled in 1964. *Fascinating.*

"You might want to go see what your boyfriend wants," Chelsea says. "He's got that puppy dog eye thing going on."

"He's not my—"

She nudges my shoulder with enough force to knock me out of line. "Teasing would be so much easier if you dropped the denials."

Solid point, except I'm in full-on avoidance mode. No question the tension between us has shifted from animosity to that awkward flirty stage. I'm trying to ignore it, but it's impossible when we're always together. His essence is everywhere.

I elbow my way to him through a crowd gathered at the other end of the room. I'm a hot sweaty mess when I finally catch up to him. I don't even know if my wig's on straight. "This better be worth it."

It totally is.

"Eleanor," he says.

Not *our* Eleanor—the movie version from *Gone in Sixty*

Seconds. The film that vaulted the Mustang back into the spotlight. Even a nonbeliever can understand her appeal—that shiny Gunmetal Gray body, the twin racing stripes that cut through the center of the hood. This car . . . it single-handedly has the power to make me rethink every negative thing I've ever said about Mustangs.

"Jesus."

Nick rubs the back of his neck. "She's a beauty, all right. I could stand here all day."

Me too, but the universe has other plans. Mat's voice pings through the earpiece. "We're moving."

I tug on Nick's sleeve. "Time to go. We have a date with George."

The brochures don't do it justice.

That's my first thought when we muscle our way for a close-up view of the Cosma Ray.

My second is that there's no way in hell we're getting out of here with this car. Forget the live—as in, it will *zap* you—security fencing and the excessive, borderline obsessive, cameras. That's bad enough. But the Barris exhibit is at the far end of the museum, and several cars block the closest exit. For a clean break, we'd have to hot-wire all of them—and we're not talking Camrys—without tripping a single alarm.

Things are about to get messy.

Mat leans close. "We need to find a security flaw."

"Look at this place," I say. "It was built not to have any."

Cameras flash-blink-flash all around us. Voices rise and fall with various degrees of awe. I hate to admit it, but for a Corvette, George is making all the right moves. "Can you hack the system?"

Mat adjusts his fake glasses. "The renovations aren't totally finished, which might leave a few gaps in their technology. I'll take a look."

An exuberant fan jostles me from behind and I pitch forward into the perimeter fence. I twist to avoid hitting the wire, but my shirt rides up, leaving the side of my stomach exposed. My skin connects and—

Nothing.

Steadying myself, I raise an eyebrow.

"Maybe they're not live during the day?" he says.

Good thing. "But they will be tonight?"

"I'd be shocked if they weren't." He grins, clearly pleased with himself.

It takes me a second to catch the pun. "Good one."

I snap off a couple of pictures while Mat keeps an eye out for Chelsea and Nick, who have wandered off to see where the Barris cars will be held overnight. I zoom in on everything from George's tires to his door handles. They're keyless.

Mat touches my shoulder. "We should go."

I follow his gaze to where two security cops have begun

weaving through the crowd toward us. They're big, burly, and determined. My pulse speeds up. "You think they made us?"

Mat lets out a breath as they pass. "Not yet. I don't know how long our luck will hold, though."

I check the time on my cell. "At least six hours. Because that's the soonest we're getting back into this building."

21

IT'S GO TIME.

Not that we can *go* far until Mat gets us inside the Petersen.

Moonlight reflects off the silver crisscrossing ribbons of steel that frame the museum's futuristic architecture. The surrounding LED lights are supposed to suggest the speed of an automobile ripping through the wind, but right now, everything moves in slow motion. My body hums with restless energy.

Nick's boot snaps a twig, causing me to jump.

He puts his hand on my back. "Deep breath."

Any second, the roving camera outside the front entrance will rotate toward us, where we'll be smack dab in the center of its lens. Busted.

"Hang tight." Mat's low murmur hums through the earpiece. "Almost there."

Move too far left or right, and we risk triggering the motion sensor alarms that dot the perimeter. I shuffle closer to Nick. His ragged breathing whispers across the top of my head. There's mere inches between us.

"Camera one, moving," Nick says.

Air traps in my lungs.

"Got it," Mat says. "You're clear."

Relief flickers over me like warm rain. "Chelsea, you're up."

Nick presses up against me to let Chelsea pass. His heartbeat pulses through our clothes. He pulls me close. It feels so good to be wrapped in his embrace that I almost forget where we are.

I put some distance between us.

The surrounding streets go quiet but I'm still uneasy. This kind of boost should take weeks, maybe months to pull off. One hour staking out the place—that's the extent of our physical recon. We did everything else online.

"I'll need more than a standard torsion wrench," Chelsea mutters. "Dammit, I forgot my ball pick."

"Men around the world are saying a prayer in thanks right now," Nick says.

"Aren't you a fucking comedian?" Before he can respond, Chelsea adds, "That was rhetorical. Jules, stop groping your boyfriend and find my Slagel pick."

I'm stunned frozen.

She sighs. "*That* wasn't rhetorical."

I grab her pack and start fishing around for what I can only assume are special lock-picking tools. They all look the

216

same. I hold one outright but she shakes her head. "That's the half-diamond."

Of course it is.

I gather all the tools in my hand like straws. "Pick a pick, any pick."

Chelsea stares at me like I'm a moron, rolls her eyes, and then yanks one of them from the bunch. "You two are meant for each other. Seriously."

Heat flushes up my neck. Embarrassed, I force myself not to look at Nick.

"No pressure guys, but we've got about twenty seconds of loop before the feed repeats," Mat says. "No guarantees it's a smooth transition."

Which means Chelsea should pick up the pace.

She fiddles with the pick, bites off a string of serious curses, and then pops off the lock. Her relief comes out in a loud *whoosh*. "We're in."

My stomach does a slow roll.

"Five seconds," Mat warns.

Nick pushes open the door and we all file through. It takes a second for my eyes to adjust to the lighting. The entire lobby is bathed in a warm blue glow. A red EXIT sign blinks in the far corner.

An army of ants scampers along my skin. I can't shake the feeling we're under surveillance, that there's something Mat missed.

The scooped overhead ceiling and rounded walls give off the illusion that you're standing under a giant dome. On the other side of the entrance, shadowed vehicle outlines begin to take shape.

Nick guides us through the virtual blueprints we've committed to memory. "Fifty paces forward."

We need to find the exhibit showroom again to make sure the car's been moved. Our best guess is that the Cosma Ray will be stored in the loading docks at the back of the building.

The Barris exhibit leaves at first light, en route to a car show on the other end of the country. This is our only opportunity to make the grab before George gets too far out of range.

Chelsea puts one hand on my shoulder and counts our steps as I follow behind Nick.

At fifty paces, we pivot right, walk thirty steps, and turn left. I shine a small flashlight on a familiar door and make like I'm about to twist the knob.

Chelsea grabs my wrist. "Wait. You're not wearing gloves."

Shit. I sling my pack off my shoulder and dig around until I find them. Amateur move.

"It's locked," Chelsea says. She quickly sets to work on the lock and seconds later, we're through.

I'm impressed. "You are a Jedi."

"Wait until you see what I can do with my ball pick."

The easy laughter fades to disappointment when my quick

218

flashlight pass over the room reveals nothing but air.

"Empty," Nick says. "Thought maybe we'd get lucky and the car would still be here."

Too easy. "It's got to be on the loading dock."

We retrace our steps, turning left, right. A second corridor up ahead steers us around a corner. The synchronized *thunk* of our footsteps echoes through the halls.

At another locked door, Nick pulls out his cell and checks the blueprints. "After this, we're home free."

Chelsea examines the lock. "It's electronic." She lowers her lips to the Bluetooth mic clipped to the collar of her jacket. "Sending you the specs now, Mat."

"On it," Mat says.

"I'm heading back," Chelsea says. I swallow hard and give her a quick hug. She braces my shoulders, holds my gaze. "You've got this."

My heart jackhammers. "We don't have a choice."

Nick and I slide through the door and aim our flashlights at the warehouse-style space. Cars are lined up on the cement floor, strategically parked in rows of eight. If the Cosma Ray is somewhere in the middle, we're screwed.

"George isn't here," Nick says.

"He has to be."

His flashlight beam bounces off the walls, reflecting off windshields and side mirrors. He's right. There's no sign of the Cosma Ray.

"The rest of the Barris cars are . . ." I pause as his flashlight beam catches a glint of orange. "Wait. Go back." The light hovers over a Stingray hood. "There you are."

Tucked behind an oversize storage crate.

We almost missed it.

I hit my mic. "Eyes on George."

"But there's no available exit," Nick says.

All hope deflates when I spot the issues. Heavy crates block the bay doors. There's only one other exit, and it leads straight to the main artery of the museum. If we can fit George through—and it's a big if—we'll have to drive through the maze of corridors to find an exit.

My limbs go limp. "It's impossible."

"Oh ye of little faith," he jokes. "Tight, yes. But doable."

He's fucking crazy.

But we've run out of options. Nick yanks the Slim Jim out of my pack, pops the lock, and motions for me to get in the car. "This is your domain."

"Hold up, are you saying I'm better at this than you?"

He winks. "Let's not push it."

I slide into the car before he can see the blush that creeps up my neck. George has one seriously tricked out interior. Walnut finish coats the steering wheel and side panels. Leather covers the seats. The upgraded, obviously modern entertainment console even has a—

Nick taps the roof. "I'm not seeing any action."

"There's a fucking TV in here."

He leans in through the window. "Huh. Well, how about you catch up on your soaps a little later?"

"Screw you, dick."

He flips me the bird but it's all in jest—which makes me think about how far we've come.

I duck under the steering wheel and start disassembling the paneling. The routine comes second nature, but I hesitate. Jesus. It almost *hurts* to take apart this car.

Shaking it off, I focus on grabbing the wires, stripping and twisting them until I feel the connection. The engine sparks before it engages, and then George roars to life.

Vibrations ricochet off the walls.

Nick gives me an enthusiastic thumbs-up and my heart skips with pride. I slide up in the seat and give the 'Vette a little gas. My adrenaline jacks.

Chelsea's *whoop!* blasts into my eardrum. "Sounds good, girl."

Nick waves me in the direction of the exit.

I inch toward him, careful not to give the car too much gas. As I creep closer, I realize we can't do it. The throughway's too small. I'm just about to give up when I hear Chelsea again. Her voice is high and panic-stricken. "Company. You guys, you've got . . . oh crap. Cops!"

My heart drops like it's falling into my chest.

Nick jogs over to the window and leans in. "You good?"

I can't even see straight through the blinding fog of fear.

Emma's face comes into focus. I gasp and press my back into the seat, my fingers wrapped tightly around the steering wheel. "This is it. We're finished."

"No, I believe in you." Nick snaps his fingers, forcing me to look at him. "You're the best at this." He tries to lighten the mood. "You've even got a nickname."

"Yeah, a stupid one."

But what I don't say aloud is that there's nothing more I'd like than to disappear. Right now.

"You're a legend," he says.

A screech builds on the tip of my tongue. "You think that's how I want to be remembered?"

He takes a step back. "None of us do, Jules."

It's the first time he's said it—the first time I've believed—he wants out just as much as me. The idea is comforting, somehow gives me the confidence to keep going. If we're busted now, there's no shot at normal. No future.

No us.

I give the engine another rev and creep forward. The front end of the car slides through the doorframe. Another inch. Again.

Scraaape.

The passenger mirror snaps off. "Shit."

Nick shakes his head. "Don't worry about it. Keep coming. You're almost through."

I tap the gas and deliver George into the hall. Holy hell.

Nick scoops up the broken mirror and hops into the passenger seat. I grip the steering wheel so tight my hands glow white through my gloves. I am freaking out.

"How are we going to get past the cops?"

"It's probably just security."

Not comforting. "They still carry guns, right?"

"Maybe, but they drive like shit." Nick slaps the dash. "Let's get out of here."

I flick on the headlights and the museum teems with cars—vehicles on pedestals and mini stages, angle parked on slabs of pavement, tucked into corners. Mat navigates us through the maze to a bay door at the side of the building.

"Disengaging the lock now," he says. "Gimme four, three. Shit. Need another route. Security is on it."

I clamp down on the steering wheel and grit my teeth. "Just open it."

He hesitates. "You sure?"

Not even close. "Do it."

The bay door lifts in slow motion. I hit the gas and shoot out of the museum—and straight into the scene of a movie. A half-dozen cars swarm toward us, blue and red lights flashing.

"Get past the gate," Nick says.

If I don't we'll be trapped.

"Gas!"

I stomp on the pedal and the Corvette shoots through the

gate. I crank the wheel left and the back end slides right. Two security cars flip a U-turn and come in hot.

"Real cops coming," Chelsea says.

My eyes widen.

Nick puts his hand on my knee. "Just drive."

George may not be the fastest car on Roger's list, but he's got enough torque to put some distance between us and the guards.

Nick leans forward to peer through the window. "Hard right."

I make the turn and we disappear behind a cluster of buildings. Right, left, another right. I duck behind a Dumpster in the alley and cut the lights.

My heart beats so fast I struggle to breathe. *Ten, Mississippi.*

Nine.

Eight.

At *five*, I crawl back onto the main street.

"Clear," Nick says.

I push the gas pedal all the way in. "Hang on!"

There's a flash of white in my rearview as one of the security cars stops, spins around, and tries to follow. He's too late.

Nick threads his fingers through my hair and squeezes the back of my neck. "Holy shit, we did it." I grin so wide my cheeks feel stretched out of shape. "*You* did it, Jules."

Mat and Chelsea echo his praise.

"Yahoo!" Chelsea yelps. "George is coming home."

That's right. I'm bringing George home.

Nick leans back in the seat and tucks his hand behind his head. Shifts a little and fake yawns.

"Don't you dare fall asleep on me."

He leans forward to flick on the TV. "Nah, I'm just going to check out what's on the boob tube. Rest my eyes a little. . . ."

22

IT'S ALMOST THREE IN THE MORNING BY THE TIME WE turn onto Kyle Canyon Road. My nerves are like frayed live wires, stripped and raw, buzzing with energy. I now know every Doors song by heart.

"You really *can't* sing," Chelsea says.

I stick out my tongue. "I wasn't joking."

Mat thumps the back of Nick's seat. "Five bucks says Roger's already waiting for us at *the Trophy Case*." He emphasizes the last part with a faux fancy accent.

"No one is going to take that fool's bet," Nick says.

Chelsea pokes her head between the two front seats and squints. She points out the window. "There's proud papa now."

I cradle the Corvette's busted side mirror in my lap. "He's going to flip."

"He'd better not," Chelsea says. "We risked our butts back there." She pauses. "Well, mostly you and Nick."

I twist around in the seat. "Everyone played their part. We're a team."

I'm surprised to realize I believe it. In less than a month, we've not only gelled as a team, but have begun to form friendships. I don't know the last time I could call someone a friend.

Nick rubs my kneecap. "You good?"

"Just exhausted." We've been up almost twenty-four hours, and Nick's the only one who hasn't had a reprieve. "You must be running on adrenaline."

"NOS, actually."

I roll down the window as we approach the gate, and Roger comes up beside me. The peppery scent of his freshly extinguished cigar lingers on the brim of his fedora. His eyes narrow in on the mirror tucked between my legs.

"We had a minor casualty," I say. His nostrils flare. "Nick can fix it," I add quickly. "It will be good as new."

Roger nods tersely. "And the rest of the car?"

"It's all here."

"Show me."

Jesus. After five boosts you'd think he'd have some faith. But I guess that's a little hypocritical, since he's the last person I'd put my trust in. I call him an asshole under my breath and hop off the truck. My left leg stings with pins and needles. I bend to stretch my back, massage the kinks out of my thighs, and then hobble to the back of the trailer.

Nick slides open the cargo door.

"Bring it down," Roger says. "I need to see the whole car."

Because we'd leave half of it in California? I could drag it out, play with him a bit, but one look at the dark circles under Chelsea's eyes and I know the team is eager to put George to rest. "Roger, Roger."

With Nick's go-ahead, I climb up onto the back of the truck and into the Cosma Ray. My fingers feather across the walnut finish on the steering wheel as I think about our narrow escape. I blow out the last remnants of fear through my nose.

Nick adjusts the ramp and gives me the signal that I'm clear.

I fire up the car.

Exhaust fumes are trapped inside the confined space of the trailer. The engine noise rattles the steel walls. As I shift the car out of neutral, the headlight beams bounce off the front panel and blind me. I flick them off, relying on the eerie glow of the reverse lights to guide me out of the trailer.

The wide tires hit the metal ramp with two slightly out-of-sync clicks.

"Keep coming," Nick shouts.

The engine sputters like it might give out, but I tap the gas and a puff of smoke blooms from the tailpipe. George settles back into an easy idle.

When all four tires hit the pavement, I stick my head out the window. "You want me to park this thing?"

"There's an empty stall at the end of the Corvettes," he says.

I drive inside the warehouse and putter past the Mako Shark. Thoughts of Kevin hit me like a bad nightmare. A shiver crawls up my spine. The sooner we finish this gig, the less chance we'll have of running into my ex and his creepy boss.

I'm not even out of the car before Roger starts petting it. A low purring sound rumbles from his mouth. Okay, I get it, the guy's got a car fetish, but I can't watch. This whole ritual makes my skin crawl.

Chelsea wraps her arm around my shoulder and tilts her head toward mine. "You did really good tonight."

"You too," I say. If not for Chelsea, there's no way Nick and I could have cracked those locks. "But there's not enough money in the world to pay for the therapy we'll need after tonight."

"Booze," she says. "Lots and lots of booze."

A grin splits her face when she catches me nervously steal a glance at Nick. The butterflies in my stomach start fluttering and I know something's changed between us. He gives me one of those lazy smiles and *KABOOM!* My insides explode.

"Or that," Chelsea says. She squeezes my shoulder. "Go get some therapy."

I feel myself blush.

Mat and Nick join Chelsea and me at the front of Corvette Row. Roger is still feeling up George, which is wrong on so many levels. I shake my head and look away. "The guy's messed up."

Even Chelsea agrees.

"I don't know about you guys," Mat says, "but I need some sleep. Let's blow this place."

Roger looks up from the hood of the car. "Before you leave, Julia, there's something I'd like to talk to you about."

I stand at unease.

"You guys go ahead," Nick says to Chelsea. "I'll stay behind with Jules. We can take my bike back to the mansion."

Chelsea hesitates. "You've been driving all day. You okay?"

His cheeks go a little pink. "It's cute that you're worried about me."

"It's disturbing you think my concern is for you," she says, giving me a pointed look.

When they leave, Roger flags me over.

I start toward him, but Nick grabs my wrist. "You don't have to do this alone."

I have a suspicion I know what Roger wants to talk about— Nick's car—but I like that he wants to protect me. Warmth spreads through my body and I get a little shy. My tongue ties into knots.

"Whatever you have to say to Julia, you can say to me too," Nick says, mistaking my nerves for fear.

Roger reaches into the front pocket of his corduroy pants and tosses us a small key. I barely catch it.

"That opens the box over there," he says. "In it, you'll find keys for any of the cars that were obtained . . . legally."

I stare at the key. "I don't get it."

"Perhaps you want to know a little more about some of the cars," Roger says, with a bit of emphasis on the last part of the sentence. "However, be advised—you're not permitted to drive them."

I'm still not quite getting what he's putting down, but my gut tells me he's giving me a hint about Nick's car. Is Vicki in the building? I scope out the first floor, skimming over the Mustangs. It's not there. Wow. He's really not good at this.

"And you probably *shouldn't* go near the third floor," he says, his eyes never wavering from mine.

Got it. Vicki's on the top level.

I nudge Nick's shoulder. "Hey, wanna go sit in a Ferrari?"

His eyebrows knit in confusion. "Uh . . . sure?"

I know he's wary, but I need him on board, so I grab his hand and drag him toward the second level of the Trophy Case. Glancing over my shoulder, I find Roger staring at us with an almost wistful expression.

"Lock up when you're done," he calls out.

I'm shocked he'd leave us alone with his precious collection of cars. But as he watches us round the corner, I wonder if he isn't thinking about his wife, and a love that ended too quickly.

What kind of man was Roger before she died? A sadness starts seeping into my bones. Maybe things could have been different for all of us.

Nick stops at the front of a modern sports car—sleek, silver, shaped almost like a bullet. Probably goes just as fast.

"What the hell is that? A rocket?"

"It's an Aston Martin One-Seventy-Seven," he says with a touch of awe.

"It's—"

"Breathtaking," he says. "Let's take it for a spin."

Before I can respond, he climbs into the unlocked car. I open the passenger door and stick my head in. "You have no intention of following the rules, do you?"

He laughs. "Probably not. But don't worry, I don't even know if I could handle this thing. Hop in." I hesitate and he rolls his eyes. "We're not going anywhere. I just want to sit in it."

"Mr. Barker! Are you asking me to park?"

His wolfish grin widens. "Well, when you put it that way . . ."

I climb into the car and settle into the seat. The leather closes in around me like a glove. Everything about the car screams expensive. The black detailing is polished, chrome gadgets buffed. There is nothing antique, nothing *classic* about this car—there's not even a stick shift—and yet, I'm mesmerized by it.

"This beast tops out at two hundred miles per hour," Nick says. "Now, that's some speed."

"Faster than Vicki?"

He frowns like he can't understand why I'd bring up his Mustang—an obviously touchy topic—and it takes me a second to realize I probably should have waited. Too late to take the words back now.

He shrugs. "Vicki's a project, but she'd never keep up with something like this."

"I guess I never thought of you as a racer."

His eyes light up. "I'd love to be. But I'd take a cross country run over a lap track any day." He shifts so we're sort of facing each other. "That kind of racing takes cash—a lot more than the hundred grand Roger's forking over. I've got more important things to worry about with that money."

A tiny frog gets trapped in my throat. "I'm sorry."

His eyebrows furrow in confusion.

"For Vicki," I say.

He lowers his chin. "Should have known you'd figure it out."

"You weren't exactly subtle about how much you hated me," I say, not without a bit of tremble in my voice. "And then Kevin—"

He opens his mouth, but I slap my hand across his lips.

"I swear I didn't know it was your car." The apology seems ridiculous because I didn't even know *him* when I stole his prized pony. "If I'd known how important she was . . ." I break off because what I'm about to say is a lie. I want to tell him that if I'd known about his parents, about what the car meant to him, I would have left her idling by the curb. But he'd see right through me because back then, the only person I cared about besides myself was Emma. "God, I'm such an ass."

Nick laces his fingers through mine. "No more than me."

I stare at my chipped fingernails pressed up against his tan skin. "Makes total sense why you held a grudge against me." He rubs his thumb across Emma's name tattooed on the inside of my wrist. "I didn't care who I hurt, you know?" I go on. "I did whatever I needed to get money for Emma."

"I understand," he says.

"She knows." It wasn't something I planned on admitting to Nick, but it's eating me up and I need to get it off my chest. "I'm, like, the worst role model in the universe." A tear trickles down my cheek. "I can't even believe how much I've let her down."

Nick rubs my cheek dry. "She's not a dumb kid, Jules. Maybe she doesn't fully understand now, but later, when this is all over, she'll figure it out."

"I have to go legit after this," I say, with a strength I don't quite believe is achievable. "She can never think this is okay, that what I've done is acceptable. I can't keep justifying my actions."

Nick looks thoughtful. "I get it. After this, I'm done too."

He flicks his tongue over his lip ring. "The Barris car changed things."

"Because we almost got caught?"

"I wish." He squeezes my hand. "But I think the love of the thrill is built into my DNA. I'm always going to crave the adrenaline rush, which is why I want to race. The whole drive back from the Petersen, I kept thinking about the car in the trailer. Barris is my fucking idol"—his voice rises—"and I stole a car from him. Not just any car, but his prized possession." He points to his chest. "How can I be okay with that? It was the biggest boost of my life and I'm not proud. I'm ashamed." He takes a deep breath. "I don't want to be that guy anymore."

"You're not *that* guy, Nick. You just hit a roadblock."

His eyes search mine. "Is that why you gave up dance?"

I chew on the end of my thumbnail. "Partly."

"So after all this is over, go back."

"That's a nice thought, but . . ." I swallow. "That dream's over now, Nick. Making money in the arts is tough. If it was just me, I could consider it, but I have Emma to think about. We couldn't survive on what I'd bring in as a dancer."

"She'd be happy knowing you're doing something you want," he says. "You'd be following your dream. What's more inspirational than that?"

It's not enough. Getting back into dance isn't the same as riding a bike. You don't just pick up where you left off. I'd have to practice for hours, retraining my muscles to obey all the tiny little commands they've long forgotten. Even if I could make my feet light again, the heaviness in my heart will always weigh me down.

"Just think about it," Nick says. "I *saw* you dance and it was . . . magical." I look away but he tilts my chin so we're eye-to-eye. "You belong on a stage, Julia. That was some of the most beautiful dancing I've ever seen."

I can't take it. The intensity. The emotion. We're moving too fast. I push away and laugh. "You're not a very good judge. I fell on my ass."

"And you got up again. Seems like you've got a pretty good track record of doing that."

I could deny everything he's saying, but we'd both be lying. I *do* miss dance. Is it possible, after all of this is over, that I could find my way back to it again? There's a flame in Nick's ice-blue eyes that lights a fire in me, makes me almost believe in the impossible.

"Careful," I say. "I'm starting to fall for you."

It's meant to be teasing, an attempt at lightening the mood, but I can tell Nick isn't joking around when he tilts his head toward me and whispers, "I think I fell for you before I even met you."

My heart skips a full beat, but I try to play it off. "Well, I *am* a bit of a legend."

"There's that, too."

"And I stole your car, which is always a great start to a relationship."

Holy shit, his car! I yank my hand out of his and shove open the passenger door. My pulse starts to race and I must look like a crazy person because Nick's entire face is creased with confusion. I have so fucked up this moment.

But my apology isn't enough.

Words come out in a gush of air. "Come with me."

I drag him around the winding corridor that leads to the third level of the Trophy Case. It doesn't matter that the RX-8 will be there—I'm becoming immune to its power over me. Everything happens for a reason, my social worker sometimes says, and it's with growing confidence I believe I was supposed to get caught.

I was supposed to realize what a dick Kevin is.

I was supposed to get Emma away from the Millers.

We were supposed to meet Roger.

And maybe, just maybe, I was even supposed to meet Nick.

I've never been a believer in that fate shit—at least not until now.

"Julia?" Nick's breath comes in heavy rasps. "What is the rush?"

And that's when we both see her.

Vicki.

Her polished Candy Apple paint shimmers under the fluorescent lights. I recognize her—and it all comes back to me. The day, the minute I took her. How easily I popped the lock and slid under the dash. How I almost stalled her trying to push her into second gear.

But it's not nostalgia that makes my pulse surge up a notch.

The expression on Nick's face yanks on the strings around my heart. Unraveling me until I am vulnerable and exposed. Pride fills my chest. I have done this. Given Nick this moment.

"How . . . ?" He shakes his head in disbelief. "Is this . . . ?"

I laugh through my tears. "You don't recognize your own car?"

Nick grabs me around the waist and scoops me into his arms. His head nestles against my neck. Shivers run down the length of my spine.

He pulls back, and quirks an eyebrow. "You didn't steal her, right?"

"She's legal."

He plants a hard kiss on my cheek. My forehead. The tip of my nose. "You're amazing! How did you pull this off?"

"I can't take all the credit." I hate that I have to admit this, but it wouldn't be right to have him think otherwise. "Roger helped."

He looks pained. "What did it cost you? If you had to give up something . . ."

I shake my head. "Shhh."

He pulls me close again. "You're amazing, you know that?"

"I'm not." A teardrop breaks free. "But I needed to do this."

Nick lifts my chin. "I forgave you a long time ago." As if

to make me believe it, he kisses me hard on the lips. I'm so shocked I don't even know how to respond. The second time is sweeter, softer. My heart begins to pound.

"I don't know what happens next," he says, and I'm surprised by the emotion in his eyes. "But I know we make a great team. Not stealing cars—for real. Tell me you feel it too."

I've tried to slough it off, pretend our chemistry isn't real. But it's impossible to ignore. The future is uncharted, an open map of unknown roads. Maybe our paths will go in opposite directions at some point, the journey will change. But for right now, in this moment and as long as it lasts, I can't think of a better travel companion.

"I'm willing to try."

Nick pulls me in to him and buries his face in my neck. His hand weaves through my hair to lightly tilt my head upward. I can't take my eyes off his lips. They move to meet mine. Tentative and sweet.

I am completely sucked in.

My bottom teeth scrape against his piercing and he groans. He pulls me closer to deepen the kiss. His tongue probes between my lips as his hand sweeps across my back.

My entire body goes numb.

"You're beautiful, Jules."

His mouth moves to my shoulder, my neck, behind my ear. Goose pimples cover my skin. Our bodies mold together. I am drowning, sinking, melting into the floor when his hands reach around my waist and scoop me off the ground. I wrap my arms around his neck and let him carry me to the hood of his car.

As he leans in to reclaim my lips, my pulse redlines.

23

The List

~~Jack-1970 Dodge Super Bee 426~~
~~José-1965 Corvette Mako Shark II~~
~~Reggie-1968 Chevy ZL1 Camaro~~
~~Adam-1970 Dodge Hemi Coronet R/T~~
~~George-1968 Corvette Cosma Ray~~
James-1964 Aston Martin DBS
Eleanor-1967 Mustang Shelby GT500

JAMES IS IN PIECES.

It's almost like someone went all Bond-action on the Aston Martin—took it out, rode it hard, and then parked it up on blocks to rot. Tragic, since based on its pictures, the car is kind of impressive.

If you're into that sort of thing.

"It's worth millions," Mat says, as if that should make me want it. He shifts forward on his stool and jabs at a picture of the car on his tablet. We all hunch over the round table in the game room. "I mean, look at it. Machine guns in the front fenders. Tire cutters on the wheels . . ."

Chelsea's eyes widen. "Wow, you are *totally* nerding out."

Everyone laughs except Nick.

The muscle in the side of his cheek flexes. "Fuck."

I get why he's pissed. We've spent the last couple of days coasting, hanging out like normal teens, acting like the Barris job was our last. Nice fairy tale while it lasted. But the truth is, we got lazy.

Mat grimaces. "Obviously I can't find another *missing* James." The Aston Martin has been missing since it was stolen more than a decade ago. "Even if I could locate the replica, Roger wouldn't go for it."

"Maybe he wouldn't notice," Chelsea says.

"Oh, he'd notice," Nick says. "The duplicate comes without all the bells and whistles. The original car was too heavy for the car chases in *Goldfinger*." At Chelsea's blank stare, he half smiles. "That's the Bond movie this car is from."

She flops down on the sofa next to Nick and puts her feet up on the coffee table. Her toenails are apricot, like the paint on the Cosma Ray. "Without going all nerd on me, how did you find the car, Mat?"

"Here's the irony," he says. "The car was stolen from an old airplane hangar back in '97. Yesterday, it turns up here"—he points to an image on the screen—"in a similar hangar just east of the city."

"Feels a bit coincidental," I say.

Nick snatches the iPad out of Mat's hand. "Let me see that."

I peer over his shoulder to take a look. Thick vines cover the outside of a rusted old building that sits on a field of over-grown grass. A forest of trees surrounds the place. "You're sure James is in there? That place looks abandoned."

And a little like a trap.

"That's the beauty of it," Mat says. "Those inside shots were taken using some sweet technology Roger hooked me up with. That's why the pictures are a bit grainy."

Chelsea glances up from where she's begun removing the polish from her toenails. "You took photos of the car from the outside?"

Mat rocks back on his heels. "Not bad, huh?"

Chelsea doesn't seem to notice the way his blush dims under the soft Tiffany light. "Okay, I'll bite. If James is shacked up in some hangar in the woods, why don't we just go get it?"

"It's not whole," Nick says.

"Roger freaked out over a busted side mirror," I remind her. "This isn't that." I squint at the image on the screen. "We're look-ing at new wheels, and for sure there's damage on the front end."

Chelsea holds up a finger. "Wait. What color is it?"

I lift an eyebrow. "Silver . . ."

She roots around in a basket tucked under the coffee table and pulls out a bottle of metallic nail polish. My eyes go wide. "Are you matching your nails to each boost?"

"Obviously." She holds the nail brush midpolish. "I'm stoked for Nightmist Blue."

Nick steers us back on topic. "We can't do anything about the state of the car. Roger will have to take it as is—or not at all."

"That's only half the problem," Mat says. "Security is tight."

Chelsea looks thoughtful. "Never broke into an airplane hangar before. That's one for the bucket list."

My lips curl into an involuntary smirk. "You have a bucket list?"

"We pulled off the Petersen," Nick says.

I can't imagine anything being more complicated than that, but if Mat has concerns, I'm worried too.

"What you don't see is the live perimeter fence." Mat traces a square around the building with his fingertip. "I can cut the alarms there, and sever the other alarm wires—which is funny, since that's exactly how the thieves ganked the car years ago."

"Good so far," Nick says.

"But accessing the property won't be easy. The owner's house is half a mile up on the road—which is surrounded by trees. Probably the closest thing we've got to a forest around here." He hesitates. "Also, there's a dog."

"Okay, let's say we get past Cujo, anything else we need to worry about?"

Mat shifts his gaze to me. "We'd need to tow it off the property."

"Tow trucks are slow," Nick says.

Not to mention about as subtle as a Volkswagen Beetle on the Autobahn.

"We should get Roger to weigh in." All eyes land on me. "Even before we plan this boost, we have to know if the car's in good enough shape. Otherwise we're spinning our wheels."

Mat points to the grainy picture of the Aston Martin. "Not those wheels."

I give him a high five. "Smart-ass."

"What if Roger doesn't want the car?" Chelsea says. "Does that mean the deal's off?" She screws the cap on the nail polish and flexes her toes in admiration. "Will he go back on his word?"

Mat's face drains of color. "Better not, or I'll have some words for that asshole. Finding my parents is the only reason I agreed to this."

Nick rolls off the coach. "He'll do right by us." He grabs my hand and squeezes. "Jules and I will make sure of it."

Music from Roger's room drifts out into the hall with loud dramatic beats and trumpets. An orchestra is playing *in* his bedroom. Either that or those are some impressive surround-sound speakers.

I toe the edge of the Persian rug covering the inlaid floor in the hallway. A massive raised panel door is inches from my fist but I can't seem to muster the courage to knock.

I've just about figured out what I'm going to say when the door swings open. Roger stands in the frame wearing nothing but a thin, short robe that barely hits mid-thigh. My gag reflux ignites. I squeeze my eyes shut. Too late. The image of his pasty white legs is burned into memory.

Annoyance flickers over his face.

"Give me a minute," he says, closing the door.

I crash into Nick's chest. "Kill me now."

Nick shakes with laughter. "That could have been so much worse."

"Don't even go there."

Seconds later, Roger comes out of his room fully dressed. His slicked-back, wet hair only accents his receding hairline. He runs his tongue along the top of his mouth in an exaggerated expression of displeasure.

I'm conscious of how close I stand to Nick.

Maybe he's pissed about our relationship or, whoops, he checked the security footage at the Trophy Case and saw the steam rising off the hood of Nick's car. I meant to ask Mat to delete that film, but I couldn't think of how to phrase it without embarrassing myself.

"I can assume you aren't foolish enough to reopen negotiations."

Part of me thought Roger and I had bonded over Vicki, but it's clear the only thing he cares about is the cars on that list. Asking him for a favor means I've used up any leverage we might have had.

"The Bond car's a bust," Nick says.

Roger blinks. "I don't understand that terminology."

"The car's in pieces," I say. "No wheels, exterior damage."

That gets his attention. "Can you salvage it?" he asks Nick.

"Impossible to know right now."

Roger grunts. "Aren't you some kind of mechanical genius? Never mind. Just get me the car."

We could have called that bet. "It's not even a showpiece car anymore. What about a substitute? Maybe another Camaro?"

"I must have the Aston Martin," Roger says. His voice cools. "That is nonnegotiable. Now, if you'll excuse me."

Roger disappears into his room.

"We'll need a tow," I whisper. The orchestra kicks up again and I raise my voice. "It's not like we can rent one."

"Or steal one," Nick says. "If we got busted, we'd have no chance of outrunning the cops."

"Know anyone with a truck?"

Nick chews on his lip. "I do—but I don't think you'll like the plan."

*　　*　　*

"This is the stupidest idea ever and you're an idiot," I say. "And I hate you."

Nick shrugs like he knows I'm joking, which is partially the truth. Mostly I'm scared. I'd tell him as much, but I can't even look at him right now. He reeks of cheap whiskey. It's in his hair, splashed across his T-shirt—there's even a giant alcohol stain on his thigh.

He's wasted.

At least, that's what we need Kevin to think.

Kevin.

At the thought of seeing him again, my stomach clenches with unease. Which is why I'm hanging outside the pub while Nick pulls off an Academy Award–worthy performance.

I make a left turn into the parking lot of the HAZE Lounge, a run-down bar where the owners don't double-check ID and scum like my ex go to suck back a few illegal drinks. A popular watering hole among Riley's crew.

A giant neon cowboy waves at us in the distance. Vegas Vic isn't really flagging us into the HAZE, but from this angle, it almost looks that way.

Nick drapes his arm across my chest and slurs. "Do you thhhink I thound drunk?"

"If the slurring doesn't work, your stench will do the trick." My nose scrunches up. "Jesus, are you sure you *didn't* down that bottle?"

"Stone-cold sober."

I'm still nervous. We're taking a huge risk and I'm not convinced the payoff will be worth it. The plan seems simple: Nick will bump into Kevin inside the bar. He'll act like we broke up and he needs a buddy to drown his sorrows. Nick will shift the conversation to shop talk, which makes sense, since boosting cars and me are the only things the two of them have in common. Nick will slip in the information about the Aston Martin. Kevin will pass the info on to his boss, because that douche bag is always looking for brownie points. If Riley takes the bait—and that's the part that worries me—his crew will boost the car for us.

And then we'll steal it from them.

"A lot could go wrong here," I say. "What if Kevin doesn't tell Riley?"

"That shit-weasel needs any piece of leverage he can get if he wants to stay in Riley's good books. I know what it's like to be on the outs." He leans across the console and kisses me on the cheek. "Trust me."

I choke on his stench and shove him away. "You're so getting in the shower after this."

"If you say so."

"Alone."

His lower lip juts out. "Tease."

I bat my eyelashes and try to look coy, but flirting still makes me feel like the only duck in a pond filled with swans. Literally every girl on the planet is better at it than me.

Nick jumps out of the car and leans in through the window. "We've got this."

"Make sure you're hooked up."

He pulls back the collar of his leather jacket to show me the Bluetooth wire taped to his neck. As I start to drive away, his low voice curls into my eardrum. "You're sexy when you're stressed out."

"Keep your head in the game, idiot."

I'm sure he can hear my smile through the wires.

I pull around to the back of the parking lot, find a spot between two beaters, and cut the lights. The Ford Escort I've chosen from Roger's selection of specialty bait cars is the least conspicuous, but it's still nicer than the rest of the vehicles around me.

A homeless guy plods from behind a Dumpster, bottle of booze dangling from his outstretched hand. If another zombie comes out, I'm activating my Apocalypse Survival Plan. For now, I lock the doors.

Another voice snake slithers through my earpiece. "Jesus, Nick. You look like hell."

Kevin.

Nick mumbles something but I can't hear over the background noise. I turn up the speaker and a high-pitched squeal bites at my eardrum. "Fuck." I turn it down and lean forward, my chest pressed up against the steering wheel like it's somehow going to help me hear.

The horn blasts.

Startled, I jump back.

Across the lot, the drunk zombie tilts his head with an inquisitive stare. I hold very still.

"Where's Ghost?"

The sneer in Kevin's tone is clear through my headset.

Nick lays it on thick. "Bitch dumped me."

According to Kevin, I wasn't worth much—certainly not getting busted over, which is why he bailed on me. He wouldn't have lasted a day in prison anyway. I don't care about him, but that doesn't mean the words don't sting.

I pull out a pair of binoculars from the glove box and train them on the windows of the bar. Bodies are everywhere, including a half-dozen women wearing not much more than bikinis. Two of them flank an oversize guy sporting a leather vest. I spot his Harley at the front entrance. He kisses the blonde on the cheek, plants one on the brunette's mouth, and then pulls them both closer to his side.

Somewhere behind him, I think I see Nick.

"Took a boost and fumbled it," he's saying. "And now I'm jammed up. Jammed real bad."

"That's the shits, man."

"You don't know the half of it," Nick says. "This car . . ."

Music from the band drowns out the rest of his sentence. Frustration shakes through me. I'm starting to think this plan isn't going to work.

"Why? So you can rat me out to your boss?"

Okay, so somehow I missed the transition, but it sounds like Nick's on track.

The interest in Kevin's voice is unmistakeable. "Nah, we got history, bro. I've got your back. You can bank on that."

"Bullshit," I spit out. I know from experience you can't believe a thing Kevin says. All trusting Kevin ever got me was a trip to the cop shop and a broken heart. I sniff. Screw that—love was never on the table.

Glasses clink together and there's some kind of murmured oath of secrecy before the band kicks in again and the conversation is drowned out by an out-of-tune bass riff trying to mimic Gene Simmons.

I can't hear a fucking word they're saying.

Two guys leave their seats at a table. Nick stumbles into view, nearly crashing into the chair. I catch him searching the parking lot for me before plunking down across from Kevin. Maybe if I zoom in enough, I can read their lips.

Their conversation cuts in and out between the guitar riffs.

". . . Bond movie . . ."

"Serious, bro?"

". . . airport hangar . . . security . . ."

I chew on my fingernails and tap the floor mat. Okay, Nick, time to wrap this up.

Across the parking lot, zombie dude slumps up against a rusted Chevy Malibu. A little paint, some TLC, the car would probably clean up nice.

Movement from the bar draws my attention. Nick stumbles into a standing position and fist-bumps Kevin. I throw the binoculars into the backseat, flick on the headlights, and drive up to the side of the bar.

A couple of guys come out and stare at me before getting into a taxi that pulls up behind me. By the time Nick trips into view, my nerves are rattled and my heart is pushing against my chest with fear.

"Well, hey there, purdy lady," he slurs. "Is it time for that shower now?"

His scent is so strong it takes my breath away. "Way past due." I wait for him to buckle up and then step on the gas. With the pulsing HAZE sign in the distance and the image of Kevin wiped clear, the tension finally drains from my shoulders. "You think he bought it?"

Nick rolls his head toward me and smirks. "Oh yeah. He practically pissed himself. I give it until morning before he spills his guts."

24

CHELSEA AND I ARE WHITE-HAIRED TWINS. I COME BY it naturally, and yet she wears it better.

The blue glow of her cell gives her tanned skin a slight neon hue that somehow looks exotic. I've never been more aware of our differences.

"Tell me again why you chose a white wig for this stakeout?"

Chelsea looks up from her Instagram feed. "Nick said we should make like we're invisible," she says. "So we're, like, sister ghosts."

Somehow I doubt that's what Nick meant.

She frowns. "Still nothing?"

"Nada." This is our third shift since Nick told Kevin about the Aston Martin. We figured Riley would have jumped on it faster, but maybe he's working through the logistics. It's not like they're working to a deadline.

Ten days.

That's what's left of our seven-week heist, and we've still got two cars to go. My confidence is beginning to wane—and that's a bad sign. I shuffle down in the seat, staying far enough above the dash so I can see what's happening.

We've parked on a side road that sits parallel to the hanger. A thick cluster of trees obstructs most of our view, but I managed to find a small clearing that allows just enough of a sight line.

Chelsea holds out a bag of popcorn. "Hungry?"

I can't eat when I'm stressed. "Go ahead."

She tosses a kernel into the air, catches it with the tip of her tongue, and curls it into her mouth. Her eating habits are a bit lizardlike tonight.

"I can't decide if that's sexy or gross."

She looks up at me from behind hooded lashes. "You'd be amazed what I can do with my tongue." To drive home the point, she licks her lips.

"Disgusting."

"So far you're the only one that thinks so."

That's probably true.

I check in with Mat, who is back at the mansion working on the trawling program. There's nothing new to report there, and Nick's asleep, so I turn on the radio to cut the silence.

Chelsea taps the dashboard clock. "I turn into a pumpkin at midnight."

"Three more hours of fun to be had."

She rolls her eyes. "Would it kill you to talk a little?"

The question takes me aback. I'm probably the worst stakeout partner, since for the past two hours, all I've done is stare through the binoculars and answer Chelsea's questions with one-line responses. Except when she asks about Nick. I pretend not to hear her.

"What, you want to gossip?"

She twists a strand of hair around her finger. "Sure, if we can gossip about you and Nick."

"No hablo Inglés."

She flicks a popcorn kernel at me. "Like hell you don't speak English. Come on. Give me something here."

I'm almost surprised it took her this long to say something. It's not like Nick and I have been hiding our . . . well, whatever we want to call it. But I'm not ready to tack a label on it. So much of our future depends on what happens in the next ten days.

But Chelsea's right. If I have any hope of building my friendship with her, I've got to open up a little. "We're taking it slow."

"I admire that," she says. "I'm more of an impulse girl."

No shit. "You ever regret those knee-jerk decisions?"

The shift in tone is unintentional, but Chelsea's body language tells me she's uncomfortable with the question. I think about dropping it when she sighs. "Are you asking if I miss my parents?"

"Do you?"

She scrunches up the empty popcorn bag and tosses it into the backseat. "Sometimes." She tilts her head. "Okay, maybe. But I don't regret leaving." She blows out a long breath. "Well, not entirely."

"Have you thought about going back?"

She shakes her head. "Not if my father came crawling on his hands and knees."

Something about the way her voice wavers tells me she isn't quite telling the truth about that, but I don't blame her for lying. Owning up after a fuck-up isn't easy.

But it's like Chelsea is the only one who hasn't really opened up.

"I've never known anyone who chose to go into the foster system," I say gently. In fact, I don't even know if that's possible.

Chelsea chews on her bottom lip. "Well, I'm not *technically* in the system." She swallows. "It's kind of complicated."

A flush of anger rides up my throat but I tamp it back. I'm a hypocrite to expect her to trust me, even after all we've been through. If there's one thing I know something about, it's how to build effective walls.

A flash of light catches my eye, and I decide to drop it. Maybe she'll tell me when she's ready.

We both peer over the dash as headlights pull up to the hangar. Seconds later, blue and reds flicker through the trees.

"That's not Riley," Chelsea says.

My stomach plummets. "Cops."

Chelsea scooches up and squints through the bug-splattered windshield. "Kind of strange how the police tracked James down after all this time."

"There are no coincidences in boosting cars."

Which means instead of taking the bait, Riley called the police. It doesn't make sense. Either he knew he'd been set up or he has a backup plan.

I zoom the binoculars in on the scene. Two officers get out of a squad car and wave flashlights at the hangar. One walks the perimeter while the other tugs on the door.

A second set of headlights cuts through the trees.

"Tow truck," Chelsea says.

"Fuck." I hand her the camera. "Zoom in on the logo as much as you can. You won't get a clear picture, but maybe Mat can work with whatever shows up."

A shadowy figure runs onto the scene on foot. That's got to be the owner. Judging by the way his fists punch the air, he clearly wasn't expecting this raid.

"They're going to take the car."

I hold the binoculars steady.

Chelsea's voice lifts. "What do we do if they take the car?"

Tension spider-webs across my neck.

"Jules!"

I snap my head toward her. "I don't fucking know." Her eyes fill with tears and I curse under my breath. "I'm sorry. I just don't . . ."

Have a clue.

Without the Aston, we've got nothing. All of our work until now, worthless.

Think, Jules. Think.

I hand Chelsea the binoculars and grab my phone. "I'm calling Nick."

One.

Two.

He picks up on the third ring. "Jules . . . ?"

"We've got a serious problem. Cops are here."

His voice tightens. "You've been made?"

"No." I blow out a deep breath. "But the police are taking James. There's a tow truck and everything. They're outside the—"

"Inside," Chelsea says. "The tow truck is backing up to the door."

"Stay calm," Nick says. His voice is muffled like he's covering the microphone, and I hear him talking to someone else—has to be Mat. "Damn it. I thought for sure Riley would take that bait."

"There's a cash reward for that car. Maybe Kevin wants that all to himself."

Money over loyalty, that's how he works. Always looking out for Number One. Jesus. How is that a lesson I didn't learn?

"James is on the flatbed," Chelsea says.

My stomach roils. "What's the plan here, Nick?"

A beat, and then, "Follow them."

The vein in my neck thickens into a tight cord. I work through the logistics, the options. There aren't any. If I don't do this, we've failed.

I've failed.

259

"They're probably going to the impound," he says. "We just need to know which one."

I can read between the lines of false optimism. It doesn't matter how experienced we are, how much our crew has gelled, stealing a car from the LVPD isn't as easy as it seems in the movies. Distracting guards, disabling cameras, using blowtorches to cut through fencing—one big Hollywood lie.

"They're leaving," Chelsea says. "What now?"

"Follow them," Nick repeats.

"And if they don't go to an impound?"

There's a chance they won't, given the car's significance.

"Follow them to wherever they park it."

Right. I hand my cell over to Chelsea. "Tell Nick we'll call him back when we have a location."

Boosting cars is one thing. This PI shit is a whole different pile of crap, and I can't afford the distraction.

I flip a U-turn and drive toward the hangar. The back roads are a maze of unmarked pavement. I stay well under the speed limit to keep off anyone's radar, but by the third intersection, I realize we're lost. I never even got close enough to tail them.

I make a left turn and double back.

Hit reverse and turn right.

Everything looks familiar, but different. There are no landmarks or street signs to gauge my location. I think I see headlights to the left, but it's just a kid on a dune buggy zipping along the ditch.

Chelsea points right. "There!"

I suck in a gasp, hoping she's right.

But as we close in, I realize it's an oversize camper trailer, not the tow truck. I veer off to the side to see in front of it. The road stretches into a dark abyss.

They're gone.

I pull over to the side of the road and slam on the brake. "Fuck!" My fist punches the dashboard, sending a fiery ball of flame through my wrist. "Fuck. Fuck. Fuck!" I'm so mad I start crying. I can barely see through the haze of my grief.

Chelsea reaches across the seat and squeezes my hand. "It's okay, girl. You don't know these roads."

But I should have.

Instead of feeling sorry for myself or gossiping about Nick, I should have been studying maps. Memorizing back roads and detours.

"I'll GPS directions to the mansion," Chelsea says.

I can't help but snort. "Maybe I should stay lost for a while. At least until I figure out how to make this up to the guys."

At this, Chelsea brightens. "You'll be fine. You're practically sleeping with one of them, right?"

My jaw drops.

"Well, if you're not going to tell me what's going on, I have to imagine it." She grins. "And boy, do I have one helluva good imagination."

25

ROGER IS *PISSED*.

Like, cartoon-character mad. He stalks across the sitting room floor with enough force to dent the wood. His eyes are glossed with rage.

He whirls on me and I flinch. Jesus. He's batshit crazy.

"Just a couple of days," Nick says.

Roger paces closer to the long sofa table. A crystal frame with a picture of his wife and some antique-looking opera glasses dot the tabletop. He clears it with one sweep, smashing the frame. The image stares up at me from the floor, somehow eerily familiar.

Chelsea gasps.

We've copped to everything—tracking down the car, trying to bait Riley, losing the tail. I didn't expect Roger to do cartwheels, but he's beyond irrational. I edge closer to Nick.

One signal from me and we'll grab Emma and run. "We'll get it back."

Roger's face goes red and he levels me with a stare that sends a shiver down my spine, eyes like deadly laser beams. "Do you have any idea what you have done?"

The question seethes from between his gritted teeth and for a second I'm stunned. Roger's crazy has always hovered just under the surface, but right now it's bubbling over. Every hair on my body stands up in alert.

"We're still checking impounds," Mat says. "No luck."

"As I understand it, your current theory is that"—he snarls at me—"your repulsive ex-boyfriend told the police about the car—*my car*—and they have towed it to a common impound lot? A car that's worth several million dollars?"

It does sound implausible when you put it that way.

"I get it. We screwed up." My muscles tense. "But if you could just give us a couple more—"

"There will be no further negotiations." He balls his hands into fists and strides toward me. I'm not the kind of girl who cowers, but this lunatic has blown a serious gasket and my whole body chills. "Find. My. Car."

Nick wedges his way between us, his face an inch from Roger's. "Back off."

I exhale hard. My T-shirt sticks to the small of my back and my heart pounds so fast I'm sure it's about to punch through my chest. We may have underestimated Roger's wrath.

Roger lowers his voice. Still menacing, but softer. Calm. "Without the Aston Martin, the entire deal is off." An icy chill crackles along my spine. "All of you—including Emma—will be out."

Emma.

I can't even remember the last time I've seen her. I've been so wrapped up in this, in all of the stuff with Nick. My chest constricts. She's the whole reason I'm doing this.

"What's the harm in waiting, Rog?" Chelsea opts for charm. "Won't it be that much sweeter?"

He whirls on her and points. "If you ever want to get into Harvard, I suggest you shut up."

Chelsea blinks in surprise.

Roger stalks to the foot of the foyer and calls up the stairs for Emma. "Would you like to come down here for a minute?"

Fear paralyzes me. "What are you doing?"

Emma peers over the railing and waves when she sees me. "Jules!" A pink tutu floats around her waist like cotton candy, and the ballet slippers Nick bought for her are snug to her feet. The ghost of my younger self glides down the stairs.

"Roger got me into dance lessons," she says.

Tears spring to my eyes and I blink-blink-blink to shut them down. This is my sister at her happiest and I'm about to strip it all away.

At the bottom of the staircase, she lifts her leg and points her toe toward Nick. "They fit!"

In my periphery, I can see Roger smirking, watching the scene unfold with calculated precision. A sense of dread forms at the base of my neck. I've met dozens of shady people in my life, but never have I gone head-to-head with someone so masterful at manipulation.

Roger is enjoying this control.

Emma looks around the room. "What's going on here?"

Chelsea swoops in with a smooth lie. "Roger said you had a surprise." She clucks her tongue. "You are totally rocking that tutu, girl."

Emma practically lifts off the ground with excitement. "You'll come to my audition, right?"

"Wouldn't miss it," Mat and I say in unison.

She beams. "It's a musical play. I'm trying out for a lead."

It's hard to hold back my surprise. Emma's anxiety has always prevented her from trying out for anything like this. I worried her nerves would keep her from dancing.

Stability.

The doctors are right. That's Emma's cure. It's more than just the roof over her head—Roger has taken an interest in her. Despite everything, I believe it's genuine, and maybe that's the hard part. None of our other foster parents have ever cared. They just wanted the paycheck.

Roger clears his throat. "I'm afraid I won't be able to make the audition," he says. "I have some important business to attend. Mr. Grasdal will make sure you arrive on time."

Emma scrunches up her nose. "In the limo?" At Roger's nod, she shakes her head. "That's okay. Melissa's mom said she would take me."

My eyebrow arches.

"I met her at registration," Emma says to me, grinning. "Her mom is a friend of Roger's."

Roger claps his hands together and avoids my curious stare. I'm happy Emma is meeting people, but shouldn't I know what's going on? Why didn't anyone tell me?

"Very well, then. Emma, dear, you should get some rest. Your first class starts quite early tomorrow."

Emma gives me a hug good night. I hold on a little longer than I should, and I feel her body tense up. She knows something isn't right. "I'm proud of you," I whisper.

It's the truth, but not what she wants to hear. I can't assure her I'm not up to no good. If anything, I am more resolved than ever to get back Roger's car—so that we can leave this place forever.

"Good night, sweet pea," I say.

Her eyes cloud over. "You know I hate when you call me that."

As she disappears up the stairs, I realize I've made a mistake. The only time I use that nickname is when I'm about to screw up.

My blood boils. I need air, a drink, something. Pushing past Nick, I half run toward the pool, blinking away the tears that mark frustration, sadness, the utter loss of being trapped.

Nick catches up with me at the edge of the waterfall. "Roger won't hurt her."

"He already has."

I know Nick understands. Roger has crafted a perfect environment for Emma, a place where she feels safe, loved, and, most important, part of a family. If we don't pull off this heist, he'll take that all away.

And this time, the loss will crush her.

Nick pulls me into his arms but even he can't stop me from trembling. "None of us really knows what Roger's capable of," I say.

He brushes his finger across my lips.

I sense Roger's approach before he appears. He gives me a tentative, almost apologetic wave. "Julia, can we talk?"

Nick holds my waist, like he thinks I might bolt. I lift my chin to meet Roger's gaze.

"I'm afraid my behavior tonight has been deplorable." He stuffs his hands into the pockets on the side of his vest. "I hope you know I would never intentionally harm Emma. Any of you, really. I admit I can get carried away when it comes to my passions."

My shoulders slump. "I know the cars are important, Roger. I just don't get why . . ." My voice trails off. Why should the reasons matter? It doesn't change the fact that we've already agreed to the job, that we're in too deep.

"I know what it feels like to lose someone," he says, and I

know he means his wife. "It leaves a hole." Sadness radiates off him, chipping away at the armor strapped to my heart. "We were supposed to celebrate our twenty-fifth anniversary this year. Silver." He blows out a breath and changes the subject. "I'd never let anything happen to Emma. Please believe that."

In spite of everything, I do. "We'll get the Aston Martin back."

He fiddles with his Rolex. "If it's more money you want . . ."

Tempting. "It's not."

Roger nods. "Again, I apologize."

"I think I just need to get out of here for a bit." I try for a smile. "We're all a little cooped up."

Nick puts his hand on my shoulder. "Stay here. I have an idea."

Alone with Roger, the awkwardness creeps back in. He kicks at a patch of grass, looking sheepish. "I've registered Emma in a good ballet school."

"I don't doubt that." Though a twinge of resentment trickles through the gratitude. I should have done that. "Emma's dream is to dance, so thank you."

"I'm not a bad man, Jules."

Nick whistles from across the yard. I look over and he waves me toward him. "I should go. . . ."

Holy hell, this is awkward.

Roger bows his head a little, sending a shockwave of guilt through me. I should say I know he's not bad—maybe just a little misguided—but the words don't come out. I offer him a pathetic finger wave instead, and then catch up to Nick, who is already in his Mustang with the window rolled down.

The engine purrs like it wants to go fast.

He leans across the console to push open the passenger door and winks. "Wanna go for a ride?"

There is suddenly nothing I want more.

"Hell yeah." I hip check the door closed and climb in through the window.

Vicki corners like she's on rails.

My shoulder bashes into the side of the car door before I'm jostled left. Right. Another left. The car picks up speed.

Everything feels so fast, but my senses are heightened by the blindfold across my eyes. Nick's idea. That, and the promise of a surprise.

His fingers skim across my knee midshift and my skin tingles. I feel everything—the rumble of his laugh, the vibrations of the car flying across the asphalt, the steady beat of my pulse.

The tires squeal as we peel around another corner.

"I think I'm going to be sick."

"Don't you dare throw up in Vicki."

I pretend to make gagging noises.

"That's it, we're taking the long way," he says. I can't see his grin, but I hear it.

I thought being on his motorcycle was the pinnacle of excitement, but I realize this is so much more. Tonight, we are not planning a boost, not sneaking away in the shadows, putting our lives at risk. For the first time since I can remember, I am free.

Nick downshifts and eases off the gas. Slowly, he comes to a stop and turns off the ignition. I wonder if my disappointment is as visible as it feels. "Do I get to take off the blindfold yet?"

He shushes me.

The passenger door opens and Nick holds on to my wrists, leading me out of the car. I'm dizzy, disoriented, but he doesn't let me stumble.

"You trust me, right?"

The question lands hard. For so long I've fought to keep my emotions in check, masking my feelings under the pretense of taking care of me and my sister. Truth is, I've been afraid to let anyone in.

But in two months, Nick and I have been thrown together under the most difficult circumstances.

I've laughed.

Cried.

Fucked up.

Nick's seen me at my best and my worst, and through it all, he's stuck by my side. It's more than boosting cars that bonds us and I'm surprised to realize . . .

"Yes, I do trust you."

He kisses my cheek and then takes my arm, guiding me along what I think is a sidewalk. He removes my blindfold.

My reflection stares back from a bank of tinted windows. The building has sandcastle beige stucco walls, with swooping architecture that reminds me of the curl of sheet music. "Where are we?"

Nick bends over the door lock with a tool that looks suspiciously like one of Chelsea's.

"Are you breaking into this place?"

The lock clicks and he yanks open the door. "We're just borrowing it for a little while." He motions for me to go inside.

Nick flicks a switch and a series of fluorescent lights flicker to life. The lobby is clean, professional, and filled with memorabilia from various famous ballets. Framed satin slippers from one version of *The Nutcracker*. A signed poster from the cast of *Romeo and Juliet*.

Tutus hang from a rack outside a small merchandise shop that's obviously closed.

I'm utterly speechless. Because even though I have never been to the Nevada Ballet Theatre, I have dreamed of dancing on this stage since I was a little girl. I'd recognize it anywhere.

"Hang tight," he says, disappearing from sight for a second. When he returns, he holds out his hand. "Come with me."

A single spotlight shines over the stage in the giant theater. The memories come rushing back. Glitter and costumes and muscles that ache with a need to be stronger, better, the best. My eyes fill with tears.

Nick pushes me gently toward the stage. "Go on."

"Oh, I couldn't. . . ."

He reaches into his jacket and pulls something out of his pocket. It's my old pink tutu, folded and squished together, somehow rescued from the trash. Impossible. "How did . . . ?" The answer dawns on me. "Emma."

He hands me the tutu. "Just stand. That's all you have to do."

Slowly, I make my way down the aisle. My fingertips brush along the tops of the velvet-covered seats. I grip the tutu so tight it crinkles.

The stage is a magnet, pulling me closer. Several times I pause, fighting the urge to turn back, resisting the need to go forward. And by the time I get to the base of the small staircase that leads to the stage, my insides are twisted into knots and my pulse thrums.

"Just once, Julia."

I take a step. And then another. Three more. I keep going until my running shoes thump against the stage. I stare at my feet under the spotlight, this strange juxtaposition of my past and present, colliding in this moment.

It's then that I notice the music weaving through overhead speakers.

I close my eyes and allow the melody to carry me far from

back alleys and dusty warehouses. I kick off my shoes and slide the tutu over my hips. It probably looks ridiculous over my jeans, but it doesn't matter. There is no one here who will judge.

Knowing this gives me confidence.

My feet move to match the rhythm as they draw tentative, and then crazy, invisible patterns on the floor. It's too much—my legs feel like lead.

"You can do it," Nick calls.

I pause, draw in a deep breath, and try again, this time gliding across the stage with confidence. The music transports me to another time and place, and if I squeeze my eyes shut, I can imagine my mother and Ms. Griffin praising my arabesque. I hear them tell me how my balance is flawless, my form impeccable. I am their little dancing ballerina princess.

I lift my leg into a pirouette, and as I spin, I'm transported back to happier times. I can feel myself glowing, as though the light that once shone inside of me has been turned on again. Shining brighter than it ever has.

For so long, I've avoided looking into a mirror, tried to run from this place. No matter what happens now, there's no looking back. There is no reason to be scared. Because for a ballerina—for me—the mirror is home.

26

MY LEG STRETCHES OVER THE BALLET BARRE IN THE basement, muscles unwinding. Even overnight, they've tensed up.

I catch Mat approaching in the reflection of the mirrors. He blinks, then grins. "Whoa. Nick told me I'd find you here, but this is . . ."

His voice trails off.

"I didn't even know this room existed, let alone that we have a prima ballerina living in *casa de* Roger."

I turn away to hide my blush, simultaneously lowering my leg and reaching for a towel to dry off. My forehead drips with sweat.

"Roger built it. Creepy, right?" Anxious to change the subject, I gather my sweats and pull them up over my tights. I start overheating right away. "What's up?"

For a second, he looks confused. "Oh. Yeah." He puffs out his chest. "We can't find James at the impound because he isn't *at* the impound."

"No shit. We've checked all of them—twice."

Five separate ones to be exact, and then we cased out another two outside the city, on the off chance we missed something. Either there's a secret compound for stolen cars in Las Vegas, or James has pulled another disappearing act.

"Riley has the car."

Impossible. "I saw the police, Mat. And the tow truck . . ." That's when it hits me. "Shit. That asshole's got cops on his payroll, doesn't he?"

"I had a hunch," he says. "So I took a look at some LVPD contracts and compared them to the picture of the logo Chelsea snagged. Turns out, Silver State Towing is one of their go-tos. I hacked into Silver's corporate profile and guess which asshole owns the joint?"

A slow smile spreads across my face. "Riley."

Nick slouches low in the front seat of a Ford Escort and adjusts his ball cap. "I can't believe I didn't think of this."

When he first started beating on himself, we all tried to make him feel better, but after another drawn-out stakeout, mine isn't the only patience ready to give out.

Mat snaps a piece of chewing gum between his teeth. "Yep. You totally should have."

"I worked for the guy," Nick goes on, like he hasn't heard a thing we've said. "I'm off my game."

"Hey, at least you've got game," Chelsea says. "What the hell have I contributed?"

Obviously she's mocking Nick's woe-is-me shtick. I crane my neck to make sure, surprised when I see she's on the brink of tears. I fumble for some kind of comforting words. "Jesus, Chelsea, you don't even realize how many jams you've gotten us out of. You've definitely done your part."

"Nah. You would have found a way in," she says. "Nick could have busted up some doors. Mat probably would have Google searched how to pick a lock. I'm kind of a tagalong."

I get where this is coming from, even if her words don't make sense. We could all kick ourselves for not considering this possibility, for making mistakes. It's tough to think positive when you're staring down the barrel of a deadline that has the potential to explode in your face. Knowing Riley has the Aston Martin should give us some comfort, but we still haven't caught a glimpse of James.

Chelsea curls up into the side of the car and yawns. "Maybe it's not even here."

"Gotta be," Nick says. "This is his garage."

A couple of rough-looking dudes in oil-stained jeans and wife-beaters loiter outside the building, smoking and tossing back some beers. We can't get close enough to see inside.

"What if this isn't his only garage?" I say. "Is it possible he's expanded?"

"Maybe." Nick holds the binoculars up to his face. "I recognize a couple of those guys, but some of the regulars are missing. Could mean something. We'll have to wait it out and see."

"Wait, wait, wait," Chelsea says with an exaggerated eye roll. "Seriously, after this gig, I am so done with crime. Half your time is spent being bored out of your mind."

I smile. "What happens when you get to Harvard and there's all that boring studying?"

She waves me off. "That's different. Med school is something I'm passionate about."

"Doctor Chelsea," I say, enjoying the way the title sounds on my lips.

"Has a nice ring to it," Mat says.

She pouts. "Are you mocking me? Because that's not funny." She shrinks lower into the seat. "I was actually thinking about doing something with chemistry. Maybe getting a PhD."

Nick twists around in his seat. "Hey, you could mix potions and stuff."

"I'm not a witch, douche bag."

Mat nudges her shoulder. "You could totally do anything you wanted." Chelsea's eyes soften and a tint of red touches Mat's cheeks. He recovers quickly. "We all could."

I never pegged Chelsea as a scientist or a doctor—but I bet she never figured me for a ballerina, either.

Nick sits upright. "Something's happening."

Chelsea and I lean forward. "Hallelujah," she says.

Nick peers through the binoculars, giving us the play-by-play. "Riley just showed up. He's handing someone a key. . . ." He waits. "Okay, now that guy and some other dude are getting into a tow truck. Shit." He hands off the binoculars. "Keep eyes on them. We'll follow and see where they lead us."

"Wait. Follow. Wait. Follow."

Mat nudges Chelsea and she grins. "Don't mind me. I'm just writing my memoirs. I'll call it *Profile of a Serial Heister*."

"What happened to giving up the life of crime to become a legitimate scientist?"

She slumps against the backrest. "Who said anything about legitimate?"

Riley's tow truck follows a maze of side streets that cross over the I-15 and into Spring Valley. When we turn onto Rainbow Road, Chelsea tenses. Even her curls seem to lose some of their bounce.

"I hate this area," she says.

"It's not all bad," Nick says. "A few of the houses on these side roads are massive." He winks at me. "I boosted a couple of hot rods from here a few years back."

"Doesn't some rich politician live around here?" Mat says. "I read about him on Twitter, Senator Lynch or something. His whole platform is built on a tourist tax."

Chelsea pales. "He thinks it will help keep teens off the streets. But he doesn't have a clue about kids—especially his own," she says.

I remember Chelsea's last name is Lynch, and that's when I realize the senator is her dad. I reach behind and grab her hand, a silent promise I won't rat her out even if I'm more sure than ever that I only know half of the story.

Nick turns left at Charleston Boulevard.

"If Riley's got the car stored out here, that's good for us," Nick says. "We're close to the Trophy Case. Less chance of getting caught."

We follow the tow truck into an industrial area, but when it veers off onto a side street, Nick goes straight and turns into a back alley. He cuts the lights and parks so that we can see through two abandoned storefronts to what looks like a small warehouse. A chain-link fence surrounds the perimeter.

One guy gets out of the truck and unlocks the gate, his hand at his hip. I can see the butt end of a gun. My shoulder blades pinch together as I stiffen up.

"There are two security cameras in the front," Mat says. He tethers his phone to his laptop and starts typing into a search engine. "A numbered company owns the building—no name. I can find out who it is, but it's going to take some time."

Nick's jaw tenses. "Don't bother. I know this is Riley. I can feel it."

"Can't you do that thing you did at the hangar?" Chelsea

says. "Take pictures from the outside like Superman or what-ever."

"Too much interference," Mat says. "The hangar was pretty much in the middle of nowhere."

"The car is here," Nick says. He grabs the binoculars. "I spot seven cameras, maybe eight, unless that's a light. Hard to tell. The gate has a triple lock on it. Might need bolt cutters."

"Too risky," Chelsea says. "Mat, if you can freeze out those cameras, I can crack this lock. I just need to buy one thing."

"I don't like the idea of you being out there exposed," Nick says. "Three locks is a long time, and this isn't a residential area."

The implications of his words send a shiver up my spine. Riley's goons don't mess around.

"Come on, you guys, you know I'm the weakest link here."

"Chelsea, stop," I say. "We're all in this together."

"Perfect. Then get me to a mall, so I can do my part."

27

IF NICK'S PLAN TO TRICK KEVIN WAS STUPID, CHELSEA'S is outright dangerous. I'm so not on board with it, but she's beyond rational thought. I keep telling her she has nothing to prove, that we'll figure out a different way.

She's convinced this is our only option.

I duck down in the backseat of the nondescript Honda we've borrowed from the Trophy Case to execute this phase of the plan. We're about a block from Riley's garage, waiting for Chelsea to work her magic. The vinyl smells like aftershave, which makes me wonder about the last person who drove this car. Was it one of the thugs Roger recruited to steal his cars? Or another random car-theft victim?

Mat strums his fingers on the steering wheel. "So, I put the clutch in and *then* step on the gas, right?"

My voice rises in surprise. "Tell me you're joking." When

he doesn't say anything, I sit up and smack him lightly across the back of the head. "You'd better not be serious."

"Relax! I know how to drive a stick." He laughs. "Get down before someone sees you."

Ha. Because that's not like trying to change the tires on a Mustang without the right lug nuts—aka impossible.

My cell buzzes. I stare at the caller ID. "It's Emma."

"You have to answer it," Mat says. "You always answer."

I bite my lower lip and accept the call, touched that he knows that. "Hey, Ems."

"Jules? Where are you?"

My throat constricts. I can't tell her what we're doing, but I'm having trouble spitting out a lie. "We're just out. Something wrong?"

She sighs. "You said you'd come to my audition."

"That's tonight?" Shit. I bash my head against the seat. "Of course I'll be there. What time?"

"You're not coming, are you?"

The tone of her voice kicks me right in the gut. "We'll be there."

"All of you?"

Mat leans over the seat and nods his head. "We'll get there," he mouths. Despite his confidence, I'm not convinced. If Chelsea completes her mission, this heist *has* to go down tonight. We'll have a narrow window of time.

"We're going to do the best we can." The answer barely

appeases Emma, but I'm relieved when she sounds more positive. We talk about staying calm, about doing her best, about how proud I am no matter if she gets the part or not.

She admits that she's nervous, but says she also hopes Melissa gets a part too, so no one goes home sad. Warmth spreads through me as I realize I'm thrilled she'd bonded with someone outside the mansion. She doesn't easily make friends.

"I love you, Jules."

"Me too, Ems." My chest swells with pride. "And hey . . . break a leg."

Emptiness fills my chest when the line goes dead. I keep telling myself it's just a few more days. What if she can't hold on?

Through the window, I catch a glimpse of a vulture flying overhead and I shudder. I'm pretty sure birds of prey are a bad omen.

Or maybe that's just crows.

"We've got three hours to do this and get to Emma's audition."

"Chelsea's in."

And so it begins. She's borrowed one of Roger's older cars, which she hopes will convince Riley's crew that she's in need of a mechanic. With her tight skirt, high heels, and a padded bra, she'll distract them enough to find what she's looking for—the key to the second garage. Riley's goons are stupid enough to fall for it, which makes me throw up a little in my mouth.

I argued against this plan, but Chelsea's right—we need this.

My hands pool with sweat. I wipe them on my jeans and exhale three times in quick succession. It still feels like my chest is filling up with air. "How long has she been in there? An hour?"

"Five minutes."

Damn it.

"How are we doing on locating the Shelby?"

Mat sighs deep. "A bunch of dead ends." He runs his hand through his hair, snagging his fingers in the curls. "Lots of chatter, but it never amounts to anything. Might have one lead, but they've got one hell of a smoke screen—I can't seem to hack under the surface." He pauses. "Yet."

"Fuck."

He squares his shoulders. "I'll get it, don't worry."

I gnaw on the inside of my cheek until I taste blood. Obviously I'm nervous about finding the GT, but I'm also worried about Mat. He's in deep—too deep for a guy looking to reform.

"You still planning to cut loose from this life?"

"More determined than ever."

His answer gives me some comfort. Part of me feels like this is my fault, like if I hadn't moved into Roger's, he'd still be looking for the fourth member of his crew. Knowing Mat's plans haven't been derailed assuages some of that guilt.

His cell rings and we both flinch. He puts the call on speaker.

"Rico," Chelsea says, using Mat's code name for this objective, "you can pick me up now. I'm at . . ." There's a pause while she

284

fake asks someone for the address in a way-too-chipper voice. "It's that mechanic's place, just past East Sunse—what's that? You're just a few blocks from here? Perfect. I owe you one."

She's babbling, which either means she got the key, or she's in trouble. Either way, we need to set the extraction plan in motion.

Mat puts the car in gear and taps the gas pedal, but takes his foot off the clutch too soon. We jerk forward and stall. He restarts the engine.

Panic starts building in my chest. "Thought you knew how to drive a standard?"

He shifts again, but I know the clutch isn't engaged.

"No problem."

I fight to stay calm. "Let me drive."

Mat refuses to give up. He fires off a string of curses and jams the gearshift up into first. This time, it clunks into place. Relief ribbons through me.

"Easy on the gas," I say. "It's a balance. Listen for the friction po—"

Mat stomps on the pedal. A cloud of black smoke comes out the car's back end, along with the strong scent of burning rubber. The engine starts to whine. "Let off the clutch!"

He should be in second right now, but if he shifts and we stall, then what? Instead, we kind of leapfrog to the front of Riley's shop.

"Scoot over to the passenger seat." It's a clunky move, but

if we need a fast getaway, Mat won't be able to pull it off. "Chelsea can drive."

He climbs awkwardly over the gearshift, shooting me an evil glare when his foot gets caught on the steering wheel. Maybe I've had too much experience maneuvering my way around car interiors, but he makes it look a lot more complicated than it needs to be. The gearshift jabs him in the groin. *"Merde!"*

I cup my hand over my mouth to stop laughing just as Chelsea flings open the door. She pauses to giggle and wave at someone inside, then slides into the seat. "Holy crap."

She jams the car into gear and peels out of the parking lot.

"Subtle." I sit up and buckle in. "Jesus, that was close."

"I did good," Chelsea says. With one hand on the steering wheel, she reaches into her padded bra with the other to retrieve a key.

To anyone else, it's a tool to open a locked door. But for the four of us, it's a much-needed symbol of hope.

Nick's knee bounces.

Up and down.

Up. Down.

The heels of his feet don't even touch the pavement. If he loses balance, I'm not strong enough to hold the bike upright, which means we're going down. This is the last place I want to fall flat on my face. The alley reeks of sewage and overripe bananas.

Nick chews on the end of his fingernail, shifts, and bounces again.

I reach around his waist and rest my hand on his knee. "Stop. You're making me crazy."

This is where Nick usually jumps in with some quip about my fragile mental state. When he doesn't, I realize his nerves are even more frazzled than mine.

Things are not going as planned.

We're tucked between two buildings at the end of the block while Mat and Chelsea wait on the other—cleaner—side of the street in another nondescript car. They're both disguised, so unless Riley's goons are specifically looking for them, they're well covered. Unfortunately, cheap costume disguises wouldn't be enough to camouflage Nick and me.

A faded full moon crests the horizon. Dusk turns the surrounding buildings into shades of gray. Pieces of litter blow around in the light wind, yanking me back to a couple of months earlier in another grungy end of town. A boost that went all wrong.

I study Nick's profile. Okay, it wasn't a complete bust.

Chelsea's voice pipes through the Bluetooth. "We've got movement."

A few minutes later, two trucks and a motorcycle pass. I count to ten in my head before checking in again. "Clear?"

Mat answers this time. "Cameras are disabled. Chelsea's at the lock."

Nick nods to let me know he heard and fires up the bike. When Chelsea gives us the all clear, we'll cruise up to the gate and hot-wire the tow truck in the lot, back it up to the shop, hook up the car, and hit the road.

No sweat.

Except we don't even know if the car's *in* there.

Chelsea's curse blasts through the earpiece. I should be used to her trucker mouth by now, but it shocks me every time. "This key's a piece of shit. Argh."

My pulse speeds up. "Are you sure you grabbed the—"

"Shut the hell up, Jules," Chelsea snaps. I shrink a little under her tone before remembering she's not always like this. By the time we drop James off at the Trophy Case she'll be back to "aw, shucks" and "you guys are so freaking cute." I can hardly wait.

Nick coughs. "You've got one minute Chelsea or else—"

"Don't you threaten me," she cuts in. "Damn it. It's not working. Bring the bolt cutters."

Nick pulls out in the alley and drops me off at the gate. I take the tool and she grabs it from me. "I got this."

"You'll break a nail."

"Then you'll owe me a manicure." She snaps the cutters around the lock. Two hard squeezes and the metal breaks.

I swing the gate wide. "Guess no spa package in your Christmas stocking this year."

Nick rides to the perimeter and over to the tow truck. The

288

plan's a little shaky from here. I'll work with Chelsea to get inside the shop, while Mat stands watch. Nick will hot-wire the truck and hook up the car. I'll drive the tow truck to Roger's, and the others will keep close to make sure I'm not being followed—or in the event I need a quick exit plan, I can catch a ride.

It's by far our least thought-out boost, and probably the most dangerous.

"I must have grabbed a bum key," Chelsea says. She nudges up against the door of the building. "Should have known it was too easy."

Unease creeps around the back of my neck. In my experience, anything simple is usually too good to be true. "You think you were made?"

She pauses long enough to make my heart stutter. "No." She shakes her head. "No way. I just got nervous and took the wrong one."

It's small comfort.

The lock clatters to the ground. "Shit," Chelsea says. "I really mangled that thing." She flashes a grin. "Not my cleanest work."

"Perfection is overrated. . . ."

She pushes open the door. I stick my flashlight inside and wave it around. The light beam lands on a shadowed form in the shape of a car. My pulse skips. "Think that's it?"

I hold the light while Chelsea rips off the gray cover. Dust flitters through the beam and lands on the silver curve of the Aston Martin's front fender. My breath hitches.

James.

Blood rushes to my head as my adrenaline jacks. *Holy shit.* Chelsea and I fist-bump.

"Go tell Nick we found James, then meet up with Mat to keep an eye on things. We don't have a lot of time."

Sixty seconds.

I pan the flashlight beam over the front of the car, lightly touching the headlights. My fingers trail along the grille. The wheels and one side mirror are missing. Scratches mark the paint. Surface flaws, easily fixed.

"Looking good, James," I murmur.

On my way to the garage door opener, I scan the shop for the missing headlight or the rear fender. Maybe an extra set of wheels.

The place is empty. Too empty.

A chill weaves its way under my skin. I shine the light on the floor. There's not a speck of oil or dirt on the concrete finish. In fact, there's nothing in this place to even hint it's a garage.

The Aston Martin is just plunked dead center of the floor, covered only by a thin tarp. Almost like it's on display.

My blood turns to ice.

I spin around and run toward the exit, moving so fast I can barely breathe. The Bluetooth isn't working so I start screaming, "You guys, get out of here, it's a tra—"

I run straight into a brick wall.

Not a wall. A chest.

My heart—

Stops.

Some goon grabs me by the wrist. I yelp and struggle to break free but then my gaze locks on the two shadowed figures behind him.

Riley.

And Nick—with a gun pointed at his head.

My chest fills with hot air.

They step from the shadows and Riley's mouth widens into a grin. "Well, I'll be damned. It really is you. Pleasure to finally meet you . . . Ghost."

28

A SHARP PULSE THUMPS AT MY TEMPLES, BLINDING ME.

I'm clearly dreaming, because this can't be real. I stumble forward, trip, and lose my balance. Everything goes—

"Jules!"

The panic in Nick's voice snaps me back to my senses. I take in a deep breath and slowly raise my head to meet Riley's stony black eyes. I can't face Nick; I'm already teetering on tears.

Riley waves the gun around. "So, Kevin says to me, 'That's the Ghost.' And I laugh, because what the hell was she ever doing with that loser? Right?"

I feel my face go hot.

"And then the loser comes to me and says this asshole"—he taps the side of Nick's head with the barrel of the gun—"took a boost he couldn't handle. And again, I laugh, because there's nothing Nick can't handle."

My skin tingles with unease.

"We both know Kevin isn't much a man of his word," Riley goes on. His mouth turns into a sneer. "But I guess you'd have a more *intimate* knowledge of that."

I glare at Riley. I've disliked a lot of people in my life, but nothing compares to the hate I feel for this man. The pit of disgust in my stomach burns hot.

Nick's jaw tenses. "Lay off, Riley. She's not part of this."

"See, that's not what Kev says." He cocks the gun and rests his finger on the trigger. "And I think this time I should believe him."

Blood drains from my face. "You can have the Aston Martin."

Riley chuckles. "That's generous of you." He nudges his chin toward the car. "But, as you know, I've already got it."

We're totally fucked. Guys like Riley don't let people who betray them walk. The best we can do is stall him until Mat and Chelsea go for help. They'll call Roger, the police . . . someone.

"What do you want, Riley?"

He licks his lips. "I thought we could have ourselves a little conversation." His teeth look fluorescent in the bright light. "Me and my guys . . . and the four of you."

My heart feels like it's being squeezed right out of my chest. I want to deny it, tell him he's too late for Chelsea and Mat. But that's when I hear her voice.

"Get your ape hands off me."

Riley's goon shoves her into the room and another walks in with a pistol aimed at Mat's head.

The rest of my hope bursts like an exploding exhaust pipe.

Riley smirks. "About that talk."

The fear in Chelsea's eyes makes my knees go weak. My gaze flits between Mat and Nick, searching for solutions, ideas, some way to get us out of this jam. I have absolutely no doubt Riley will kill us if we don't deliver what he wants.

That's my only leverage.

Riley leans up against the wall, adjusting the gun so it practically sticks to the side of Nick's head. One sudden move and he's a dead man. I stand very still, like I'm rooted to the ground, but my insides are a writhing mess.

"It don't make sense." Riley waves the gun back and forth between Mat and Chelsea. "These two are a couple of idiots, so maybe I can see how they thought they'd get away with this." His eyes land on Chelsea's chest. "Nice work with the fake tits, I'll give you that."

He turns back to me. "But you and Nick are pros." Is that supposed to be a compliment? "You know better. Which got me thinking that maybe there's more to this than the Aston Martin."

I swallow hard. "It's worth millions."

Riley nods thoughtfully. "It sure is, and I'm going to make a mint off your great detective work." He nudges his chin toward Mat. "Nice job there, *paco*—or is that Ringo?"

Mat's lips press into a firm line.

"I heard you're all living up in that big mansion on the hill. What's his name?" Riley snaps his fingers twice. "Rick. Richard. Roger. That's it. Roger Montgomery. Seen his name in the paper a few times."

I straighten my back. "You going to shoot the shit all night, or get on with it?"

"That's fair," he says. "Bottom line is, we've been scanning the airwaves and I admit, you kids got balls. Covering up the fact that—not counting the Aston, because that was my good work—the four of you did five major boosts in as many weeks. I figure they gotta be connected."

I open my mouth but he shuts it with a wave of his finger.

"Things'll go much smoother if we're honest with each other going forward," he says. "Let's start with this. Who are you working for?"

"Why? You offering me a job?"

I'm stalling, but Riley's too smart to fall for it.

"A few months ago, sure. But after a mistake like this? You've lost your edge, kid."

I don't know why the words sting. I blink away a tear that's more fear than anything else.

"A piece of whatever job you're working," Riley says. I blink, surprised. Maybe I should have expected this. "Give me that, and we're square."

Nick shakes his head with such subtlety I almost miss it.

"The Aston Martin was the last car on the list," I say.

Riley arches an eyebrow. "I'd like to believe you, Ghostie. I really would. But . . ." He presses the gun harder against Nick's temple. "I've got like this sixth sense, you know? A feeling there's more to this gig. A lot more."

Nick's Adam's apple bobs.

Riley points the gun at the guy holding my wrist. "Take her phone."

I don't bother arguing. My cell's password protected, and even if he finds the list of cars, they're all in code. The goon yanks it out of the front pocket of my leather jacket and tosses it at Riley. He enters the password with one thumb and flashes me the screen.

Emma.

Her face is my background picture, and her name is my password—which means Kevin didn't just tell Riley about me, he also told him about my sister. Bastard.

"Cute kid," Riley says.

My knees threaten to give out.

He starts thumbing through the phone and I know the exact moment he lands on the list because he lets out a low whistle. "What's this? Keeping track of all your exes? Looks more like a shopping list to me."

"Reggie—gotta be the Camaro that got picked." He sticks his tongue into the side of his cheek. "George. That's clearly the Cosma Ray grabbed during the Barris show." He leans toward

Nick. "That one had you written all over it, Barker."

"Just fucking get on with it," I snap.

He looks up from the phone and grins. "Eleanor. Come on, guys. That's the best you could come up with?" He chucks my cell aside. The glass shatters and sprinkles onto the concrete. "I'll give you points for creativity on the others. But this isn't even a challenge—who doesn't want a '67 Shelby? Your buyer's got good taste."

It's at this moment I realize we've caught a small break, because while he might know the make and model we're after, he doesn't know the specifics—the fact that it's Jim Morrison's long-lost car we need. We could pass off any of the three in Roger's garage for the last car on the list.

Roger might not even miss one of those Mustangs.

Riley digs a cigar out of his front pocket. He lights it and takes a long pull. "All right, this is starting to get a bit boring. I'm sure we're all looking forward to some sleep—big days ahead of us."

My nostrils flare. "Quit dicking around."

Maybe I should make like the rest of my team and keep my mouth shut, but I'm pretty sure the guy's going to blow our heads off anyway. I'm sick of waiting for the inevitable.

"You're going to steal Eleanor," Riley says. "For me. And then I want an introduction to your boss."

Yeah, like that's happening. My lips turn up in a smirk. "You expect me to believe you're going to let us go?"

"Oh, I have a feeling you'll believe anything I tell you." He waves one of his men over with two fingers.

"Yeah, why's that?"

"Because I have something you want."

The goon dials a number and then hands over the phone. Riley puts it on speaker. Kevin answers on the third ring.

"Kev, why don't you fill your ex-girlfriend in?"

The line crackles a bit before a young girl's voice whimpers in the background. "Jules?"

I feel the blood rush through my veins and my heart picks up pace. My knees buckle. Oh God, no . . .

Emma.

29

"RUN IT AGAIN."

Mat flinches. I've totally snarked at him, but at this point, I'm desperate. Emma's been missing for twelve hours and we're no closer to finding her, Eleanor, or frankly *any* Shelby—aside from the three in the Trophy Case. We might be able to leverage one of those to get Emma back, but how the hell are we supposed to break into that fortress?

Every nerve in my body feels thin, stripped.

I've gnawed my pen cap down to a twisted mess. Blisters have formed on my heels with all my pacing. I should have been at Emma's audition. We all should have been—together. Like the family she expects us to be. Deserves us to be.

"Run. It. Again."

Mat's fingers fly over the keyboard. "It just keeps coming back to the same thing."

I grab a pillow off my bed and fling it at my dresser. It bounces off the lampshade and skids across the surface, taking down two picture frames before hitting the floor.

The monitor *pings*.

I hold my breath, waiting for Mat to say something, to tell me he's wrong. He has to be, because I can't take it if he's right. I wrap my arms around myself to stop the shudder. Everything comes rushing back, sending my senses into overdrive—the scent of Riley's cigar, the fear in Nick's eyes when the gun was pointed at his head, the sound of Emma's voice. That's already too much. But if Mat's right, we're all screwed.

Because it means Roger has had Eleanor all along.

Mat takes a deep breath. "Same result."

Blood shoots to my temples and I feel my face go hot. I scream out in frustration and slam my fist into my bedroom door. The wood splinters on impact. Pain radiates up my arm.

Mat tosses his laptop onto the bed and springs off his chair to pull me into a hug. "There's got to be a logical explanation for this." He turns my hand over in his—the skin is scuffed, but not broken.

Yeah, I dropped my guard. Trusted Roger when I should have known better.

I choke back a series of cries. My shoulders shake. I bury my face deep into Mat's chest, drawing comfort from his warmth. He's safe.

Family.

Mat grabs the back of my neck and pulls me closer. He's trying to stop me from worrying, but his voice cracks when he says, "We'll find her. I'm good at what I do."

Except Mat doesn't have a special trawling program that will find people. Nothing that will pinpoint Emma's exact location, let me know she's safe. Unharmed. Even if we could get our hands on the car, it's only half the puzzle: Riley won't let Emma go until we set up a meet between him and Roger.

Tears stream down my face. "Run the program again." I'm almost whimpering now. "Please, Mat. Just one more time."

We gather at a park a few miles from Roger's mansion, cobbling together a plan, some kind of next step. I'm only half listening. Emma's voice whispers in my head about how I've fucked up, how I should have been there with her. How she *knew* I was up to no good.

I press my lips together, holding firm to the last of my worry. I can't break now. Emma needs me.

Where is she? Has she suffered another anxiety attack? God, how could she not? Being kidnapped by my ex-boyfriend is not exactly the definition of stability.

Nick reaches under the picnic table and takes my hand, his skin cool to the touch. I know he's shouldered some guilt of his own on this.

"We could go to the police," Chelsea says.

The tips of her chrome fingernails are chipped and torn.

I haven't bothered to see if she's changed the color on her toes to Nightmist Blue.

"Going to the cops means owning up to what we've done," Mat says. "We'll go to jail." His eyes meet mine. "But if it means saving Emma, I'll do it. I'll do whatever it takes, just so that's clear."

It's this combined love for my sister that holds me together.

Nick shakes his head. "Riley isn't afraid of the police."

"And some of them are on his payroll," I say, thinking back to when the Aston Martin was taken from the airplane hangar. "We have no evidence to link back to any of this."

But there's a mountain of it that could bring the four of us down. I can't help but think the rest of them are paying for my mistakes—especially my sister.

Nick rubs the top of my knee. "Riley's a thug, but he won't hurt Emma. Not as long as we stick to the plan."

When it comes to his former boss, Nick's instincts have backfired, but I have to believe Riley is more interested in his business than in hurting a kid. "It's different now that we know Roger has had Eleanor all along."

Saying the words makes my stomach roil. I've worked through every possible scenario, but none of them explains it. I suck in a breath to stop from crying. To think I almost started trusting Roger.

"Go through it again," Nick says. "How did you find Eleanor, Mat? Maybe it will give us some perspective."

Mat sets an old laptop on the picnic table. I stand behind

him to block the sun from hitting the screen. A smiley-face sticker mocks me from the corner of the computer case.

"I started noticing weird patterns whenever I entered key words into the trawling program." He powers up the screen. "No matter what I typed into the search, I got the same six dead ends. Like I'd been blocked or something."

Technology shit usually goes over my head, but even I understand that there should be more than a half-dozen combinations, especially given the extensive list of key words we came up with. "Roger?"

Mat shrugs. "I had no reason to think so at the time."

"Why would you?" Chelsea picks at the peeling blue paint on the picnic table. "Far as we knew, we were supposed to find the car for him."

"I thought maybe my IP had been tracked," Mat says. "So I switched computers. Twice. I got the same dead ends. I figured it had something to do with the laptops Roger bought, so I went back to old faithful." He taps the top of his screen. "After shit went down last night, I installed the trawler and tried again."

"Smart," Nick says.

"I started a new scan, using some of the same key words . . . plus a few extras," Mat says.

"Like *asshole* and *dickhead*?" Everyone looks at me and I shake my head to stop from blubbering. This isn't the first time I've felt betrayed, but it doesn't make sense that Roger could be so cruel. Why send us on this wild goose chase? "What could you have added?"

"Hacking isn't always about exploiting technology," Mat says with a slight grin. "It's also about exploiting humans. I dug around in Roger's virtual files"—he raises an eyebrow—"and his password to almost everything is the title of a Doors song. I also found this."

He points to a picture on the screen. It's old and faded, probably taken in the late sixties. Just two guys standing next to Eleanor. The first guy is Jim Morrison—I recognize him from the poster in the basement. The second . . .

"Dude. Is that Roger?"

"That mustache," Chelsea says with an exaggerated shudder.

"Okay, so he's clearly had a boner for this car for a long time," Nick says. "But that doesn't mean he *has* that car."

"Every car has a VIN number," Mat says. "A unique code that includes a serial number for tracking. I hacked into his personal files and found a spreadsheet listing the VIN numbers of the cars he owns. There's no description of the cars, so at first glance, it looks kind of random, but I plugged in the VIN for Eleanor and it popped up right away."

My entire body goes limp with defeat.

"That car is *not* in the Trophy Case," Nick says. "I'd have remembered the color. So, where is he keeping it?"

"The garage," I say quietly. "It's the one place Roger has

banned us from." A sliver of hope cuts through the gloom. Busting into the Trophy Case for one of the Shelbys might be a challenge, but breaking into the garage would be child's play for Chelsea.

"It's not in the garage," she says. All eyes land on her. "You think I didn't tap that lock? Come on, guys."

My optimism hits a dead end. "Anything in there we can use?"

She rubs her temples. "Nothing I can think of. It wasn't even a satisfying break-in—some junk, a bunch of movie memorabilia . . ."

I scrunch up my nose. "Jesus. What's the deal with that, anyway?"

"He likes to collect things, but . . ." Chelsea's eyes brighten. "Holy crap, that's it!" She stands and begins to pace. "Something has always bugged me about the props in the house. How they looked out of place, but somehow familiar."

"Maybe they're from well-known movies," Mat says. "Why else would Roger collect them?"

"Nah. That mask in the games room? That's from a super B-grade horror flick from the seventies. I don't even know why *I* remember it," Chelsea says.

I pull out my phone and Google search the movie, scrolling through the pictures of the actors. I point to an image that looks somewhat familiar. "This actress . . . she was in that knight movie with what's his name? Hugo? Harry."

"Henry!" Nick says. "I think it was called *White Knight Tale*."

Chelsea makes a face. "That's the most ludicrous title I've ever heard."

"Holy shit." Mat turns his screen around so we can all see. "Check this out. According to IMDb, the actress who played alongside that guy is Eloise. Eloise Montgomery."

My stomach clenches as I recognize her picture from the living room. "Roger's wife?"

Mat calls up a search engine and types in her name. Her IMDb listing credits her with more than a dozen obscure films. He scrolls through a series of articles written about her until we're all sure Eloise is Roger's wife.

Nick leans over Mat's shoulder, reading. "Check out her bio. The Trophy Case was hers. She loved muscle cars."

I pull out my cell phone and type her name into Google. The first item is an article about her death. I zoom in on the picture of the car, a blue and white Chevelle similar to the one in Roger's driveway, except the one on my screen is totaled. The hair on the back of my neck stands on end. "She died in a car crash."

"That's terrible." Chelsea peers over my shoulder. "What else does the article say about her?"

I skim the text until I land on a paragraph that sticks out like a flashing burlesque sign. My mouth dries to desert sand. "You guys . . ." A sick sensation creeps across my skin. "Eloise Montgomery was supposed to be the next Bond girl."

Nick's eyes go big. "As in James . . . Bond?"

I nod. "It was her dream role, but she died before they started filming."

Mat whistles low. "It makes sense . . . why he wanted the car."

"She never had the chance to act in her dream role," I whisper. "Giving her the Bond car was probably Roger's way of honoring her."

Chelsea presses her hand to her chest. "That's so sad."

I blink to stop the tears from coming, thinking of the few times Roger talked about Eloise. The way he sometimes looks at Nick and me together, as if remembering his own love that was cut too short. He wasn't over losing her—not without finishing the Trophy Case. Maybe not even then.

"Check the date she died," Mat says.

I know the answer before he reads it out loud. Eloise Montgomery, aspiring actress, Roger's beloved wife, was killed five years ago, one week from today, which would have been their twenty-fifth—silver—wedding anniversary.

The same day as our deadline.

My emotion squeaks out in a strangled cry. "I need to talk to him."

Nick grabs my wrist. "And tell him what? That we know about Eleanor? About Eloise? How will that help us get Emma back?"

"He cares for her," I say, desperate to believe that, amid all the lies, I can trust in that truth. "Maybe if we tell him everything, he'll let us have the Shelby, or one of them in the Trophy Case—at least to get Emma back."

There would be other consequences, but we can deal with them.

Mat's eyes gloss over. "I don't doubt he loves Emma, Jules. But how can we trust him? Not after he kept Eleanor a secret. What else is he hiding?"

"We need to get our hands on a Shelby," Nick says. "And if we can't get into the Trophy Case, then we need to find Eleanor."

"I don't even know where to start," Chelsea says. "The information about that car could be anywhere."

"There has to be a reason the garage is off-limits," I say. "Maybe among those props and other memorabilia, we'll find a clue?"

"Good thinking," Chelsea says.

I sure hope so. Because it's not my life that depends on it—it may be our only shot at saving Emma.

"It's daylight," Chelsea whispers. "Shouldn't we wait until night?"

No time. So far we've managed to hide Emma's disappearance with a tall tale about her sleeping over at Melissa's house for a couple of days. Roger made it clear it's an unsanctioned move, but when we reminded him that it gives us the freedom to boost the last cars on his list, he let it drop and retreated to his sitting room with a tumbler of whiskey and a new hot rod magazine. Now I just pray he won't call Melissa's mom. Somehow he doesn't strike me as the type.

"Maybe we should just tell Roger," Chelsea says.

"Nick's right. I can't trust him anymore."

She puts her hand on my arm. "My dad . . . he's connected. I could call him."

Fresh tears spring to my eyes. The significance of the offer carves into my heart, the lengths she'd go to for me—for my sister. I pull her into a hug and squeeze so hard I'm afraid she might snap in half. "That means . . . everything."

"This whole thing has made me realize . . ." She blinks away a tear. "I really took my parents for granted."

"You should call them. Their life's probably been boring since you left."

Chelsea laughs. "Dad's a politician, what could possibly be more boring than that?" She exhales and I'm shocked by the sense of peace that falls across her face. "I'm not really a foster kid, you know."

My lip curls into a half smile. "I'm shocked."

She ducks her head a little. "Roger didn't press charges when I broke into his warehouse because of who my dad is. When I screwed up, Roger offered to take me in, some hush-hush deal between high-powered aquaintances."

The idea makes my stomach roil, the thought that Chelsea's dad would so easily give her up.

"Senator Lynch is one of Roger's charities," Chelsea says. "Political stuff. You know?"

I don't, but I understand that's not the real issue here. Chelsea misses her family, even if she's not ready to admit it.

"When this is over . . . ," she says.

I squeeze her arm. "They'll be thrilled to have you home."

"Aw." Mat's voice *pings* through my earpiece. "You two need more time, or are we doing this?"

I clear my throat. "Stop eavesdropping, you creeper."

He can't risk cutting the security cameras, so he's shifted the lens enough so we can access the garage door. But if things go as planned, Roger won't even know we've been here.

Chelsea glances over her shoulder. "What if one of the staff sees us?"

Definite possibility. "That's why we need to be quick."

Seconds later, we're in.

I head straight to the boxes of memorabilia and start rooting through them. Nothing. Chelsea takes the posters off the wall and checks behind the frames. She comes up blank.

My shoulders sag. "Fuck, Chelsea, I thought for sure we'd find something here."

"He's too smart to be that obvious."

I look around the garage. "There's nothing else in here, right?"

Chelsea reassembles the pictures and starts to hang them on the wall, concentrating hard to keep the order the same. "His file cabinet. But I already went through that."

I switch two of the posters back to their original placement. "No raised flags?"

She shakes her head. "Info on each of us, some property deeds, blah blah." Her eyes widen. "Wait. I did see a set of blueprints for the Trophy Case before I knew what they were."

I think of the secret room he built for my small ballet studio. Could he have done the same for Eleanor? "Do your thing."

Chelsea crosses to the other side of the garage. "Damn, he's good." She digs around in her pockets for the right tool and unlocks the file cabinet. After a quick flip through the files, she pulls out a rolled-up piece of paper.

I spread it across the top of the cabinet.

The plans are hardly detailed, with only the key rooms identified. I'm no engineer, but it doesn't look to me like the Trophy Case even has a basement level, let alone a secret room. "Damn it. Anything else in there?"

"Empty."

Is it possible we're wrong? That Roger doesn't have Eleanor at all?

No. Mat tracked the VIN number.

But if not in the warehouse with the other three Shelbys—

Three.

Identical except for color.

Switch the paint and—

My heart starts picking up speed. I hold on to Chelsea for balance. "This is going to sound crazy, but I think Eleanor is *at* the warehouse. She's been hiding in plain sight."

30

The List

~~Jack-1970 Dodge Super Bee 426~~
~~José-1965 Corvette Mako Shark II~~
~~Reggie-1968 Chevy ZL1 Camaro~~
~~Adam-1970 Dodge Hemi Coronet R/T~~
~~George-1968 Corvette Cosma Ray~~
James-1964 Aston Martin DBS
Eleanor-1967 Mustang Shelby GT500

I'VE CHEWED MY FINGERNAILS TO THE QUICK AND TURNED the inside of my cheek into raw hamburger. Adrenaline pumps through my veins.

Everything rests on tonight.

At any other time, the steady rumble of Nick's Mustang would provide comfort. Now it just heightens my anxiety. I can't shake the feeling that Roger's onto us, that this is all going to blow up in our faces.

Nick shines the headlights on the first gate of the Trophy Case. Chelsea has already started working on picking the lock.

"I can't do it." Her voice is pained, like she's teetering on tears.

If she cries, I'm done too. It's building up, the weariness in my muscles, the monotonous pounding of a never-ending migraine. I'm now almost thirty-six hours without sleep and I still have no idea if Emma's alive. Hurt.

Dead.

"I know I said there wasn't a lock I couldn't pick . . ." Chelsea breaks off with a string of curses. "But fuck, you guys, I think this is it."

"You can do it," I croak out.

Behind us, Mat has abandoned trying to disarm the alarms and moved on to disabling the cameras. The plan must be executed with pinpoint precision—one slipup and the domino effect will be catastrophic.

Nick takes my hand.

The warmth helps, but my entire body still trembles. "What if we can't get Emma?"

He squeezes.

A single tear burns a trail down my cheek.

Even he'd admit our plan's shaky at best. Roger will head to the warehouse when we tell him we've got the Aston Martin.

But getting Riley there before Roger realizes we've duped him is going to take a timing miracle. And perhaps the scariest part is convincing Riley to let Emma go before things get crazy.

Unless Mat and Chelsea find her first—which is the plan.

Mat has hacked into Kevin's cell phone and downloaded his GPS coordinates—we tracked him to a small house owned by Riley's cousin on the outskirts of town. Nick says the guy is a long-haul trucker and isn't home much. It's a stretch, but Mat figures Riley is keeping Emma there with Kevin. Riley will bring reinforcements to the warehouse and Kevin won't expect Mat to have found him. Kevin doesn't do well with surprises.

Nick takes my chin in his fingertips and gently turns my face to his. For one perfect moment, I almost believe everything can be okay. He touches my cheekbone, my jawline, studying me like this is our last moment together. As though somehow, tonight marks the end. I don't know, maybe it does.

"We can do this, Jules."

I'm not convinced. Breaking into the Trophy Case is our biggest challenge yet.

He leans forward and brushes his lips against mine. They're sweet like cotton candy, feather-soft. "Nick . . ."

Chelsea's voice breaks through the moment. "Holy fuck, you guys, I did it!"

I shake it off. "We're up."

Nick kisses me again. "Good luck."

I slide into the driver's seat and wait while Nick and Mat

cut the perimeter alarms. Listen for anything unusual. I keep my eyes trained to the rearview, watching for headlights, surprise guests. There's no real reason Roger should suspect anything, except, as we've already figured out, he's a crafty SOB.

Chelsea unlocks the second gate and I drive through. Mat takes the second car and parks it around the corner by the Dumpster outside the fence. Hidden, but not camouflaged.

I meet Chelsea at the front door.

She digs a pick out of her pack and holds it up into the light. "Behold, the Slagel."

It looks the same as the rest of her tools, a slender metal rod with a jagged-edged tip. "Sounds like something out of *Lord of the Rings*."

"That's Smeagol." She gives me a look that suggests I'm an idiot for not knowing the difference. "This is for electronic locks—designed by James Slagel, a security guru for IBM."

"Still lost."

Chelsea inserts the tool into the keyhole and grunts. "It works by . . . shit . . . by selectively pulling internal parts of the . . ." There's a loud snap. "Fuck."

The hair on the back of my neck stands on end. "Tell me you didn't break it."

"Of course I broke it," she says. "And I just fixed this stupid nail."

The tension bunched between my shoulder blades loosens a bit.

315

Seconds later, the lock disengages.

"Holy crap, Chelsea, it worked!"

She blows on the end of the Slagel like it's a loaded pistol and strikes a pose. "I am totally rocking this lock picker shit."

From the corner of my eye, I catch Nick and Mat jogging toward us. "Yeah, you are." My voice goes soft and I work hard not to cry. "Find Emma, okay?"

She pulls me into a hug. "Be safe."

I hang on a little longer, seeking assurance, comfort, a sign that this is all going to work out. It means trusting everyone to do their part—and I've never been very good at that.

"You're set," Mat says, as Chelsea and I break apart. "Alarms are down. Cameras too."

I press my hand against his cheek. "You're a genius."

He tries to shrug it away, but I can see the emotion trapped behind his dark eyes. They shimmer just like mine. I look away to chase the tears.

"This is it, guys," I say. "No turning back from here."

Mat squeezes my hand. "I should stay."

"No. You and Chelsea need to find Emma." I inhale a shaky breath. "Please, bring my sister home."

"We'll bring *our* sister home," Mat says. He pushes a piece of paper into the palm of my hand. "This is the VIN number for Eleanor. You know where to find the VIN, right?"

I must look annoyed because he rolls his eyes. "Jesus. Of course you do."

"It won't matter," Nick says. "Riley doesn't know anything about the Morrison angle. Any of those Shelbys will work."

He's right, but stealing the Morrison car from right under Roger's nose feels justified, a little payback for betraying us, for having the car all along. If I have time, that's the one I'll take.

We gather in a circle for a moment of silence. A chance to think, plan, pray . . . to believe. I don't know what happens next, whether we can pull off what needs to be done, but I'm struck by the overwhelming sense that after so many years chasing the ghosts of my past, I'm finally right where I belong.

I bounce on the tips of my toes and shake out the nerves.

Blood rushes through my veins.

"It's go time," I say.

When they're back in a cell reception zone, Chelsea will call Roger and say we've recovered the Aston Martin. Three minutes after that, Mat will message Riley and confirm that we have the Shelby, and that we've arranged a meeting with our buyer—at a secret location we'll reveal only *when* he releases Emma.

Mat has Photoshopped a series of pictures showing Nick with one of the Shelbys to show to Riley as proof. If I hadn't seen him do it, I would have thought them real.

Finally, Chelsea will call the police.

It's this last part that makes me the most nervous, and the

reason the timing must be in sync. For it to work, everyone—including the cops—must converge at the Trophy Case around roughly the same time. Hopefully, the police will provide enough of a distraction for Nick and me to make a clean getaway, while still bringing both Riley and Roger to justice.

Nick and I run through the hallways, yanking open doors that have been disarmed thanks to Mat's mad hacking skills. I'm nervous and scared, but there's something else too. The rush of adrenaline that makes me wonder if, when this is all over, I can truly give it up.

We push through the last door and flick on the main lights. The overhead fluorescents flicker and buzz to life. As soon as my eyes adjust, I spot the three Mustangs.

My heart feels like it's falling into my stomach.

"I can't believe he painted it," I say, running my hand along the hood of the first car. It's not Eleanor.

"Over here," Nick says. "The numbers match."

The real Eleanor is a magnet, pulling me to her. I touch the doors, the headlights, the bumper, the tires. My fingers trail along the twin racing stripes up the center of the hood, and then the single line of white along the side.

My pulse thrums with the need to drive her.

To hear the roar of the engine and feel the torque from three hundred twenty solid pounds of horse.

Nick twirls me around and kisses me hard on the lips. "Stay in one piece."

I hate that we have to separate, but one of us has to keep watch. If Riley arrives with the Aston Martin first, Nick will lead him to me and the car to negotiate a trade-off. If it's Roger, he'll distract him. Somehow. And if, by some terrible turn of events, the police are first to arrive on the scene . . .

We're screwed.

Without working cell phones, there's no logical way to manage the timing.

"Go," I say, pushing him toward the door. It's too hard to think with him around anyway.

He nods. "If anything happens . . ."

I blink to stop the tears. "I know."

The alarm on my stopwatch beeps three times. Any minute now, Roger, Riley, maybe both, should arrive. I listen for sounds, but the only thing I hear is the *thump-thump-thump* of my heart.

My walkie-talkie crackles to life. "Jules, someone's here."

I start to pace.

The countdown begins in my head. I estimate less than a minute from where Nick would have seen the car approach to the gates. Everything's unlocked, which Mat says will "look" like a malfunction. He'll be so pissed—panicked?—he won't bother to lock the gates behind him.

The walkie-talkie sizzles again, but Nick's voice cuts in and out. I can't make out anything he's saying. I push the talk button and hold the device close to my lips. "Nick? I can't hear you. Is it Riley?"

No answer.

"Nick? Are the police here?"

Still nothing. I pound on the front of the walkie-talkie, like I can beat it into working properly. Try again. "Tell me it's Roger."

The hairs on the back of my neck stand on end as I sense a presence behind me.

I turn slowly and my stomach bottoms out.

"It's Roger," Roger says.

31

I HOLD MY HANDS UP AND TAKE THREE GIANT STEPS back, aware I have nothing to protect myself with. I don't have a weapon, no source of communication. It's just me and Roger.

"I really thought we had a deal," he says.

"Funny, me too." Fear makes me cocky, so I straighten my spine and lift my chin with false defiance. "But then you lied." He takes a step forward. I move back and hold up one hand. "Stop right there."

Roger stills. "I never lied to you, Julia. I had planned to honor all of your requests. Chelsea's Harvard application is already in progress. Nick's money. Finding Mat's family." He raises his hands. "All to be yours, when the four of you finished the job."

"Except you set us up to fail."

His eyebrows knit. "I gave you everything you asked for."

"Stop playing games." Exasperation makes my voice lift. "The car. Eleanor. She was here all along."

His face blanks and that's when I realize he doesn't know. It's the only explanation that makes sense. Roger was collecting Shelbys in search of Morrison's ride, but never knew he'd been in possession of the original vehicle all along. But how could he not?

Roger shakes his head. "It can't be. . . . Eloise would have known." His skin pales. "Dear God . . . before she died, there was a secret . . . something about 'the perfect anniversary gift.' I never gave it another thought. But now . . . this must have been her secret, the gift she never had a chance to give me."

My heart softens at his sheer look of defeat and loss. I can't help it—I care. "We know why the Bond car was so important." His eyes lift to meet mine and I swear I see tears. "And I get the deadline now." A pained expression flashes across his face. "But Jim's car . . ."

"My wife was always such a fan of his," he says. "We met through him at a concert, had our first date in a replica Shelby. The Doors played on the radio. It was so important to both of us." His voice trails off. "When she opened this place, she said it felt empty without that car. So much I couldn't give her. . . ." His bottom lip trembles. "And I couldn't even give her that."

Instead, she found it herself.

I gather my hair into a ponytail and squeeze the back

322

of my neck. Of course his confession touches me; I'm not a monster.

My walkie-talkie crackles, startling us both. Another thread of relief weaves its way through my bloodstream.

"Jules. Are you there? Roger's in the building—I repeat, Roger is in—shit, and someone else is coming. It's Riley."

Panic flickers across Roger's face.

"Shit, Jules, another set of headlights, I think it's—fuck."

I punch on the talk button. "What is it?"

"Cops." He cuts out and then back in. "It's the fucking police. Shit. It's too early. I'm going to draw them away—get out of there, Jules. Get out!"

I'm so startled I drop the walkie-talkie. Broken pieces scatter across the warehouse floor.

Get out.

The command repeats over and over in my mind as I try to process the next steps.

Think, Jules. Think.

"You have to leave, Roger."

"Eloise would want me to protect this—her cars. I have to at least do that."

A strangled cry releases from my throat. "Did you hear what Nick said? The police are coming—and Riley." I swallow hard. "He's not a nice man, Roger. He'll bring reinforcements, guns. Some of the police are on his payroll. It's not safe here."

"I won't leave."

My chest wrenches like someone's yanked out my heart. There's no way I can stay, not without Emma. I jab my finger at Roger. "Fine. But don't blame me if you get shot."

I spin around and start running toward the door. He calls out my name, but I don't—can't—stop. He had his chance. I race toward the bay door and yank on the handle. It's stuck. I run back to the Mustangs, fueled by adrenaline and determination.

Only one other exit, and it's the garage on the main floor. On foot, I'll never make it.

Eleanor.

Using the butt end of the broken walkie-talkie, I bust the glass on the passenger side window, reach inside, and pop the locks. Somewhere in the back of my mind, I hear Roger protest. A blade of glass slices into my skin. I see the blood, but it doesn't hurt. Nothing hurts. I'm numb.

Focused.

My fingers tremble like it's the first time I've hot-wired a car. I bust into the steering column. A drop of my blood hits the floor. *Breathe.* Grab the wires from under the dash. *Inhale.*

The wires are already stripped. *Exhale.*

I twist them together and a bolt of electricity fires off a series of short sparks. The engine kicks over and I stomp on the gas pedal to flow fuel through the injector. Eleanor sputters. Please God, no . . .

Another shot of gas and the Mustang hits idle. The engine echoes like a panther ready to chase its prey.

I can do this.

Steadying myself, I look up over the dash, prepared to run straight through Roger if he gets in my way. I freeze.

It's Emma.

My little sister stands in the middle of the warehouse, looking so small and vulnerable, she's almost a doll. Red blotches cover her neck and cheeks, the front of her chest. Her anxiety is taking control.

I blink-blink-blink until I'm sure she's not a mirage.

Tears stream down her face.

I jump out of the car.

"Jules?"

Her voice is so tiny, it's almost a squeak.

"How did you—?"

She races toward me, throwing herself into my waist. Her hands hold tight. "I was so scared. . . ." I press my hand against her head, keeping her close. Her heart beats fast through her shirt. "If not for Roger . . ."

"But how?" I can't process her words. Everything moves in slow motion. Realization hits. Roger called Melissa's mom and knows we lied. I look to my left, then right, double check again. But Roger is gone. A loud bang outside snaps me out of my trance. "We'll talk about that later. Ems, we have to do something really scary right now, okay?"

Her small nod transports me back to when our mother

first left. To when my sister was just six years old, confused and frightened. It's the same now, only this time, the stakes are so much higher. Our lives hang in the balance.

"I need you to get in the car."

As she does, I punch in a code on the keyboard attached to the side of the garage. The bay door doesn't open. *Fuck.* I try again, punching random numbers until I realize it won't work. Mat has disabled all of the alarms and door locks.

I'm going to have to do it manually.

The broken walkie-talkie crackles on the floor. I kick it aside and get back in the car. With a trembling hand, I shift the car into gear. "Buckle up, Ems."

I hit the gas and the car shoots forward. The back tires squeak on the pavement. *Holy shit.*

I take the corner slow to the main floor, put the car in neutral, get out, and yank on the bay door handle. It inches open.

Sirens squawk from every direction.

There's an explosion, followed by a series of gunshot blasts. I can't see what's going on. My adrenaline spikes.

Emma screams.

I heave on the door with everything in me. It gets stuck midway, but it's enough for me to get through.

There's another gunshot.

Sirens wail as more cop cars approach. Tires screech, more gunfire, a series of commands and shouts.

And . . . fuck me. A helicopter in the distance.

My stomach hurts, my heart pounds. Adrenaline rushes into my blood.

I get back in the car and slam the door shut. "Hang on, sweet pea!"

Ready.

Strap in.

Set.

Go!

I jam the car into first and hit the gas, shifting to second before I even clear the bay door. The car hits the uneven road and shoots toward the back gate. My head slams forward when the tires hit the ground and I involuntarily crank the wheel.

Eleanor spins a one-eighty.

Everything goes in slow motion.

Police cars close in on the Trophy Case. If they get any closer, they'll block the only exit—I'll be trapped. We all will.

Get out.

Nick's voice propels me forward. I turn the corner and slam on the brakes. It's Riley.

I can't get through. There's not enough room to pass.

My stomach plummets as I realize my only option. I have to reverse. Riley gets out of the car and aims a gun at the windshield—he doesn't even seem to care who's betrayed him. He's pissed and no one is safe, not even Roger.

"Emma, duck!"

I skulk lower in the seat and slide Eleanor into gear. A bullet *pings* off the side mirror.

Emma's high-pitched scream reverberates through the car.

I step on the gas but the gear hasn't engaged.

Through the windshield, I see Riley smirk.

Reverse, Jules. Reverse.

I inhale deep and focus. Slide the gear back, left, and up. The clutch engages. I stomp on the gas and the car shoots back. I yank on the e-brake and spin the wheel. Step on the gas.

In my rearview, a dark sedan vaults toward Riley from out of nowhere. *Roger.* His front bumper slams into Riley's car and the front tires go flat, rendering his car useless. I turn around in my seat just as Riley pivots at Roger, the gun leveled at his windshield.

I have to go back.

Roger saved Emma, saved me. I owe him this.

I crank the wheel to spin a one-eighty and charge toward Riley. Emma pokes her head up over the dash and I yell at her to stay down. I floor it. Riley spins around to shoot at me, but the bullet goes wide. He dives sideways to avoid the front end of my car and hits the ground. The gun skips across the pavement.

Eleanor and Roger's sedan are nose to nose. Our eyes meet through the windshield and I see his emotion—the apology, the regret. We both know things could have been different.

An incoming siren grows louder. Shit. I can't risk getting caught.

I flip another U-turn, quick-shift to third, and step on the gas. The wheels bounce along the bumpy road. In the distance ahead, I catch a flash of red and I know it's Nick.

Using Nick's Mustang as a marker, I hit fourth gear and fly through the gates, scraping the side mirror on the metal. It hangs limply against the side of the car. Fuck.

A fiery explosion bursts in my rearview.

Tears spring to my eyes when I realize there's no one on my tail. This is it, the homestretch. We're almost free.

I crest the hill at almost a hundred and fifty miles an hour. The car lifts off, then slams back onto the ground with enough force to knock my teeth against each other. I spin the wheel, slam on the brakes, and slide to a stop right next to Nick.

This time, I let the tears fall.

Nick gives me the thumbs-up and takes off. I pull up behind him, keeping pace. The warehouse fades into the distance.

Emma slumps in the seat beside me, her body limp. Her eyelids are so heavy she's almost asleep. I reach across and rub her leg. "We're going to be okay now, Ems."

It's almost a shock to realize I mean it.

We pull over at the edge of Kyle Canyon Road as two more police cars turn down the dirt road. Nick rolls down his window. His eyes are red, his cheeks streaked with dirt. "You have Emma?"

My sister leans forward and waves.

Relief spreads across his handsome face. "You've got to stop running away like that."

Emma sticks out her tongue. She's putting on a brave front, but the sweat from her palms leaves imprints on her jeans.

"Chelsea and Mat?"

"Safe," he says. "Once they knew Roger had Emma, it made more sense to stay clear of the showdown. They worked the scene from afar. Mat intercepted the police scanners and called off the chopper—otherwise we'd never have gotten out of there. But we should go before more cops arrive."

"But how did they know?" I say, grateful. "And how did Roger get to Emma first?"

"Mat will explain it fully, but it seems not all of our communication was as private from Roger as we thought. Should have known. He got to Riley's cousin's house before Mat and Chelsea—which was probably for the best."

I widen my eyes. "Kevin must be scared crapless . . . losing Emma to Roger. Riley won't be impressed."

"I suspect he's halfway to Mexico by now."

The whole situation is almost ironic, but there's something deeper too—Roger knew we'd betrayed him, and he still came to the Trophy Case. He still tried to make it right, even though he could have been in danger. *Is* in danger. I don't know what to make of that.

The Shelby rumbles under me. "This car doesn't like to sit around."

Nick juts his chin. "Think you've got more under the hood than me?"

"It's not the horsepower that matters."

His eyes burn with mischief. "Challenge you to a race, Ghost?"

This time the nickname doesn't bother me—it's a part of who I am. In this moment, I'm no longer invisible, no longer a ghost of the past. Nick sees me—really sees me—and with my new family and Emma by my side, I am invincible.

I shift into first, rev the engine, and flash Nick a smile that tells him I'm more than happy. I'm home. "I dare you to keep up."

32

Six Months Later

NICK'S FEET STICK OUT FROM UNDER A '67 CAMARO. I'd recognize his camouflage boots anywhere. Jazz music pulses through the garage.

It's after hours, but I can tell he's been busy. An old GTO is parked in the far bay and a Corvette is wedged between a Chevelle and Vicki. Nick says he specializes in muscle cars, but I guess even he'll make exceptions. Corvette status is still up for debate.

Emma sneaks up on him and tugs loose one of his laces.

There's a sharp *thunk*, followed by a curse of pain. Emma cups her hand over her mouth to stop from laughing.

"When I get my hands on the imp that . . ." Nick slides out from under the car and fake scowls. "Should have known it was you."

Grease smudges both of his cheeks and there's a fresh

scrape on his forehead—probably from hitting his head on the oil pan after Emma startled him. Even dirty, he still makes my heart race.

I hold out my hand. "Want help up?"

His eyes undress me. "And get you all greasy?"

"You've got showers in here, right?"

He lifts an eyebrow. "On second thought."

Emma claps her hands over her ears. "Gross, you guys."

My sister pretends that we disgust her, but just the other day she made it clear we're never allowed to break up. She hops up onto one of the workbenches in Nick's shop and picks up a wrench. Barely a week old and already chipped from use. Business has been steady since he opened Nick's Garage last month.

He stands, brushes off his coveralls, and taps Emma's nose. "Aren't you supposed to be in dance?"

I reach into my purse to pull out a small bottle of champagne. "We're celebrating."

Nick's eyes brighten. "The deal closed?"

"Today."

I am now the proud co-owner of a small dance studio in a complex right across the street from the small two-bedroom apartment I rent. Using the rest of the money Roger gave us, I've hired a senior ballet instructor while I retrain my muscles. Roger will remain on as a silent partner, at least until I graduate and turn eighteen.

Roger carried through on his promises—every single one.

Nick pulls me into his arms for a congratulatory hug and light kiss. My stomach flutters.

"I guess we better pop the cork on that bottle," he says, scooping it out of my hand. He inspects the label. "Sounds fancy."

"Courtesy of Roger."

I'd stopped by the mansion earlier to pick up the rest of our things. It's not the first time since everything happened that I've seen him, but it's less awkward. Baby steps. He's promised to send money for Emma every month, at least until she's an adult, but I get the sense he'd hoped for something more. Friendship? I guess a part of me doesn't mind the idea.

Nick raises an eyebrow, impressed. "Straight life seems to be agreeing with him."

With all of us, so far. We have Chelsea's dad to thank for that. After the police raided the warehouse, Riley and his crew—including Kevin, who they found trying to cross into Mexico—ended up in jail. Roger might have been as well if Chelsea's dad hadn't used his influence to keep Roger out of the slammer—his way of saying thanks for taking Chelsea in. And, in his own way, making up for the fact that he let her leave so easily. I thought I'd be envious that she has that, a family that wants her, but mostly I'm just happy she's home.

A chunk of the cars from the Trophy Case were confiscated and returned to their rightful owners. Roger says he plans to reopen it someday. Legally. Regardless of whether he can get his hands on any of the dream vehicles on his wife's list. It's not as easy as handing over some cash. I was wrong before—not everyone has a price.

Nick presses his fingers against the champagne cork and points the bottle to the ceiling. Emma puts her hands over her ears. The cork explodes and hits the flickering NICK'S GARAGE sign over the workbench.

"Holy crap, you guys making enough racket in here or what?"

"Chelsea!" Emma jumps off the end of the workbench and goes running. She stops before hugging her. "Wow. I love that dress!"

Not surprising, Chelsea looks like she's stepped off the runway rather than the hospital halls where she's volunteering for extra credit. Roger used his pull to get her into Harvard next year, but now that she's back living with her parents, she spends most of her time studying. Senior year promises to be a big year—for all of us.

Chelsea crouches down to Emma's level. "And you, Miss Diva, are still adorable." She stands to give me a hug. "I hear we've got some celebrating to do."

"Jules started her dance studio," Emma says. "And I'm her very first client."

Chelsea raises an eyebrow. "Except you don't have to pay."

Ems laughs. "That's true." Her eyes turn wistful. "I wish Matty could be here."

My sentiments are the same. It hasn't been the same since he left last week, chasing the lead Roger gave him on the where-abouts of his family. Much as I want him to find them, it worries me to think he may never come back. We—I—feel a little lost without him.

"I'm here," comes a muffled reply.

Nick peers around the corner, but the shop's empty. "Am I hearing things?"

"Oh!" Chelsea pulls her cell out from the wire trappings of her bra and turns the screen so we can all see. Mat's face swims into view. "He's on FaceTime."

I decide not to comment on the fact that Mat's face has been smooshed between Chelsea's breasts for an undetermined amount of time. Nick and I have a bet on how long it will take the two of them to admit they like each other as more than friends.

We all gather around the phone.

Emma leans in close. "Where are you?"

"Mexico," he says, panning the screen across a stretch of white sand beach.

Nick hands each of us a disposable red cup topped up with bubbling champagne. "Have you found them yet?"

"No, but I'm getting closer."

Emma grabs the phone and kisses the screen with a loud smack of her lips.

Mat blinks. "What was that for?"

Emma beams. "Good luck."

Mat's dimples grow bigger. "I'm sorry to miss out on the celebration."

"When you get back, we'll do it again," Nick says.

"And we'll have something else to toast to," Chelsea says, holding up her glass. "To you finding your family."

My chest swells with emotion and I blink away the tears. I look around at my sister, the wide smile on her face, and pull Nick to my side. "I'll toast to that right now."

Acknowledgments

My love of muscle cars began long before I saw *Gone in 60 Seconds*, though I admit, it was this movie that inspired my '67 Shelby GT 500 obsession.

I took my driver's test on a stick shift, hoping—praying?—that this would convince my stepdad I was worthy of driving his rusted old Camaro, the Silver Bullet. Sadly, I drove it only once before he sold it. That was enough.

It should come as little surprise then that *Overdrive* is not only a true book of my heart, but one fueled by the adrenaline of everything that I love—a true dream project. I have a lot of people to thank for helping me bring it to fruition.

To Agent Awesome, Mandy Hubbard, who dreamed up a story conceit that even today feels too good to be true. Thank you for trusting me with it. In this crazy industry, filled with highs and lows, I am so grateful to have you standing at my side. Sometimes I still pinch myself. I couldn't ask for a more amazing agent and friend. Truly.

I am so thankful to the entire team at Simon Pulse for believing in me and supporting this story, in particular Karina Granda, who created a brilliant cover (you nailed what this book is about), and to my wonderful editor, Jennifer Ung. Thank you for "getting" this book, for pushing me to write better, for being a beacon of hope at the end of writerly self-doubt, and for loving this story (and Jules) as much as I do. You took this book to a level I didn't even realize was possible. Also a nitrous-oxide injected thanks to copyeditor and proofreader extraordinaires, Beth Adelman and Stacey Sakal, whose keen eyes kept me from much future embarrassment.

Several brave and kind souls read various drafts of this book. Without their insight, words of encouragement, and tough love, I might still be stuck in first gear. Thank you, Sue Worobetz (the numbers are safer now!), Hailey Pelletier, Izzy Jones, Kyle Kerr (multiple, impossible-to-count thank-you's!), Karen Dyck, Rocky Hatley, Denise Jaden, Louise Gorenall, Megan Grimit, Claire Donnelly, Nancy Traynor, Anne Tibbets (🍉 ♥), and my soul sister, Jessica Bell.

Thank you, Kitty Keswick, for reading the terrible first draft and telling me you loved it. Thank you for reading the slightly less-terrible second draft, and still loving it. And thank you for reading the third, fourth, and fifth drafts. For dropping everything to read, even when you had projects of your own to complete. For investing in these characters, in me, and in our friendship with absolute abandonment. And for being the kind of critique partner every writer needs, and I honestly don't deserve. Thank you. I don't know a life before you.

Publishing my debut novel, *Anne & Henry*, was a magical experience, not only because it fulfilled my lifelong dream of seeing my name on a hardcover book in an actual bookstore, but also because I met so many wonderful people. Thank you,

Kathy Coe, for being my first fan and an unwavering pillar of support. Our friendship began with *Anne & Henry*, but continues with brilliant TV, wine, and a full slate of adventures ahead. To Anthony Franze (go read his book, *The Advocate's Daughter*—it's so good!) and Barry Lancet (his Jim Brodie series is classic thriller!) for taking me under your wings at *The Big Thrill*, and becoming more than mentors, but dear friends. Cheers to many beers at Thrillerfest! And to Nancy "Remarkably Raven"—a fan, a confidant, fellow Canadian, and kick-ass friend. Thank you for always waving your pom-poms for me.

Speaking of cheerleaders, I have an impressive squad—Kyle (you get another mention because no one works as tirelessly to boost me up, promote my writing, and put up with my fragile ego as you. I love you.), James Grasdal, Bessie McLaughlan, Betty Morris, Kate Cosgrove, Carolyn Adams, my awesome sister-in-law (♥) Trisha Dalton, and my number one fan (sorry, Jeff), Jessica Driscoll. It's true that you can't choose your family, but even if I had the power, I couldn't pick a more amazing sister. Thank you for inspiring, encouraging, and loving, but most of all, for believing. I love you to the moon and back.

As always, I thank my mentors Gary Braver, Steve Berry, Jacqueline Mitchard, and James Rollins, who believed in me when I didn't, and taught me to write often, write tight (thanks, Steve!), and write well. I am forever in your debt.

Of course, none of this would be possible without the love of my very large family (sorry, Dad, not a millionaire yet! I'll keep trying . . .), and the continued support of my readers. Thank you. You are all infinitely awesome.

And last, but never least, to my amazing husband, who not only bought me a sporty RX-8 to commemorate *Anne & Henry*, but who also raises only one eyebrow when the (occasional) speeding ticket arrives in the mail. Fast cars may feed my adrenaline, babe, but it's you—always—that makes my heart race. I love you.

About the Author

DAWN IUS is a short-story author, novelist, screenwriter, professional editor, and communications specialist. She is the cofounder and senior editor of *Vine Leaves Literary Journal*, developmental editor and marketing director of Vine Leaves Press, managing editor of the International Thriller Writers (ITW) Association e-zine, *The Big Thrill*, and the author of fifteen educational graphic novels. When she's not slaying fictional monsters or swooning over book boyfriends, she can be found geeking out over things like fairy tales, true love, Jack Bauer, Halloween, sports cars, and all things that go bump in the night. She lives in Alberta, Canada, with her husband, Jeff, and their giant English Mastiff, Roarke. Visit her online at dawnius.com.